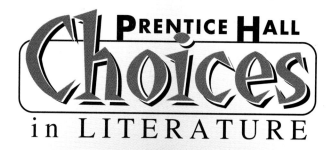

PRENTICE HALL

Choices

in LITERATURE

The Adventure of Me
Joining Hands
It's Up to You
Conflict and Resolution
The World of "What if . . . ?"

The Me You See
Where Paths Meet
Deciding What's Right
You Are the Solution
Communication Explosion

Myself, My World
American Tapestry
Justice for All
Making a Difference
Charting Your Own Course

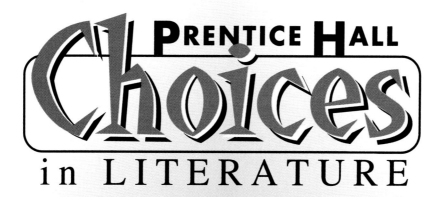

The Me You See

PRENTICE HALL
Upper Saddle River, New Jersey
Needham, Massachusetts

ISBN 0-13-411448-5

1 2 3 4 5 6 7 8 9 10   00 99 98 97 96

Cover: Student Art Untitled, Tomas Sanchez, The Scholastic Art and Writing Awards

Art credits begin on page F181.

PRENTICE HALL
Simon & Schuster Education Group
A VIACOM COMPANY

Staff Credits for Prentice Hall Choices in Literature

(In Alphabetical Order)

Advertising and Promotion: Alfonso Manosalvas, Rip Odell

Business Office: Emily Heins

Design: Eric Dawson, Jim O'Shea, Carol Richman, AnnMarie Roselli, Gerry Schrenk

Editorial: Ellen Bowler, Megan Chill, Barbara W. Coe, Elisa Mui Eiger, Philip Fried, Rebecca Z. Graziano, Douglas McCollum

Manufacturing and Inventory Planning: Katherine Clarke, Rhett Conklin, Matt McCabe

Marketing: Jean Faillace, Mollie Ledwith

Media Resources: Libby Forsyth, Maureen Raymond

National Language Arts Consultants: Kathy Lewis, Karen Massey, Craig A. McGhee, Vennisa Travers, Gail Witt

Permissions: Doris Robinson

Pre-press Production: Carol Barbara, Katherine Dix, Marie McNamara, Annette Simmons

Production: Margaret Antonini, Christina Burghard, Greg Myers, Marilyn Stearns, Cleasta Wilburn

Sales: Ellen Backstrom

Acknowledgments

Grateful acknowledgment is made to the following for permission to reprint copyrighted material:

Algonquin Books of Chapel Hill
From the "Introduction" of *Poetry Out Loud* by James Earl Jones. Copyright © 1993 by Algonquin Books of Chapel Hill. Reprinted by permission of Algonquin Books of Chapel Hill, a division of Workman Publishing Company, New York, NY.

Susan Bergholz Literary Services
"My Name" from *The House on Mango Street* by Sandra Cisneros. Copyright © 1984 by Sandra Cisneros. Published by Vintage Books, a division of Random House, Inc., New York and in hard cover by Alfred A. Knopf in 1994. Reprinted by permission of Susan Bergholz Literary Services, New York.

Berkley Publishing Group
From "Was Tarzan a Three-Bandage Man?" from *Childhood* by Bill Cosby. Copyright © 1991 by William H. Cosby, Jr. Reprinted by permission of Berkley Publishing Group.

BOA Editions, Ltd.
Li-Young Lee. "The Gift," copyright © 1986 by Li-Young Lee. Reprinted from *Rose* by Li-Young Lee, with the permission of BOA Editions, Ltd., 92 Park Avenue, Brockport, NY 14420.

(Continued on page F181.)

The Me You See
Contents

WHO IS THE REAL ME?

Looking at Literary Forms: The Short Story

WHO GIVES ME INSPIRATION?

Looking at Literary Forms: Biography and Autobiography

HOW DO I SHOW WHAT I CAN DO?   F131

About This Program

What makes reading exciting?

Reading is a great way to learn more about the world and about yourself. Reading gives you the chance to make a movie in your mind and experience adventures you might never be able to actually live. Words can take you to faraway lands, tell you about important discoveries and courageous people, make you laugh and cry, or let you look at your world in a new way.

How will reading pay off in your future?

Beyond being entertaining, reading is important. As you learn more, you increase your choices in life. The skills and strategies you practice today will help you to become a life-long learner—someone who has questions, reads to answer them, and develops more questions!

How will this book help you get more out of what you read?

This book and your teacher will help you become a better reader. The selections included will grab your attention and help you practice specific skills valuable to the reading process.

Questions and activities at the beginning of selections will help you relate the reading to your own life; questions at the end will help you expand on what you learned. Activities and projects throughout the book will help you generate and explore new pathways of learning.

What features make this book a great learning tool?

Artwork to Spark Your Interest Fine art, student art, photography, and maps can give you clues about the writing and direct the way you read.

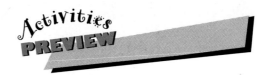
Activities PREVIEW

Exciting Activities to Get You Into the Selection A preview page for each selection asks a question to get you thinking. Stop and consider your own responses to this question. Talk with classmates to get their ideas. As you read, you may find your own opinions changing. Reading can do that, too.

 The **Reach Into Your Background** feature will always give you ideas for connecting the selection to your own experience. In many cases, you may know more than you think you do. Try the activities in this section for a jump start before you read. Don't expect to be in your seats all the time! You'll learn more about your ideas by role-playing, debating, and sharing what you know with others.

Useful Strategies to Help You Through the Selection This program will teach you essential techniques for getting more out of your reading.

In **Read Actively** you'll find hands-on approaches to getting more out of what you read. Here's your chance to practice the skills that will bring you reading success. You'll learn to make inferences, gather evidence, set a purpose for reading, and much more. Once you've learned these skills, you can use them in all the reading that you do . . . and you'll get more out of your reading.

Some of the strategies you'll learn include:

Identifying Problems
Making Judgments
Asking Questions
Visualizing Characters
Setting a Purpose for Reading
Recognizing a Sequence of Events
Connecting Nonfiction to Your Own Experience
Responding to Literature

Activities
MAKE MEANING

• Thought-Provoking Activities to Generate New Ideas Following each selection, you'll have the chance to explore your own ideas and learn more about what you read.

Explore Your Reading takes you into, through, and beyond the actual selection to help you investigate the writing and its ideas more closely.

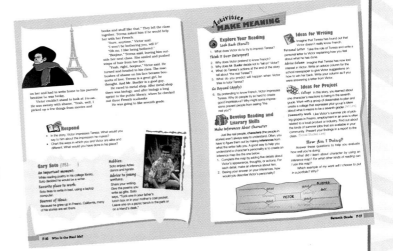

Develop Reading and Literary Skills expands your knowledge of literary forms, terms, and techniques. Following up on the Read Actively activities and strategies, you will learn more about how writing communicates.

Ideas for Writing and **Ideas for Projects** offer you the chance to create your own answers to your own questions. How does the selection relate to you? Where can you learn more? What cross-curricular connections can you make? These ideas features help you try things out yourself.

Enjoy this book!

All the features of this program fit together to develop your interest, skills, and, ultimately, your ability to learn.

Have fun with the time you spend with this book. Look at the art, plan for unit level projects, look for connections between selections. Pay attention to your own questions—finding the answers to those may be the most rewarding of all.

The Me You See

Gemini I Lev T. Mills, Evans-Tibbs Collection

"I celebrate myself and sing myself" —**Walt Whitman**

Get the Picture Think about what Walt Whitman said as you look at the portrait of the young girl. Like her, you are unique and your interests and ideas are worth celebrating. What gives you *your* identity? In answering this question, you may ask yourself questions like the following:

- **Who Is the Real Me?**
- **Who Gives Me Inspiration?**
- **How Do I Show What I Can Do?**

The authors in this unit have asked themselves the same questions, and their answers will help you find new ones of your own. Keep a journal for "The Me You See." As you go through the unit, you can use your journal to write your own questions, answer them, and reflect on what you've read and learned.

Activities
In a Group With several classmates, discuss how each of the following makes a person similar to and different from others: family; name or nickname; friends; gender; ethnic, regional, and national background; appearance; talents; and personal style. Rank each item to show its importance.

Activities
On Your Own Write your name in the center of a piece of paper. Create a web around it by drawing a number of lines to the left and to the right. On the left, show what makes you similar to your friends and classmates and on the right, what sets you apart.

Project Preview ....

You can also respond to questions about identity by working on exciting projects. Preview the following projects and choose one that you might like to do. For more details, see page F162.

- **Scientific Report on The Real You**
- **Your Inspirations in Multimedia**
- **Book of International Names**
- **Class Yearbook**
- **School Survey on Role Models**
- **Community Project**

Read Actively

How does my reading relate to my world?

How can I get more from what I read?

The answer to questions like these is to be an active reader, an *involved* reader. As an active reader, *you* are in charge of the reading situation!

The following strategies tell how to think as an active reader. You don't need to use all of these strategies all of the time. Feel free to choose the ones that work best in each reading situation.

BEFORE YOU READ

PREVIEW
What do the title and the pictures suggest? What will the selection say about "The Me You See"?

GIVE YOURSELF A PURPOSE
What is the author communicating? What will you learn about the theme? How will the selection relate to your life?

REACH INTO YOUR BACKGROUND
What do you know already?

WHILE YOU READ

ASK QUESTIONS

What's happening? Why do the characters do what they do? Why does the author give you certain details or use a particular word? Your questions help you gather evidence and make inferences.

PREDICT

What do you think will happen? Why? You can change your mind as you read along.

VISUALIZE

What would these events and characters look like in a movie? How would the writer's description's look in a photograph?

CONNECT

Are characters like you or someone you know? What would you do in a similar situation?

AFTER YOU READ

RESPOND

Talk about what you've read. What did you think?

ASSESS YOURSELF

How did you do? Were your predictions on target? Did you find answers to your questions?

FOLLOW UP

Show what you know. Get involved! Do a project. Keep learning.

The model that begins on the next page shows Kimberly Akuna's thoughts while actively reading "Was Tarzan a Three-Bandage Man?"

Read Actively Model

My name is Kimberly Akuna. I'm a student at Harriet Eddy Middle School in Elk Grove, California. I wrote the notes you see in the margin of this selection, as I read this funny story by Bill Cosby. I liked the way he used the names of people I knew to tell about growing up. *Kimberly Akuna*

What is a three-bandage man? Will the article have anything to do with the title? [Purpose]

Was Tarzan a Three-Bandage Man?

Bill Cosby

I can relate to his imitations of people. People I know of all ages imitate the people they believe in. [Connection]

He uses lots of dialogue in the beginning, which pulls me in. I want to keep reading. [Response]

In the days before athletes had learned how to incorporate themselves, they were shining heroes to American kids. In fact, they were such heroes to me and my friends that we even imitated their walks. When Jackie Robinson,[1] a pigeon-toed[2] walker, became famous, we walked pigeon-toed, a painful form of locomotion unless you were Robinson or a pigeon.

"Why you walkin' like that?" said my mother one day.

"This is Jackie *Robinson's* walk," I proudly replied.

"There's somethin' wrong with his shoes?"

"He's the fastest man in baseball."

"He'd be faster if he didn't walk like that. His mother should make him walk right."

A few months later, when football season began, I stopped imitating Robinson and began to walk bowlegged[3] like a player named Buddy Helm.

"Why you always tryin' to change the shape of your legs?" said my mother. "You keep doin' that an' they'll fall off—an' I'm not gettin' you new ones."

---

1. Jackie Robinson: First African American to play major league baseball, Robinson began his career with the Brooklyn Dodgers in 1945.

2. pigeon-toed (PIJ uhn tohd) *adj.:* Having the feet turned in toward each other.

3. bow-legged (BOH leg guhd) *adj.:* Having legs that are curved outward.

Jackie Robinson
Brooklyn Dodgers, 1948

I wonder why the author and the men in both the pictures are African Americans. [Question]

Although baseball and football stars inspired us, our real heroes were the famous prize fighters, and the way to emulate a fighter was to walk around with a Band-Aid over one eye. People with acne walked around that way too, but we hoped it was clear that we were worshipping good fists and not bad skin.

He talks about imitating his heroes. I can relate to this. Fievel from American Tale was once my idol. [Connection]

I think this will be about him growing up and all the different people he idolized. [Prediction]

The first time my mother saw me being Sugar Ray,[4] not Jackie Robinson, she said, "What's that bandage for?"

Words to Know

incorporate (in KOR puhr ayt) *v.*: To form into a legal business

locomotion (loh kuh MOH shuhn) *n.*: Movement

emulate (in KOR puhr ayt) *v.*: To imitate a person one admires

---

4. **Sugar Ray Robinson:** Boxer who was world welterweight champion 1945–1951, defending his title five times.

Sugar Ray Robinson

"Oh, nuthin'," I replied.

"Now that's a new kinda stupid answer. That bandage gotta be coverin' somethin'—besides your entire brain."

"Well, it's just for show. I wanna look like Sugar Ray Robinson."

"The fastest man in baseball."

"No, that's a different one."

"You doin' Swiss Family Robinson[5] next?"

"Swiss Family Robinson? They live in the projects?"

"You'd know who they are if you read more books instead of makin' yourself look like an accident. Why can't you try to imitate someone like Booker T. Washington?"[6]

"Who does he play for?"

"Bill, let's put it this way: you take off that bandage right now or I'll have your father move you up to stitches."

The following morning on the street, I dejectedly told

This sounds realistic. I can see a mother and a son talking this way. She's probably got her hands on her hips. [Visualization]

His mom sounds like she cares. [Connection]

the boys, "My mother says I gotta stop wearin' a bandage. She wants my whole head to show."

"What's wrong with that woman?" said Fat Albert. "She won't let you do *nuthin'*."

"It's okay, Cos," said Junior, "'cause one bandage ain't enough anyway. My brother says the really tough guys wear two."

"One over each eye?" I asked him.

"Or one eye and one nose," he said.

"Man, I wouldn't want to mess with no two-bandage man," said Eddie.

And perhaps the toughest guys of all wore tourniquets around their necks. We were capable of such attire, for we were never more ridiculous than when we were trying to be tough and cool. Most ridiculous, of course, was that our hero worshipping was backwards: we should have been emulating the men who had *caused* the need for bandages.

---

5. Swiss Family Robinson: Fictional family stranded on a desert island.
6. Booker T. Washington (1856–1915): African American educator and author.

Maybe the one who is less understanding is the son. [Response]

I like how the writer looks back and is able to rethink what he did in the past. Realizing his mistakes makes him sound human. [Response]

aMy original question was answered although not the way I'd expected. Tarzan might have been a three-bandage man. It does make you wonder. Was Tarzan the kind of person to hurt or be hurt? Was he someone I should admire? [Assessment]

Words to Know

dejectedly (dee JEK tuhd lee) *adv.*: Sadly; showing discouragement

tourniquets (TER nuh kuhtz) *n.*: Any devices used to stop bleeding in an emergency, as a bandage twisted tightly to stop the flow of blood

Then: As a child, **Bill Cosby** (1937–   ) was already showing signs of a budding comedy career. His sixth grade report card called him, "an alert boy who would rather clown than study." In addition to idolizing Jackie Robinson and Buddy Helm, Cosby was himself a gifted athlete. He earned a track-and-field scholarship to Temple University in his hometown of Philadelphia, Pennsylvania.

Now: Cosby has drawn from his boyhood experiences in a wide variety of projects. He created Saturday morning cartoon characters based on his neighborhood friends. Also, his television series, *The Cosby Show,* was based in part on his own family experiences.

Respond
- What "heroes" do you imitate? What is it about these people that you find appealing?
- Take a poll of five or six of your classmates to see whom they admire and imitate.

Explore Your Reading

Look Back (Recall)

1. Name two ways in which Cosby and his friends imitated their heroes.

Think it Over (Interpret)

2. How do you know Cosby's mother is not a sports fan?
3. Why does Cosby's mother make him stop wearing bandages?
4. What is funny about the boys imitating the bandaged boxers?

Go Beyond (Apply)

5. What qualities do you admire in a person?

Develop Reading and Literary Skills

Understand Humor

Some people, like Bill Cosby, are natural clowns. However, even a "natural" relies on specific techniques to create **humor**, or amusement, in a piece of writing. One device that comic writers use is exaggeration—drawing out and emphasizing silly words or actions. Cosby does this when he describes how he tried to walk "pigeon-toed, a painful form of locomotion unless you were . . . a pigeon."

Another device is showing a contrast, or difference, between what is silly and what is more usual. Cosby contrasts his mother's normal idea about walking with his own silly devotion to walking "pigeon-toed."

1. Identify another scene in which Cosby uses exaggeration and contrast to increase the humor of his writing.
2. Explain how he uses each device in the scene you choose.

Ideas for Writing

Bill Cosby and his childhood friends imitated men they admired. What if you could actually change places for a day with one of your heroes?

Persuasive Letter Persuade your hero to change places with you. Point out the advantages of the switch for each of you.

Humorous Story Make up a funny story about a teenager who trades places for a day with a hero. Use exaggeration and contrast to increase the humor of your story.

Ideas for Projects

Comic Strip Bill Cosby's humorous essay is based on a series of scenes from his childhood. Choose an incident from your own life and present it humorously in comic-strip form.

Stand-up Routine Study your favorite comedians by watching videos, or reading their comic writing. See what techniques of comedy they use. Deliver a short original comedy routine or perform an already published one to see how it feels to make people laugh.

How Am I Doing?

Take a moment to answer these questions in your journal:

Which active reading strategy helped me the most?

Which strategy do I need to practice?

Who Is the Real Me?

Student Art *Possibilities* Jennifer Vota
St. Johns, Holmdel, New Jersey

Student Writing Linda Sue Estes
New York, New York

I am the sum
Of all the people I have ever met,
All the things I have ever done,
All the places I have ever seen.
Bits, pieces, and fragments.
You thought it was me you saw
yesterday,

but you were wrong.
Excuse me,
I am not myself today,
Or yesterday,
Or tomorrow.
Are you who you think
you are?

Activities PREVIEW
Seventh Grade by Gary Soto

What would you do to impress someone you wanted to get to know?

El Pantalón Rosa 1984, César Martínez, DagenBela Graphics

Reach Into Your Background

At some time in your life, you probably have tried to impress someone. Maybe you wore a special outfit or bragged about something you'd done. Tap your memory of that experience by trying one or more of these activities with a partner:

- Discuss something you've done to make a strong impression.
- Take turns role-playing a situation in which you try to impress someone. Discuss whether the impression you made represents who you are.

Read Actively
Make Inferences

When you try to figure out the meaning behind a person's words, actions, or appearance, you're making an **inference.** Try making inferences about the person in the portrait on this page. In your journal, list the things he's wearing. Next to each item, describe what it "says" about him. For example, what do his sunglasses tell you about him?

Making inferences about the characters in the story will help you get involved in your reading. As you read "Seventh Grade," note the characters' important thoughts, words, and actions. What do these details tell you about the characters' personalities?

F-10   Who Is the Real Me?

Seventh Grade

GARY SOTO

On the first day of school, Victor stood in line half an hour before he came to a wobbly card table. He was handed a packet of papers and a computer card on which he listed his one elective, French. He already spoke Spanish and English, but he thought some day he might travel to France, where it was cool; not like Fresno, where summer days reached 110 degrees in the shade. There were rivers in France and huge churches, and fair-skinned people everywhere, the way there were brown people all around Victor.

Besides, Teresa, a girl he had liked since they were in catechism classes at Saint Theresa's, was taking French, too. With any luck they would be in the same class. Teresa is going to be my girl this year, he promised himself as he left the gym full of students in their new fall clothes. She was cute. And good in

📖 Read Actively

Predict how he will get Teresa to be his girl.

Words to Know

elective (el EK tiv) *n.*: An optional course or subject in a school or college curriculum

scowl (SKOWL) *v.*: Lower eyebrows and corners of the mouth; look angry or irritated

ferocity (fuh RAHS uh tee) *n.*: Fierceness; wild force

math, too, Victor thought as he walked down the hall to his homeroom. He ran into his friend, Michael Torres, by the water fountain that never turned off.

They shook hands, *raza*-style, and jerked their heads at one another in a *saludo de vato*.[1] "How come you're making a face?" asked Victor.

"I ain't making a face, *ese*.[2] This *is* my face." Michael said his face had changed during the summer. He had read a *GQ* magazine that his older brother had borrowed from the Book Mobile and noticed that the male models all had the same look on their faces. They would stand, one arm around a beautiful woman, and scowl. They would sit at a pool, their rippled stomachs dark with shadow, and *scowl*. They would sit at dinner tables, cool drinks in their hands, and *scowl*.

"I think it works," Michael said. He scowled and let his upper lip quiver. His teeth showed along with the ferocity of his soul. "Belinda Reyes walked by a while ago and looked at me," he said.

Victor didn't say anything, though he thought his friend looked pretty strange. They talked about recent movies, baseball, their parents, and the horrors of picking grapes in order to buy their fall clothes. Picking grapes

---

1. *raza*-style, *saludo de vato* (sah LUD oh day VAH to) *Spanish*: Gestures of greeting between friends.
2. *ese* (AY say) *Spanish*: Man.

was like living in Siberia,[3] except hot and more boring.

"What classes are you taking?" Michael said, scowling.

"French. How 'bout you?"

"Spanish. I ain't so good at it, even if I'm Mexican. "

"I'm not either, but I'm better at it than math, that's for sure."

A tinny, three-beat bell propelled students to their homerooms. The two friends socked each other in the arm and went their ways, Victor thinking, man, that's weird. Michael thinks making a face makes him handsome.

On the way to his homeroom, Victor tried a scowl. He felt foolish, until out of the corner of his eye he saw a girl looking at him. Umm, he thought, maybe it does work. He scowled with greater conviction.

In homeroom, roll was taken, emergency cards were passed out, and they were given a bulletin to take home to their parents. The principal, Mr. Belton, spoke over the crackling loudspeaker, welcoming the students to a new year, new experiences, and new friendships. The students squirmed in their chairs and ignored him. They were anxious to go to first period. Victor sat calmly, thinking of Teresa, who sat two rows away, reading a paperback novel. This would be his lucky year. She was in his homeroom, and would probably be in his English and math classes. And, of course, French.

Words to Know

conviction (kun VIK shun) *n.:* Belief
lingered (LIHN gerd) *v.:* Stayed around; delayed leaving
portly (PORT lee) *adj.:* Large and heavy; dignified

---

3. Siberia (sī BIR ee uh): A region in northern Asia known for its harsh winters.

The bell rang for first period, and the students herded noisily through the door. Only Teresa lingered, talking with the homeroom teacher.

"So you think I should talk to Mrs. Gaines?" she asked the teacher. "She would know about ballet?"

"She would be a good bet," the teacher said. Then added, "Or the gym teacher, Mrs. Garza."

Victor lingered, keeping his head down and staring at his desk. He wanted to leave when she did so he could bump into her and say something clever.

He watched her on the sly. As she turned to leave, he stood up and hurried to the door, where he managed to catch her eye. She smiled and said, "Hi, Victor."

He smiled back and said, "Yeah, that's me." His brown face blushed. Why hadn't he said, "Hi, Teresa," or "How was your summer?" or something nice?

As Teresa walked down the hall, Victor walked the other way, looking back, admiring how gracefully she walked, one foot in front of the other. So much for being in the same class, he thought. As he trudged to English, he practiced scowling.

> 📖 **Read Actively**
> Make an **inference** about Victor's personality.

In English they reviewed the parts of speech. Mr. Lucas, a portly man, waddled down the aisle, asking, "What is a noun?"

"A person, place, or thing," said the class in unison.

"Yes, now somebody give me an example of a person—you, Victor Rodriguez."

"Teresa," Victor said automatically. Some of the girls giggled.

They knew he had a crush on Teresa. He felt himself blushing again.

"Correct," Mr. Lucas said. "Now provide me with a place."

Mr. Lucas called on a freckled kid who answered, "Teresa's house with a kitchen full of big brothers."

After English, Victor had math, his weakest subject. He sat in the back by the window, hoping that he would not be called on. Victor understood most of the problems, but some of the stuff looked like the teacher made it up as she went along. It was confusing, like the inside of a watch.

After math he had a fifteen-minute break, then social studies, and, finally, lunch. He bought a tuna casserole with buttered rolls, some fruit cocktail, and milk. He sat with Michael, who practiced scowling between bites.

Girls walked by and looked at him.

"See what I mean, Vic?" Michael scowled. "They love it."

"Yeah, I guess so."

They ate slowly, Victor scanning the horizon for a glimpse of Teresa. He didn't see her. She must have brought lunch, he thought, and is eating outside. Victor scraped his plate and left Michael, who was busy scowling at a girl two tables away.

The small, triangle-shaped campus bustled with students talking about their new classes. Everyone was in a sunny mood. Victor hurried to the bag lunch area, where he sat down and opened his math book. He

moved his lips as if he were reading, but his mind was somewhere else. He raised his eyes slowly and looked around. No Teresa.

He lowered his eyes, pretending to study, then looked slowly to the left. No Teresa. He turned a page in the book and stared at some math problems that scared him because he knew he would have to do them eventually. He looked to the right. Still no sign of her. He stretched out lazily in an attempt to disguise his snooping.

San Pachuco Tony Ortega, Courtesy of the artist

Then he saw her. She was sitting with a girlfriend under a plum tree. Victor moved to a table near her and daydreamed about taking her to a movie. When the bell sounded, Teresa looked up, and their eyes met. She smiled sweetly and gathered her books. Her next class was French, same as Victor's.

They were among the last students to arrive in class, so all the good desks in the back had already

La Morena Bakery Tony Ortega, Courtesy of the artist

been taken. Victor was forced to sit near the front, a few desks away from Teresa, while Mr. Bueller wrote French words on the chalkboard. The bell rang, and Mr. Bueller wiped his hands, turned to the class, and said, *"Bonjour."*[4]

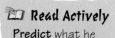

📖 Read Actively

Predict what he might do in class to impress her.

"Bonjour," braved a few students.

"Bonjour," Victor whispered. He wondered if Teresa heard him.

Mr. Bueller said that if the students studied hard, at the end of the year they could go to France and be understood by the populace.

One kid raised his hand and asked, "What's 'populace'?"

"The people, the people of France."

Mr. Bueller asked if anyone knew French. Victor raised his hand, wanting to impress Teresa. The teacher beamed and said, *"Très bien. Parlez-vous français?"*[5]

Victor didn't know what to say. The teacher wet his lips and asked something else in French. The room grew silent. Victor felt all eyes staring at him. He tried to bluff his way out by making noises that sounded French.

"La me vave me con le grandma," he said uncertainly.

Mr. Bueller, wrinkling his face in curiosity, asked him to speak up.

Great rosebushes of red bloomed on Victor's cheeks. A river of nervous sweat ran down his palms. He felt awful. Teresa sat a few desks away, no doubt thinking he was a fool. Without looking at Mr. Bueller, Victor mumbled, "Frenchie oh wewe gee in September."

Mr. Bueller asked Victor to repeat what he said.

"Frenchie oh wewe gee in September," Victor repeated.

Mr. Bueller understood that the boy didn't know French and turned away. He walked to the blackboard and pointed to the words on the board with his steel-edged ruler.

4. **bonjour** (BOHN zhoor) *French:* Hello, good day.

5. **Très bien. Parlez-vous français?** (TRAY bee YEN PAR lay voo fran SAY) *French:* Very good. Do you speak French?

"*Le bateau,*" he sang.

"*Le bateau,*" the students repeated.

"*Le bateau est sur l'eau,*"[6] he sang.

"*Le bateau est sur l'eau.*"

Victor was too weak from failure to join the class. He stared at the board and wished he had taken Spanish, not French. Better yet, he wished he could start his life over. He had never been so embarrassed. He bit his thumb until he tore off a sliver of skin.

The bell sounded for fifth period, and Victor shot out of the room, avoiding the stares of the other kids, but had to return for his math book. He looked sheepishly at the teacher, who was erasing the board, then widened his eyes in terror at Teresa who stood in front of him. "I didn't know you knew French," she said. "That was good."

📖 Read Actively
Connect Victor's feelings to your own experience.

Words to Know

sheepishly (SHEEP ish lee) *adv.:* In a shy or embarrassed way

---

6. ***Le bateau est sur l'eau.*** (le ba TOH AY soor LOW) *French:* The boat is on the water.

Mr. Bueller looked at Victor, and Victor looked back. Oh please, don't say anything, Victor pleaded with his eyes. I'll wash your car, mow your lawn, walk your dog—anything! I'll be your best student and I'll clean your erasers after school.

Mr. Bueller shuffled through the papers on his desk. He smiled and hummed as he sat down to work. He remembered his college years when he dated a girlfriend in borrowed cars. She thought he was rich because each time he picked her up he had a different car. It was fun until he had spent all his money

Vatos Parados 2 Tony Ortega, Courtesy of the artist

on her and had to write home to his parents because he was broke.

Victor couldn't stand to look at Teresa. He was sweaty with shame. "Yeah, well, I picked up a few things from movies and books and stuff like that." They left the class together. Teresa asked him if he would help her with her French.

"Sure, anytime," Victor said.

"I won't be bothering you, will l?"

"Oh no, I like being bothered."

"Bonjour," Teresa said, leaving him outside her next class. She smiled and pushed wisps of hair from her face.

"Yeah, right, *bonjour,*" Victor said. He turned and headed to his class. The rosebushes of shame on his face became bouquets of love. Teresa is a great girl, he thought. And Mr. Bueller is a good guy.

He raced to metal shop. After metal shop there was biology, and after biology a long sprint to the public library, where he checked out three French textbooks.

He was going to like seventh grade.

Respond

- In the story, Victor impresses Teresa. What would you say to him about the impression he makes?
- Chart the ways in which you and Victor are alike and different. What would you have done in his place?

Gary Soto (1952–   )

An important moment:
While reading poetry in his college library, Soto decided he would be a writer.

Favorite place to work:
Soto likes to write in bed, using a laptop computer.

Sources of ideas:
Because he grew up in Fresno, California, many of his stories are set there.

Hobbies:
Soto enjoys Aztec dance and karate.

Advice to young writers:
Share your writing. Give the poems you write as gifts. Soto says, "Tuck one in your father's lunch box or in your mother's coat pocket. Leave one on a picnic bench in the park or on a friend's desk."

Explore Your Reading

Look Back (Recall)

1. What does Victor do to try to impress Teresa?

Think It Over (Interpret)

2. Why does Victor pretend to know French?
3. Why does Mr. Bueller decide not to "tell on" Victor?
4. What do Teresa's actions at the end of the story tell about "the real Teresa"?
5. What do you predict will happen when Victor tries to tutor Teresa?

Go Beyond (Apply)

6. By pretending to know French, Victor impresses Teresa. Why do people try so hard to create good impressions? Why might some impressions prevent people from seeing "the real you"?

Develop Reading and Literary Skills

Make Inferences About Character

Just like real people, **characters** (the people in stories) aren't always easy to understand. Often, you have to figure them out by making **inferences** from what the writer tells you. A good way to help you understand a character's personality is to create an inference map like the one below.

1. Complete the map by adding five details about Victor's appearance, thoughts, or actions. For each detail, make an inference about him.
2. Basing your answer on your inferences, how would you describe Victor's personality?

Ideas for Writing

Imagine that Teresa has found out that Victor doesn't really know French.

Personal Letter Take the role of Teresa and write a personal letter to Victor explaining how you feel about what he has done.

Advice Column Imagine that Teresa has now lost interest in Victor. Write an advice column for the school newspaper to give Victor suggestions on how to win her back. Write your column as if you were answering a letter from Victor.

Ideas for Projects

Collage In this story, you learned about one character's reactions to being in the seventh grade. Work with a group of classmates to plan and create a collage that expresses your group's ideas about what it means to be a seventh grader. [Art Link]

Community Work Like Victor's summer job of picking grapes in Fresno, employment in an area is often related to a local product or industry. Find out about the kinds of summer jobs that are available in your community. Present your findings in a report to the class. [Social Studies Link]

How Am I Doing?

Answer these questions to help you evaluate how well you're doing:

What did I learn about character by using an inference map? For what other kinds of reading can I use this map?

Which example of my work will I choose to put in a portfolio? Why?

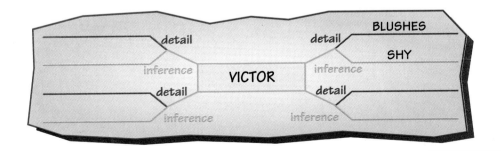

Have you ever felt that no one knew "the real you"?

Reach Into Your Background

Believe it or not, reading a poem can help you answer questions about "the real you." How can poets do so much with just a few words? One way is by making comparisons that surprise you into a new way of thinking. Gary Hyland does this when he compares the names that parents give children with the names they give themselves.

Poets can also challenge you to ask a what-if question and then see where the answer takes you. In "A Story That Could Be True," William Stafford invites you to ask such a question about yourself: What if you were really different from the way everyone thinks you are?

- In a journal, write your thoughts about this what-if question.
- With a small group, list the nicknames teenagers might like to have.

Read Actively
Read Poetry Aloud

A poem is not just words on a page. Like a song, a poem comes to life when it's heard. Read these poems aloud to a partner, pausing where the poet has used end punctuation, like periods and colons. Also pause between the groups of lines called stanzas.

To help you with your performance, try imagining that each of these poems is a popular song and that each group of lines is a new verse of the song.

Their Names

Gary Hyland

Scrawny Bumper Zip
names more alive
than parents' labels:
Lawrence Russell Marvin

5 terms to cringe at
chosen for reflected fame
or family pride
affixed like talismans:
George Stanley Albert

10 Deke Magoo Fet
handles casually acquired
from playgrounds and poolhalls
the namers now unknown
the occasions obscure

15 names taboo to teachers
sure to repel parents
earned by them
conferred by them

their names

Respond

What is your favorite nickname from "Their Names"? Why?

Gary Hyland (1940–) is a street-smart poet, as the reference to "playgrounds and poolhalls" in his poem suggests. In fact, this Canadian refers to streets in a number of his book titles: *Home Street* (1975), *Just Off Main* (1982), and *Street of Dreams* (1984).

Words to Know

talismans (TAL is muhnz) *n.*: Any things thought to have magic power (line 8)
obscure (ahb SKYOOR) *adj.*: Not clear, hidden (line 14)
taboo (tuh BOO) *adj.*: Forbidden (line 15)

A Story That Could Be True

William Stafford

William Stafford (1914–1993) used the what-if method not only in his poetry but in his life as well. His son Kim says that he and his father would sometimes go out looking for arrowheads (Stafford had ancestors who were Native American). When they reached a likely place, Stafford would say, "Now what if I were an arrowhead, where would I be hiding?" Then he would bend down and find one.

If you were exchanged in the cradle and
your real mother died
without ever telling the story
then no one knows your name,
5 and somewhere in the world
your father is lost and needs you
but you are far away.

He can never find
how true you are, how ready.
10 When the great wind comes
and the robberies of the rain
you stand on the corner shivering.
The people who go by—
you wonder at their calm.

15 They miss the whisper that runs
any day in your mind,
"Who are you really, wanderer?"
and the answer you have to give
no matter how dark and cold
20 the world around you is:
"Maybe I'm a king."

Respond

What is "a story that could be true" about you?

Activities
MAKE MEANING

Explore Your Reading
Look Back (Recall)

1. In "Their Names" what are the names that parents give children? What are the names that children give one another?
2. In your own words, tell the "story" of "A Story That Could Be True."

Think It Over (Interpret)

3. Compare the nicknames in "Their Names" with the names that parents give.
4. Why does the poem say that the names children give themselves are "more alive / than parents' labels"?
5. How is "A Story That Could Be True" like a fairy tale?
6. Which line or lines of "A Story That Could Be True" sum up the poem's message? Explain.

Go Beyond (Apply)

7. How is the last line of each poem an answer to the question "Who is the real me?" Compare and contrast these answers.
8. Find out if your own name has any special meanings that you don't know about. Ask a family member or a friend about this, or look up your name in a dictionary or a book on names.

Develop Reading and Literary Skills
Read Aloud to Appreciate Stanza Form

As you read these poems aloud, you probably paused where groups of lines are separated by a space. These groups, called **stanzas**, are like paragraphs in prose or verses in a song. Each stanza can develop an idea, express a feeling, or tell another part of a story.

With a partner, take turns reading these poems aloud again. First read the poems without pausing at the ends of stanzas. Then read them again, stopping briefly to show where a stanza ends. Notice how each stanza adds something new to the poem.

1. Which of these poems uses stanzas to tell parts of a story? Which uses stanzas to develop a comparison? Explain your answer.
2. Write a brief stanza that you can insert in one of these poems. Then include your stanza as you read the poem aloud to your partner. Ask your partner if the new stanza adds to the comparison the poet is making or the story he is telling.

Ideas for Writing

Think of some positive trait you have that others don't know about or tend to overlook. Then challenge yourself with a what-if question, just as William Stafford does in his poem: What if people were more familiar with this side of you? How would your life be different from the way it is now?

Class-Book Feature Write a prediction for your class book. Tell readers how your life would change if people knew this positive trait.

Tall Tale In a tall tale—an exaggerated story—for your school literary magazine, show how you use this positive trait to conquer impossible odds.

Ideas for Projects

Billboard Working with a small group, design a billboard that expresses the spirit of your neighborhood, town, or city. Include a variety of names or nicknames to help convey that spirit.
[Art Link]

Storyboard Create a comic strip that tells about a person "exchanged in the cradle" who is really "a king."

Pantomime Routine Using gestures but not language, express a hidden positive side of your personality.

How Am I Doing?

Respond to these questions in your journal:
How did reading these poems aloud help me to understand them better?
What other kinds of literature could I read aloud?

Activities PREVIEW

My Name Mi Nombre by Sandra Cisneros
All Names Are American Names by Kie Ho

What name would you choose to fit "the real you"?

Latinoamerica 1993, Orlando Agudelo-Botero
Engman International Fine Art, Coral Gables, Florida

Reach Into Your Background

Where did you get your name? Some children are named for their great-grandparents, others for family friends, religious figures, or famous people from history. Also, different cultures have different ways of naming children. For instance, taking the family name of both parents is common in Spanish-speaking countries and communities.

Share what you know about names with a group of classmates by doing one or more of the following activities:

- Create a name book listing your favorite names.
- Tell the story of how you got your name.
- Discuss the naming customs of different groups of people.

Read Actively
Respond to the Connotations of Words

Names, like other words, can call up feelings and images in you. Such feelings and images, called **connotations,** can vary from person to person. By keeping aware of the connotations of words, you will be able to respond to a piece of literature emotionally.

As you read these selections, for instance, listen to the sounds of the names. In a chart like the one shown, jot down the connotations the names have for you and those they have for the narrators.

Name	Connotations for the Narrators	Connotations for Me
Esperanza		
Magdalena		
Kie Ho		

MY NAME

from *The House on Mango Street*

SANDRA CISNEROS

In English my name means hope. In Spanish it means too many letters. It means sadness, it means waiting. It is like the number nine. A muddy color. It is the Mexican records my father plays on Sunday mornings when he is shaving, songs like sobbing.

It was my great-grandmother's name and now it is mine. She was a horse woman too, born like me in the Chinese year of the horse—which is supposed to be bad luck if you're born female—but I think this is a Chinese lie because the Chinese, like the Mexicans, don't like their women strong.

My great-grandmother. I would've liked to have known her, a wild horse of a woman, so wild she wouldn't marry. Until my great-grandfather threw a sack over her head and carried her off. Just like that, as if she were a fancy chandelier. That's the way he did it.

And the story goes she never forgave him. She looked out the window her whole life, the way so many women sit their sadness on an elbow. I wonder if she made the best with what she got or was she sorry because she couldn't be all the things she wanted to be.

Esperanza. I have inherited her name, but I don't want to inherit her place by the window.

At school they say my name funny as if the syllables were made out of tin and hurt the roof of your mouth. But in Spanish my name is made out of a softer something, like silver, not quite as thick as my sister's name—Magdalena—which is uglier than mine. Magdalena who at least can come home and become Nenny. But I am always Esperanza.

I would like to baptize myself under a new name, a name more like the real me, the one nobody sees. Esperanza as Lisandra or Maritza or Zeze the X. Yes. Something like Zeze the X will do.

Words to Know

chandelier (shan duh LEER) *n.*: A lighting fixture hung from the ceiling with branches for several lights
inherited (in HER uh tuhd) *v.*: Received by custom, law, or genetics from parents or an older generation
baptize (BAP tīz) *v.*: Give a name

MI NOMBRE

de *La Casa en Mango Street*

SANDRA CISNEROS

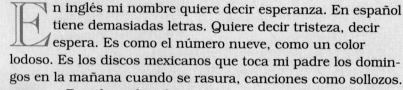

En inglés mi nombre quiere decir esperanza. En español tiene demasiadas letras. Quiere decir tristeza, decir espera. Es como el número nueve, como un color lodoso. Es los discos mexicanos que toca mi padre los domingos en la mañana cuando se rasura, canciones como sollozos.

Era el nombre de mi bisabuela y ahora es mío. Una mujer caballo nacida como yo en el año chino del caballo—que se supone es de mala suerte si naces mujer—pero creo que esa es una mentira china porque a los chinos, como a los mexicanos, no les gusta que sus mujeres sean fuertes.

Mi bisabuela. Me habría gustado conocerla, un caballo salvaje de mujer, tan salvaje que no se casó sino hasta que mi bisabuelo la echó de cabeza a un costal y así se la llevó nomás, como si fuera un candelabro elegante, así lo hizo.

Dice la historia que ella jamás lo perdonó. Toda su vida miró por la ventana hacia afuera, del mismo modo en que muchas mujeres apoyan su tristeza en su codo. Yo me pregunto si ella hizo lo mejor que pudo con lo que le tocó, o si estaba arrepentida porque no fue todas las cosas que quiso ser. Esperanza. Heredé su nombre, pero no quiero heredar su lugar junto a la ventana.

En la escuela pronuncian raro mi nombre, como si las sílabas estuvieran hechas de hojalata y lastimaran el techo de la boca. Pero en español mi nombre está hecho de algo más suave, como la plata, no tan grueso como el de mi hermanita—Magdalena—que es más feo que el mío. Magdalena, que por lo menos puede llegar a casa y hacerse Nenny. Pero yo siempre soy Esperanza.

Me gustaría bautizarme yo misma con un nombre nuevo, un nombre más parecido a mí, a la de a de veras, a la que nadie ve. Esperanza como Lisandra o Maritza o Zezé la X. Sí, algo así como Zezé la X estaría bien.

All Names Are American Names
KIE HO

At a recent seminar that my company sponsored, where many of the participants came from our overseas offices, a gentleman from the Netherlands looked at my name tag and said, "I see that you are from our division in California, but your name does not sound American." I told him that mine is indeed a Chinese name; however, I am an American citizen.

I should have told him that my name is as American as Lucille LeSueur or Margarita Carman Cansino before they became Joan Crawford and Rita Hayworth. My name does sound as foreign as the name of the Japanese slugger Sadaharu Oh, but does it not also sound as American as Joe DiMaggio?

I have already simplified my name for Yankee ears. I was born Kie Liang Ho, which means Ho the First-Class Bridge. I skip the name Liang because it is so difficult for many to pronounce correctly. Even so, the short name has caused much confusion. Some secretaries write it as Keyhole. Others, deciding that such a short last name is impossible, change it arbitrarily to something more common, like Holm or Holt.

When I was sworn as an American citizen, I could have become Keith Ho, or Kenneth Ho, or even Don Ho. I decided to keep my Chinese name; this is one privilege that my new country gives me— the right to maintain my ethnic identity—and I cherish it.

Having a Chinese name does not necessarily mean that culturally I am a Chinese. I was born in Indonesia (which a lot of people misunderstand to be Indochina), and I do not write or speak Chinese. The only Chinese characters[1] I can write are my name and my father's. Still, to everyone I am a Chinese. When somebody in my office has a birthday and we are all signing a card, people often say, "Come on, Kie, write something in Chinese." What I write is my dad's name, and I tell them that it means "Abundance of Fortune and Long Life." Actually, my father's name means Ho the Gold Fish.

Many people are confused by Asian names and nationalities. One day, my wife and I asked a patio contractor to give us a reference. He turned over page after page of his reference book and at

---

1. **characters** *n.*: Picture symbols used in Chinese writing.

Words to Know

seminar (SEM uh nahr) *n.*: A training session or group discussion

last, with a friendly, victorious smile, he said, "Here you are, this one is a Chinese lady, Mrs. Nguyen." I hated to disappoint him by telling him that Nguyen is a Vietnamese name, and, since we do not speak Vietnamese at all, she might not be the best to call.

When our daughter was born, we did not give her a Chinese name. We thought that the name should be selected for the child, not for the parents' sake. We would have liked to name her May Hoa Ho, "Ho the Pretty Flower," but imagine the problems that she would face in school among children who like to make fun of "funny" names. So we gave her a "common" American name: Melanie. We hope that she will be as gentle as Melanie Wilkes in "Gone With the Wind." I wonder if Melanie Wilkes' mother ever knew that "Melanie" refers to something black: Would she still have named her so? Only Margaret Mitchell could tell.

So what's in a name? Benjamin Kubelsky changed his name (Jack Benny). Zbigniew Brzezinski[2] did not. I will not, either.

_____
2. **Zbigniew Brzezinski** (zuh BEEG nyev breh ZHEEN skee): National security adviser to President Carter, 1977–1981.

Respond

- How were your responses to the names similar to and different from Esperanza's?
- What advice would you give Kie Ho about his name?

KIE HO was a businessman living in Laguna Hills, California when this article was published in 1982.

SANDRA CISNEROS (1954–)
Family Math:
Having six brothers and a father was more like having "seven fathers," as Cisneros saw it.
Childhood Memories:
She remembers moving very often, being new at school frequently, and feeling shy.
Books She Uses for Writing:
Cisneros consults mail-order catalogs and the San Antonio (Texas) phone book. Can you guess why?
Outlook on the Future:
"I'm looking forward to the books I'll write when I'm seventy," Cisneros says.

Explore Your Reading

Look Back (Recall)

1. How does Esperanza describe her great-grandmother before and after marriage?

Think It Over (Interpret)

2. Why does Esperanza distinguish between the Spanish and English meanings of her name?
3. What does she mean when she says that she doesn't "want to inherit" her great-grandmother's "place by the window"?
4. What is Esperanza's main reason for wanting to change her name?
5. What is Kie Ho's main reason for not wanting to change his name?

Go Beyond (Apply)

6. Both Esperanza and Kie Ho believe their names help define them. How do other people's names influence the way you see them?

Develop Reading and Literary Skills

Appreciate Connotation and Denotation

You may not have agreed with Esperanza or Kie Ho about the feelings and images suggested by their names. The **connotations** of words, the emotions they call up, are not as exact as their **denotations,** or dictionary meanings. Different people may have different connotations for the same word.

For example, Esperanza means "hope" in Spanish, and some people might have good feelings about that meaning. Esperanza, however, associates her name with her great-grandmother who hoped but never achieved her goals.

1. What images does the name Kie Ho suggest?
2. Read aloud the following words from "My Name" and write down the images and emotions they suggest to you: *silver, Sunday, tin.* Share your responses with others.
3. What are the differences between your responses and the dictionary meanings of each word?

Ideas for Writing

These selections show you narrators who feel strongly about their names.

Persuasive Letter Do you think Esperanza should change her name? Write a letter to her that explains your feelings. In defending your view, refer to the sounds of the different names. You might want to write to Kie Ho, expressing your ideas about his desire to keep his name.

Dialogue Create a conversation between Esperanza and Kie Ho as they advise each other about the importance of names. Would they come to agree about the value of their names? Work with a partner to write and perform your dialogue.

Ideas for Projects

Book of Names Read dictionaries and books about naming to discover the meaning of different names. Use what you've learned to create a book of names for new parents. [Social Studies Link]

Dance Esperanza talks about the feelings that her name calls up and renames herself Zeze the X. Create a dance that expresses the meaning of her new name.

Stage Name Report Kie Ho tells you how Benjamin Kubelsky changed his name to Jack Benny before he became famous. Find out which of today's celebrities changed their names for fame. Share your findings with the class.

How Am I Doing?

Spend a moment writing your answers to these questions:

What did I learn about the connotations, or feelings, of words? How can I use what I learned in reading poetry?

What did I learn about how names help define someone?

Who are the legends and heroes of our time?

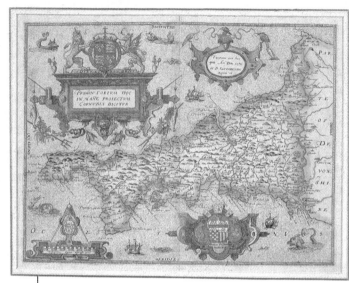

Map of Arthur's kingdom

Reach Into Your Background

Every time has its legendary characters, real people whose achievements inspire amazing stories. King Arthur, who united warring kingdoms in England about 1,500 years ago, became such a legend. Even today, movies, books, and cartoons recount tales of Arthur, Merlin the magician, and the Knights of the Round Table. With a small group, do one or both of the following activities.

- Share what you know about this legendary king. Recall movies you've seen and books you've read about Arthur and his knights.
- Look at the map of Arthur's kingdom on this page and locate his capital city of Camelot. Discuss what the decorations on the map tell you about medieval England.

Read Actively
Connect Literature to Social Studies

You can better understand certain pieces of literature by connecting them to what you've learned in social studies. In social studies classes, for instance, you've probably discussed what makes a good leader. You've also read history books and seen movies about legendary leaders like Robin Hood and George Washington.

Share what you know about such leaders with a group and list the qualities that they have in common. As you read this legend, check off the qualities that Arthur shares with the other leaders you discussed. Also, look for details that tell you what life was like in medieval England.

King Arthur
The Marvel of the Sword
Mary MacLeod

hen Uther[1] Pendragon, King of England, died, the country for a long while stood in great danger, for every lord that was mighty gathered his forces, and many wished to be king. For King Uther's own son, Prince Arthur, who should have succeeded him, was but a child, and Merlin, the mighty magician, had hidden him away.

Now a strange thing had happened at Arthur's birth.

Some time before, Merlin had done Uther a great service, on condition that the King should grant him whatever he wished for. This the King swore a solemn oath to do. Then Merlin made him promise that when his child was born it should be delivered to Merlin to bring up as he chose, for this would be to the child's own great advantage. The King had given his promise so he

MERLIN TAKETH THE CHILD ARTHVR INTO HIS KEEPING

Drawing from an 1894 edition of Sir Thomas Malory's *Le Morte D'arthur*
Aubrey Beardsley, The Granger Collection, New York

---

1. Uther (YOO thuhr)

was obliged to agree. Then Merlin said he knew a very true and faithful man, one of King Uther's lords, by name Sir Ector,[2] who had large possessions in many parts of England and Wales, and that the child should be given to him to bring up.

On the night the baby was born, while it was still unchristened, King Uther commanded two knights and two ladies to take it,

📖 Read Actively
Predict how Arthur will be raised.

wrapped in a cloth of gold, and deliver it to a poor man whom they would find waiting at the postern gate of the Castle. This poor man was Merlin in disguise, although they did not know it. So the child was delivered unto Merlin and he carried him to Sir Ector, and made a holy man christen him, and named him Arthur; and Sir Ector's wife cherished him as her own child.

Within two years King Uther fell sick of a great malady, and for three days and three nights he was speechless. All the Barons[3] were in sorrow, and asked Merlin what was best to be done.

"There is no remedy," said Merlin. "God will have His Will. But look ye all, Barons, come before King Uther tomorrow, and God will make him speak."

So the next day Merlin and all the Barons came before the King, and Merlin said aloud to King Uther:

"Sir, after your days shall your son Arthur be King of this realm and all that belongs to it?"

---

2. Ector (EK tawr)

3. Barons (BAR uhnz) *n.*: Members of the lowest rank of British nobility.

Words to Know

malady (MAL uh dee) *n.*: Illness; disease
remedy (REM uh dee) *n.*: A medicine or treatment that cures illness
strife (STRĪF) *n.*: Trouble; conflict; struggle
ordained (or DAYND) *v.*: Ordered; decreed

Then Uther Pendragon turned and said in hearing of them all: "I give my son Arthur God's blessing and mine, and bid him pray for my soul, and righteously and honorably claim the crown, on forfeiture of my blessing."

And with that, King Uther died.

But Arthur was still only a baby, not two years old, and Merlin knew it would be no use yet to proclaim him King. For there were many powerful nobles in England in those days, who were all trying to get the kingdom for themselves, and perhaps they would kill the little Prince. So there was much strife and debate in the land for a long time.

When several years had passed, Merlin went to the Archbishop of Canterbury[4] and counseled him to send for all the lords of the realm,[5] and all the gentlemen of arms, that they should come to London at Christmas, and for this cause—that a miracle would show who should be rightly King of the realm. So all the lords and gentlemen made themselves ready, and came to London, and long before dawn on Christmas Day they were all gathered in the great church of St. Paul's to pray.

When the first service was over, there was seen in the churchyard a large stone, four-square, like marble, and in the midst of it was like an anvil of steel, a foot high. In this was stuck by the point a beautiful sword, with naked blade, and there were letters written in gold about the sword, which said thus:

Whoso pulleth this sword out of this stone and anvil is rightly King of all England.

Then the people marveled, and told it to the Archbishop.

"I command," said the Archbishop, "that you keep within the church, and pray unto

---

4. Canterbury (KAN tuhr ber ee) *n.*: A cathedral and sacred shrine in Canterbury, a town southeast of London. In medieval times, many English people made pilgrimages or journeys to Canterbury.

5. realm (RELM) *n.*: Kingdom.

God still; and that no man touch the sword till the service is over."

So when the prayers in church were over, all the lords went to behold the stone and the sword; and when they read the writing some of them—such as wished to be king—tried to pull the sword out of the anvil. But not one could make it stir.

"The man is not here, that shall achieve the sword," said the Archbishop, "but doubt not God will make him known. But let us provide ten knights, men of good fame, to keep guard over the sword."

So it was ordained, and proclamation was made that everyone who wished might try to win the sword. And upon New Year's Day the Barons arranged to have a great tournament, in which all knights who would joust[6] or tourney[7]

---

6. joust (JOWST) *v.*: To take part in a combat with lances between two knights on horseback.

7. tourney (TOOR nee) *v.*: To compete; to take part in a tournament.

How Arthur drew forth ye Sword, 1903 Howard Pyle
The Granger Collection, New York

might take a part. This was ordained to keep together the Lords and Commons, for the Archbishop trusted that it would be made known who should win the sword.

On New Year's Day, after church, the Barons rode to the field, some to joust, and some to tourney, and so it happened that Sir Ector, who had large estates near London, came also to the tournament; and with him rode Sir Kay, his son, with young Arthur, his foster brother.

As they rode, Sir Kay found he had lost his sword, for he had left it at his father's lodging, so he begged young Arthur to go and fetch it for him.

"That will I, gladly," said Arthur, and he rode fast away.

But when he came to the house, he found no one at home to give him the sword, for everyone had gone to see the jousting. Then Arthur was angry and said to himself:

"I will ride to the churchyard, and take the sword with me that sticketh in the stone, for my brother, Sir Kay, shall not be without a sword this day."

When he came to the churchyard he alighted,[8] and tied his horse to the stile, and went to the tent. But he found there no knights, who should have been guarding the sword, for they were all away at the joust. Seizing the sword by the handle he lightly and fiercely pulled it out of the stone, then took his horse and rode his way, till he came to Sir Kay his brother, to whom he delivered the sword.

As soon as Sir Kay saw it, he knew well it was the sword of the Stone, so he rode to his father Sir Ector, and said:

"Sir, lo, here is the Sword of the Stone, wherefore[9] I must be King of this land."

---

8. alighted (a LĪ tuhd) *v.*: Dismounted; got down off a horse.
9. wherefore: Why.

When Sir Ector saw the sword he turned back, and came to the church, and there they all three alighted and went into the church, and he made his son swear truly how he got the sword.

📖 **Read Actively**

Respond to Sir Kay's action. What kind of person do you think he is?

"By my brother Arthur," said Sir Kay, "for he brought it to me."

"How did you get this sword?" said Sir Ector to Arthur.

And the boy told him.

"Now," said Sir Ector, "I understand you must be King of this land."

"Wherefore I?" said Arthur. "And for what cause?"

"Sir," said Ector, "because God will have it so; for never man could draw out this sword but he that shall rightly be King. Now let me see whether you can put the sword there as it was, and pull it out again."

"There is no difficulty," said Arthur, and he put it back into the stone.

Then Sir Ector tried to pull out the sword, and failed; and Sir Kay also pulled with all his might, but it would not move.

"Now you shall try," said Sir Ector to Arthur.

"I will, well," said Arthur, and pulled the sword out easily.

At this Sir Ector and Sir Kay knelt down on the ground.

from
A Connecticut Yankee

Imagine you could be a time traveler. How would King Arthur's England seem to you? American humorist Mark Twain asked himself that question and wrote a novel about a nineteenth-century American who gets knocked out in a fight. When he wakes up, he is no longer where he thinks he is.

hen I came to again, I was sitting under an oak tree, on the grass, with a whole beautiful and broad country landscape all to myself—nearly. Not entirely; for there was a fellow on a horse, looking down at me—a fellow fresh out of a picture book. He was in old-time iron armor from head to heel, with a helmet on his head the shape of a nail keg with slits in it; and he had a shield, and a sword, and a prodigious spear; and his horse had armor on, too, and a steel horn projecting from his forehead, and gorgeous red and green silk trappings that hung down all round him like a bed quilt, nearly to the ground.

"Fair sir, will ye just?" said this fellow.

"Will I which?"

"Will ye try a passage of arms for land or lady or for—"

"What are you giving me?" I said. "Get along back to your circus, or I'll report you."

Now what does this man do but fall back a couple of hundred yards and then come rushing at me as hard as he could tear, with his nail keg bent down nearly to his

"Alas," said Arthur, "mine own dear father and brother, why do you kneel to me?"

"Nay, nay, my lord Arthur, it is not so; I was never your father, nor of your blood; but I know well you are of higher blood than I thought you were."

Then Sir Ector told him all, how he had taken him to bring up, and by whose command; and how he had received him from Merlin. And when he understood that Ector was not his father, Arthur was deeply grieved.

Words to Know

grieved (GREEVD) *adj.*: Saddened; overcome by grief

"Will you be my good, gracious lord, when you are King?" asked the knight.

"If not, I should be to blame," said Arthur, "for you are the man in the world to whom I am the most beholden, and my good lady and mother your wife, who has fostered and kept me as well as her own children. And if ever it be God's will that I be King, as you say, you shall desire of me what I shall do, and I shall not fail you: God forbid I should fail you."

"Sir," said Sir Ector, "I will ask no more of you but that you will make my son, your foster brother Sir Kay, seneschal[10] of all your lands."

---

10. **seneschal** (SEN uh shuhl) *n.*: A person in charge of household arrangements.

in King Arthur's Court
Mark Twain

horse's neck and his long spear pointed straight ahead. I saw he meant business, so I was up the tree when he arrived.

He allowed that I was his property, the captive of his spear. There was argument on his side—and the bulk of the advantage—so I judged it best to humor him. We fixed up an agreement whereby I was to go with him and he was not to hurt me. I came down, and we started away, I walking by the side of his horse. We marched comfortably along, through glades and over brooks which I could not remember to have seen before—which puzzled me and made me wonder—and yet we did not come to any circus or sign of a circus. So I gave up the idea of a circus, and concluded he was from an asylum. But we never came to any asylum—so I was up a stump, as you may say. I asked him how far we were from Hartford. He said he had never heard of the place; which I took to be a lie, but allowed it to go at that. At the end of an hour we saw a faraway town sleeping in a valley by a winding river; and beyond it a hill, a vast gray fortress, with towers and turrets, the first I had ever seen out of a picture.

"Bridgeport?" said I, pointing.

"Camelot," said he.

"That shall be done," said Arthur, "and by my faith, never man but he shall have that office while he and I live."

Then they went to the Archbishop and told him how the sword was achieved, and by whom.

On Twelfth Day all the Barons came to the stone in the churchyard, so that anyone who wished might try to win the sword. But not one of them all could take it out, except Arthur. Many of them therefore were very angry, and said it was a great shame to them and to the country to be governed by a boy not of high blood, for as yet none of them knew that he was the son of King Uther Pendragon. So they agreed to delay the decision till Candlemas, which is the second day of February.

But when Candlemas came, and Arthur once more was the only one who could pull out the sword, they put it off till Easter; and when Easter came, and Arthur again prevailed in the presence of them all, they put it off till the Feast of Pentecost.

Then by Merlin's advice the Archbishop summoned some of the best knights that were to be—such knights as in his own day King Uther Pendragon had best loved, and trusted most—and these were appointed to attend young Arthur, and never to leave him night or day till the Feast of Pentecost.

When the great day came, all manner of men once more made the attempt, and once more not one of them all could prevail but Arthur. Before all the Lords and Commons there assembled he pulled out the sword, whereupon all the Commons cried out:

"We will have Arthur for our King! We will put him no more in delay, for we all see that it is God's will that he shall be our King, and he who holdeth against it, we will slay him."

And therewith they knelt down all at once, both rich and poor, and besought pardon of Arthur, because they had delayed him so long.

📖 **Read Actively**

Connect your reading to Social Studies. What qualities of leadership is Arthur demonstrating?

And Arthur forgave them, and took the sword in both his hands, and offered it on the altar where the Archbishop was and so he was made knight by the best man there.

After that, he was crowned at once, and there he swore to his Lords and Commons to be a true King, and to govern with true justice from thenceforth all the days of his life.

King Arthur

A legend never dies. Although Arthur may have reigned in the Middle Ages, stories about him continue to entertain 20th century audiences. Some examples are

Arthur, from Lancelot du Lac MS. Rawl. Q.b. 6, fol. 50r (detail)
Bodleian Library, Oxford

- *The Once and Future King* (1958) a novel based on the legend.
- *Camelot* (1960), a hit musical version of his life.
- *First Knight* (1995), a movie about Arthur's court.

Mary MacLeod (died 1914) devoted herself to updating for readers the great works of early English literature.

Respond

- If you were Arthur, how would you feel about discovering you were king? Why?
- Imagine you could travel back in time to King Arthur's England. With a group, brainstorm a list of details from the story that would surprise you.

Activities

MAKE MEANING

Explore Your Reading

Look Back (Recall)

1. Why does Merlin give Arthur to Sir Ector rather than proclaim him King?
2. Trace the events that lead up to Arthur's first pulling the sword from the stone.

Think It Over (Interpret)

3. Why doesn't Merlin tell Arthur his true identity?
4. Why does Sir Ector ask Arthur to pull out the sword again and again?
5. Why do the Barons also make this request?
6. Once Arthur knows the truth, does he behave in a kingly way? Explain.

Go Beyond (Apply)

7. Arthur is recognized as king after pulling a magic sword from a stone. In what ways do we choose and test our leaders today?

Develop Reading and Literary Skills

Connect Social Studies to Legend

Like other legendary leaders, Arthur accomplishes a deed no one else can equal. He pulls a magical sword from a stone. **Legends,** filled with marvelous deeds, are exaggerated stories based on real people and events.

Legends often are told about popular leaders like King Arthur. They express, through the leader's qualities, what a nation or group of people valued most. This legend suggests that the medieval English valued modesty because Arthur doesn't boast about pulling the sword from the stone.

1. Name two things about the test of the sword that might be exaggerated or untrue. Explain.
2. Basing your answer on Arthur's personality, identify two qualities other than modesty that the English might have valued in their rulers.

Ideas for Writing

Arthur became king of England by pulling a sword from a stone. However, he might have been able to prove he was king in another way.

Advertising Copy As a nobleman of England, write a newspaper advertisement for a king. Describe a test the applicant will have to pass, and give your ad the right flavor by imitating the language of the legend.

Legend Write your own Arthurian legend by describing how Arthur passes a different kind of test.

Ideas for Projects

Newscast With a group of classmates, present an on-the-spot, live news broadcast on the day that Arthur removes the sword. The interviewer should talk to Sirs Ector and Kay, Merlin, and Arthur himself. [Social Studies Link]

Debate Role-play the debate the Barons may have had while deciding if Arthur could really be king. One side should support him and the other argue against him. Present your debate to a small group of classmates. [Social Studies Link]

Coat of Arms Now that Arthur is king, he has asked you to create a coat of arms for him—a decoration that he can wear on his shield. Choose the objects you will include and draw them on a shield for his approval. [Art Link]

How Am I Doing?

Share your responses to these questions with a group of classmates:

What information about history did I relate to this selection? How can I use my knowledge of history to help me with future readings?

What did I learn about legends?

Was there a moment in your life when you suddenly saw "the real you"?

Untitled Pamela Chin Lee, Courtesy of the artist

Reach Into Your Background

In many movies, characters suddenly learn something new about themselves, something that changes how they think and feel. For instance, a soldier in a battle might realize he is disgusted by all the killing and decide to get transferred out of his unit.

- With a partner, list all the movies you can remember in which characters suddenly look at themselves in new ways. Think about the reason for this insight and describe how their behavior changes.
- As an alternative, write in your journal about a time when you learned something new about yourself.

Read Actively
Observe A Character's Growth

Like people in movies, characters in stories can also surprise you by thinking about themselves differently and changing how they act or feel. Your reading will be more meaningful when you recognize moments in which characters grow or see themselves in new ways.

In "Two Kinds," the daughter suddenly sees herself in a different way. Although this change occurs in a single dramatic moment, it results from a gradual buildup of pressure. Identify her moment of insight by filling in a diagram like the one shown. In each box, note a way in which she is feeling pressure. Then, on the line beneath the boxes, describe the moment when she suddenly thinks about herself differently.

Moment of Growth: _____

Two Kinds
from The Joy Luck Club
AMY TAN

My mother believed you could be anything you wanted to be in America. You could open a restaurant. You could work for the government and get good retirement. You could buy a house with almost no money down. You could become rich. You could become instantly famous.

"Of course you can be prodigy, too," my mother told me when I was nine. "You can be best anything. What does Auntie Lindo know? Her daughter, she is only best tricky."

America was where all my mother's hopes lay. She had come here in 1949 after losing everything in China: her mother and father, her family home, her first husband, and two daughters, twin baby girls. But she never looked back with regret. There were so many ways for things to get better.

We didn't immediately pick the right kind of prodigy. At first my mother thought I could be a Chinese Shirley Temple.[1] We'd watch Shirley's old movies on TV as though they were training films. My mother would poke my arm and say, "*Ni kan*"[2]—You watch. And I would see Shirley tapping her feet, or singing a sailor song, or pursing her lips into a very round O while saying, "Oh my goodness."

"*Ni kan*," said my mother as Shirley's eyes flooded with tears. "You already know how. Don't need talent for crying!"

Soon after my mother got this idea about Shirley Temple, she took me to a beauty training school in the Mission district[3] and put me in the hands of a student who could barely hold the scissors without shaking. Instead of getting big fat curls, I emerged with an uneven mass of crinkly black fuzz. My mother dragged me off to the bathroom and tried to wet down my hair.

"You look like Negro Chinese," she lamented, as if I had done this on purpose.

The instructor of the beauty training school had to lop off these soggy clumps to make my hair even again. "Peter Pan is very popular these days," the instructor assured my mother. I now had hair the length of a boy's, with straight-across bangs that hung

Words to Know

prodigy (PRAH di jee) *n.*: A child of unusually high talent

---

1. Shirley Temple: American child star of the 1930's, she starred in her first movie at age three and won an Academy Award at age six.

2. Ni kan (NEE KAHN)

3. Mission district: A residential district in San Francisco, California.

at a slant two inches above my eyebrows. I liked the haircut and it made me actually look forward to my future fame.

In fact, in the beginning, I was just as excited as my mother, maybe even more so. I pictured this prodigy part of me as many different images, trying each one on for size. I was a dainty ballerina girl standing by the curtains, waiting to hear the right music that would send me floating on my tiptoes. I was like the Christ child lifted out of the straw manger, crying with holy indignity. I was Cinderella stepping from her pumpkin carriage with sparkly cartoon music filling the air.

In all of my imaginings, I was filled with a sense that I would soon become *perfect*. My mother and father would adore me. I would be beyond reproach. I would never feel the need to sulk for anything.

But sometimes the prodigy in me became impatient. "If you don't hurry up and get me out of here, I'm disappearing for good," it warned. "And then you'll always be nothing."

Every night after dinner, my mother and I would sit at the Formica kitchen table. She would present new tests, taking her examples from stories of amazing children she had read in *Ripley's Believe It or Not*, or *Good Housekeeping, Reader's Digest*, and a dozen other magazines she kept in a pile in our bathroom. My mother got these magazines from people whose houses she cleaned. And since she cleaned many houses each week, we had a great assortment. She would look through them all, searching for stories about remarkable children.

The first night she brought out a story about a three-year-old boy who knew the capitals of all the states and even most of the European countries. A teacher was quoted as saying the little boy could also pronounce the names of the foreign cities correctly.

"What's the capital of Finland?" my mother asked me, looking at the magazine story.

All I knew was the capital of California, because Sacramento was the name of the street we lived on in Chinatown. "Nairobi!"[4] I guessed, saying the most foreign word I could think of. She checked to see if that was possibly one way to pronounce "Helsinki"[5] before showing me the answer.

The tests got harder—multiplying numbers in my head, finding the queen of hearts in a deck of cards, trying to stand on my head without using my hands, predicting the daily temperatures in Los Angeles, New York, and London.

One night I had to look at a page from the Bible for three minutes and then report everything I could remember. "Now Jehoshaphat had riches and honor in abundance and . . . that's all I remember, Ma," I said.

---

4. Nairobi (nī ROH bee): The capital of Kenya, a country in east central Africa.

5. Helsinki (hel SIN kee)

And after seeing my mother's disappointed face once again, something inside of me began to die. I hated the tests, the raised hopes and failed expectations. Before going to bed that night, I looked in the mirror above the bathroom sink and when I saw only my face staring back—and that it would always be this ordinary face—I began to cry. Such a sad, ugly girl! I made high-pitched noises like a crazed animal, trying to scratch out the face in the mirror.

And then I saw what seemed to be the prodigy side of me—because I had never seen that face before. I looked at my reflection, blinking so I could see more clearly. The girl staring back at me was angry, powerful. This girl and I were the same. I had new thoughts, willful thoughts, or rather thoughts filled with lots of won'ts. I won't let her change me, I promised myself. I won't be what I'm not.

So now on nights when my mother presented her tests, I performed listlessly, my head propped on one arm. I pretended to be bored. And I was. I got so bored I started counting the bellows of the foghorns out on the bay while my mother drilled me in other areas. The sound was comforting and reminded me of the cow jumping over the moon. And the next day, I played a game with myself, seeing if my mother would give up on me before eight bellows. After a while I usually counted only one, maybe two bellows at most. At last she was beginning to give up hope.

Two or three months had gone by without any mention of my being a prodigy again. And then one day my mother was watching *The Ed Sullivan Show*[6] on TV. The TV was old and the sound kept shorting out. Every time my mother got halfway up from the sofa to adjust the set, the sound would go back on and Ed would be talking. As soon as she sat down, Ed would go silent again. She got up, the TV broke into loud piano music. She sat down. Silence. Up and down, back and forth, quiet and loud. It was like a stiff embraceless dance between her and the TV set.

Storefront Window, Chinatown, N.Y., 1993 Don Jacot
Courtesy Louis K. Meisel Gallery, New York

6. The Ed Sullivan Show: A popular variety show hosted by Ed Sullivan that ran from 1955 to 1971.

Words to Know

reproach (rih PROHCH) *n.*: Disgrace; blame

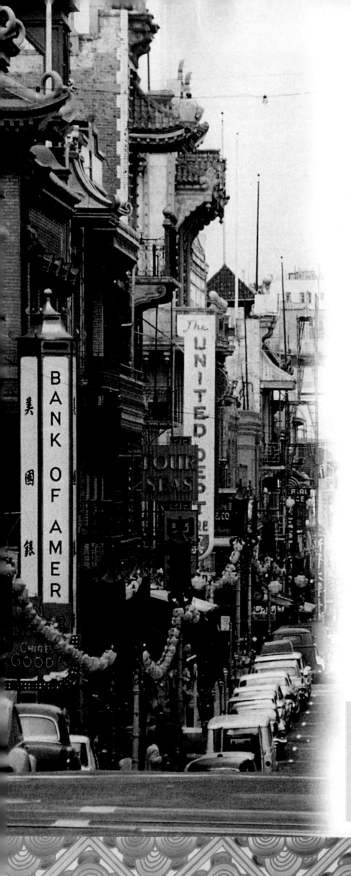

Finally she stood by the set with her hand on the sound dial.

She seemed entranced by the music, a little frenzied piano piece with this mesmerizing quality, sort of quick passages and then teasing lilting ones before it returned to the quick playful parts.

"*Ni kan,*" my mother said, calling me over with hurried hand gestures. "Look here."

I could see why my mother was fascinated by the music. It was being pounded out by a little Chinese girl, about nine years old, with a Peter Pan haircut. The girl had the sauciness of a Shirley Temple. She was proudly modest like a proper Chinese child. And she also did this fancy sweep of a curtsy, so that the fluffy skirt of her white dress cascaded slowly to the floor like the petals of a large carnation.

In spite of these warning signs, I wasn't worried. Our family had no piano and we couldn't afford to buy one, let alone reams of sheet music and piano lessons. So I could be generous in my comments when my mother bad-mouthed the little girl on TV.

"Play note right, but doesn't sound good! No singing sound," complained my mother.

"What are you picking on her for?" I said carelessly. "She's pretty good. Maybe she's not the best, but she's trying hard." I knew almost immediately I would be sorry I said that.

"Just like you," she said. "Not the best. Because you not trying." She gave a little huff as she let go of the sound dial and sat down on the sofa.

Words to Know

frenzied (FREN zeed) *adj.*: Wild; frantic; hurried; fast
mesmerizing (MEZ muh rīz ing) *adj.*: Hypnotizing
sauciness (SAW see nes) *n.*: Liveliness; boldness; spirit

The little Chinese girl sat down also to play an encore of "Anitra's Dance" by Grieg.[7] I remember the song, because later on I had to learn how to play it.

Three days after watching *The Ed Sullivan Show*, my mother told me what my schedule would be for piano lessons and piano practice. She had talked to Mr. Chong, who lived on the first floor of our apartment building. Mr. Chong was a retired piano teacher and my mother had traded house-cleaning services for weekly lessons and a piano for me to practice on every day, two hours a day, from four until six.

When my mother told me this, I felt as though I had been sent to hell. I whined and then kicked my foot a little when I couldn't stand it anymore.

"Why don't you like me the way I am? I'm *not* a genius! I can't play the piano. And even if I could, I wouldn't go on TV if you paid me a million dollars!" I cried.

My mother slapped me. "Who ask you be genius?" she shouted. "Only ask you be your best. For you sake. You think I want you be genius? Hnnh! What for! Who ask you!"

"So ungrateful," I heard her mutter in Chinese. "If she had as much talent as she has temper, she would be famous now."

Mr. Chong, whom I secretly nicknamed Old Chong, was very strange, always tapping his fingers to the silent music of an invisible orchestra. He looked ancient in my eyes. He had lost most of the hair on top of his head and he wore thick glasses and had eyes that always looked tired and sleepy. But he must have been younger than I thought, since he lived with his mother and was not yet married.

---

7. Grieg (GREEG): Edvard Grieg (1843–1907), Norwegian composer.

I met Old Lady Chong once and that was enough. She had this peculiar smell like a baby that had done something in its pants. And her fingers felt like a dead person's, like an old peach I once found in the back of the refrigerator; the skin just slid off the meat when I picked it up.

I soon found out why Old Chong had retired from teaching piano. He was deaf. "Like Beethoven!"[8] he shouted to me. "We're both listening only in our head!" And he would start to conduct his frantic silent sonatas.

Our lessons went like this. He would open the book and point to different things, explaining their purpose: "Key! Treble! Bass! No sharps or flats! So this is C major! Listen now and play after me!"

And then he would play the C scale a few times, a simple chord, and then, as if inspired

Mother and Daughter Leaf from a Manchu family album Unidentified artist, Ch'ing dynasty, The Metropolitan Museum of Art

by an old, unreachable itch, he gradually added more notes and running trills and a pounding bass until the music was really something quite grand.

I would play after him, the simple scale, the simple chord, and then I just played some nonsense that sounded like a cat running up and down on top of garbage cans. Old Chong smiled and applauded and then said, "Very good! But now you must learn to keep time!"

So that's how I discovered that Old Chong's eyes were too slow to keep up with the wrong notes I was playing. He went through the motions in half-time. To help me

keep rhythm, he stood behind me, pushing down on my right shoulder for every beat. He balanced pennies on top of my wrists so I would keep them still as I slowly played scales and arpeggios. He had me curve my hand around an apple and keep that shape when playing chords. He marched stiffly to show me how to make each finger dance up and down, staccato like an obedient little soldier.

He taught me all these things, and that was how I also learned I could be lazy and get away with mistakes, lots of mistakes. If I hit the wrong notes because I hadn't practiced enough, I never corrected myself. I just kept playing in rhythm. And Old Chong kept conducting his own private reverie.

So maybe I never really gave myself a fair chance. I did pick up the basics pretty quickly, and I might have become a good pianist at that young age. But I was so determined not to try, not to be anybody different that I learned to play only the most ear-splitting preludes, the most discordant hymns.

Over the next year, I practiced like this, dutifully in my own way. And then one day I heard my mother and her friend Lindo Jong both talking in a loud bragging tone of voice so others could hear. It was after church, and I was leaning against the brick wall wearing a dress with stiff white petticoats. Auntie Lindo's daughter, Waverly, who was about my age, was standing farther down the wall about five feet away. We had grown up together and shared all the closeness of two sisters squabbling over crayons and dolls. In other words, for the most part, we hated each other. I thought she was snotty. Waverly Jong

---

8. Beethoven (bay TOH vuhn): Ludwig von Beethoven (1770–1827), German composer who began to lose his hearing in 1801. By 1817 he was completely deaf. Some of his greatest pieces were written during this time.

had gained a certain amount of fame as "Chinatown's Littlest Chinese Chess Champion."

"She bring home too many trophy," lamented Auntie Lindo that Sunday. "All day she play chess. All day I have no time do nothing but dust off her winnings." She threw a scolding look at Waverly, who pretended not to see her.

"You lucky you don't have this problem," said Auntie Lindo with a sigh to my mother.

And my mother squared her shoulders and bragged: "Our problem worser than yours. If we ask Jing-mei wash dish, she hear nothing but music. It's like you can't stop this natural talent."

And right then, I was determined to put a stop to her foolish pride.

A few weeks later, Old Chong and my mother conspired to have me play in a talent show which would be held in the church hall. By then, my parents had saved up enough to buy me a secondhand piano, a black Wurlitzer spinet[9] with a scarred bench. It was the showpiece of our living room.

For the talent show, I was to play a piece called "Pleading Child" from Schumann's[10] *Scenes from Childhood.* It was a simple, moody piece that sounded more difficult than it was. I was supposed to memorize the whole thing, playing the repeat parts twice to make the piece sound longer. But I dawdled over it, playing a few bars and then cheating, looking up to see what notes followed. I never really listened to what I was playing. I daydreamed about being somewhere else, about being someone else.

The part I liked to practice best was the fancy curtsy: right foot out, touch the rose on the carpet with a pointed foot, sweep to the side, left leg bends, look up and smile.

My parents invited all the couples from the Joy Luck Club[11] to witness my debut. Auntie Lindo and Uncle Tin were there. Waverly and her two older brothers had also come. The first two rows were filled with children both younger and older than I was. The littlest ones got to go first. They recited simple nursery rhymes, squawked out tunes on miniature violins, twirled Hula Hoops, pranced in pink ballet tutus, and when they bowed or curtsied, the audience would sigh in unison, "Awww," and then clap enthusiastically.

When my turn came, I was very confident. I remember my childish excitement. It was as

Twenty-one Ancestors with Spirit Tablet
Ch'ing Dynasty (1644–1912), Unidentified artist
The Metropolitan Museum of Art

Words to Know

reverie (REV uh ree) *n.*: Daydream; imaginings
conspired (kuhn SPĪRD) *v.*: Planned together secretly
debut (day BYOO) *n.*: First performance in public

---

9. spinet (SPIN it) *n.*: A small upright piano.
10. Schumann (SHOO mahn): Robert Alexander Schumann (1810–1856), German composer.

---

11. Joy Luck Club: Four Chinese women who have been meeting for years to socialize, play games, and tell stories from the past.

if I knew, without a doubt, that the prodigy side of me really did exist. I had no fear whatsoever, no nervousness. I remember thinking to myself, This is it! This is it! I looked out over the audience, at my mother's blank face, my father's yawn, Auntie Lindo's stiff-lipped smile, Waverly's sulky expression. I had on a white dress layered with sheets of lace, and a pink bow in my Peter Pan haircut. As I sat down I envisioned people jumping to their feet and Ed Sullivan rushing up to introduce me to everyone on TV.

And I started to play. It was so beautiful. I was so caught up in how lovely I looked that at first I didn't worry how I would sound. So it was a surprise to me when I hit the first wrong note and I realized something didn't sound quite right. And then I hit another and another followed that. A chill started at the top of my head and began to trickle down. Yet I

Mandarin Square: Badge with peacock-insignia—3rd civil rank Yale University Art Gallery, New Haven, Conn.

couldn't stop playing, as though my hands were bewitched. I kept thinking my fingers would adjust themselves back, like a train switching to the right track. I played this strange jumble through two repeats, the sour notes staying with me all the way to the end.

When I stood up, I discovered my legs were shaking. Maybe I had just been nervous and the audience, like Old Chong, had seen me go through the right motions and had not heard anything wrong at all. I swept my right foot out, went down on my knee, looked up and smiled. The room was quiet, except for Old Chong, who was beaming and shouting, "Bravo! Bravo! Well done!" But then I saw my

mother's face, her stricken face. The audience clapped weakly, and as I walked back to my chair, with my whole face quivering as I tried not to cry, I heard a little boy whisper loudly to his mother, "That was awful," and the mother whispered back, "Well, she certainly tried."

And now I realized how many people were in the audience, the whole world it seemed. I was aware of eyes burning into my back. I felt the shame of my mother and father as they sat stiffly throughout the rest of the show.

We could have escaped during intermission. Pride and some strange sense of honor must have anchored my parents to their chairs. And so we watched it all: the eighteen-year-old boy with a fake mustache who did a magic show and juggled flaming hoops while riding a unicycle. The breasted girl with white makeup who sang from *Madama Butterfly* and got honorable mention. And the eleven-year-old boy who won first prize playing a tricky violin song that sounded like a busy bee.

After the show, the Hsus, the Jongs, and the St. Clairs from the Joy Luck Club came up to my mother and father.

"Lots of talented kids," Auntie Lindo said vaguely, smiling broadly.

Words to Know

devastated (DEV uh stay tid) v.: Destroyed; completely upset
fiasco (fee AS koh) n.: A complete failure

"That was somethin' else," said my father, and I wondered if he was referring to me in a humorous way, or whether he even remembered what I had done.

Waverly looked at me and shrugged her shoulders. "You aren't a genius like me," she said matter-of-factly. And if I hadn't felt so bad, I would have pulled her braids and punched her stomach.

But my mother's expression was what devastated me: a quiet, blank look that said she had lost everything. I felt the same way, and it seemed as if everybody were now coming up, like gawkers at the scene of an accident, to see what parts were actually missing. When we got on the bus to go home, my father was humming the busy-bee tune and my mother was silent. I kept thinking she wanted to wait until we got home before shouting at me. But when my father unlocked the door to our apartment, my mother walked in and then went to the back, into the bedroom. No accusations. No blame. And in a way, I felt disappointed. I had been waiting for her to start shouting, so I could shout back and cry and blame her for all my misery.

I assumed my talent-show fiasco meant I never had to play the piano again. But two days later, after school, my mother came out of the kitchen and saw me watching TV.

"Four clock," she reminded me as if it were any other day. I was stunned, as though she were asking me to go through the talent-show torture again. I wedged myself more tightly in front of the TV.

"Turn off TV," she called from the kitchen five minutes later.

I didn't budge. And then I decided. I didn't have to do what my mother said anymore. I wasn't her slave. This wasn't China. I had listened to her before and look what happened. She was the stupid one.

She came out from the kitchen and stood in the arched entryway of the living room. "Four clock," she said once again, louder.

"I'm not going to play anymore," I said nonchalantly. "Why should I? I'm not a genius."

She walked over and stood in front of the TV. I saw her chest was heaving up and down in an angry way.

"No!" I said, and I now felt stronger, as if my true self had finally emerged. So this was what had been inside me all along.

"No! I won't!" I screamed.

She yanked me by the arm, pulled me off the floor, snapped off the TV. She was frighteningly strong, half pulling, half carrying me toward the piano as I kicked the throw rugs under my feet. She lifted me up and onto the hard bench. I was sobbing by now, looking at her bitterly. Her chest was heaving even more and her mouth was open, smiling crazily as if she were pleased I was crying.

"You want me to be someone that I'm not!" I sobbed. "I'll never be the kind of daughter you want me to be!"

Myself
Abigail Friedman

So small, disheveled.
I never knew it was there.
Always, in New York,
I must be like the others
5   Like the cool kids.
That is why I didn't know it existed—
That I could be . . . myself.

"Only two kinds of daughters," she shouted in Chinese. "Those who are obedient and those who follow their own mind! Only one kind of daughter can live in this house. Obedient daughter!"

"Then I wish I wasn't your daughter. I wish you weren't my mother," I shouted. As I said these things I got scared. It felt like worms and toads and slimy things crawling out of my chest, but it also felt good, as if this awful side of me had surfaced, at last.

"Too late change this," said my mother shrilly.

And I could sense her anger rising to its breaking point. I wanted to see it spill over. And that's when I remembered the babies she had lost in China, the ones we never talked about. "Then I wish I'd never been born!" I shouted. "I wish I were dead! Like them."

It was as if I had said the magic words. Alakazam!—and her face went blank, her mouth closed, her arms went slack, and she backed out of the room, stunned, as if she were blowing away like a small brown leaf, thin, brittle, lifeless.

It was not the only disappointment my mother felt in me. In the years that followed, I failed her so many times, each time asserting my own will, my right to fall short of expectations. I didn't get straight As. I didn't become class president. I didn't get into Stanford. I dropped out of college.

For unlike my mother, I did not believe I could be anything I wanted to be. I could only be me.

And for all those years, we never talked about the disaster at the recital or my terrible accusations afterward at the piano bench. All that remained unchecked, like a betrayal that was now unspeakable. So I never found a way

to ask her why she had hoped for something so large that failure was inevitable.

And even worse, I never asked her what frightened me the most: Why had she given up hope?

For after our struggle at the piano, she never mentioned my playing again. The lessons stopped. The lid to the piano was closed, shutting out the dust, my misery, and her dreams.

So she surprised me. A few years ago, she offered to give me the piano, for my thirtieth birthday. I had not played in all those years. I saw the offer as a sign of forgiveness, a tremendous burden removed.

"Are you sure?" I asked shyly. "I mean, won't you and Dad miss it?"

"No, this your piano," she said firmly. "Always your piano. You only one can play."

"Well, I probably can't play anymore," I said. "It's been years."

"You pick up fast," said my mother, as if she knew this was certain. "You have natural talent. You could been genius if you want to."

"No I couldn't."

"You just not trying," said my mother. And she was neither angry nor sad. She said it as if to announce a fact that could never be disproved. "Take it," she said.

But I didn't at first. It was enough that she had offered it to me. And after that, every time I saw it in my parents' living room, standing in front of the bay windows, it made me feel proud, as if it were a shiny trophy I had won back.

Last week I sent a tuner over to my parents' apartment and had the piano reconditioned, for purely sentimental reasons. My mother had died a few months before and I had been getting things in order for my father, a little bit at a time. I put the jewelry in special silk pouches. The sweaters she had knitted in yellow, pink, bright orange—all the colors I hated—I put those in moth-proof boxes. I found some old Chinese silk dresses, the kind with little slits up the sides. I rubbed the old silk against my skin, then wrapped them in tissue and decided to take them home with me.

After I had the piano tuned, I opened the lid and touched the keys. It sounded even richer than I remembered. Really, it was a very good piano. Inside the bench were the same exercise notes with handwritten scales, the same secondhand music books with their covers held together with yellow tape.

I opened up the Schumann book to the dark little piece I had played at the recital. It was on the left-hand side of the page, "Pleading Child." It looked more difficult than I remembered. I played a few bars, surprised at how easily the notes came back to me.

And for the first time, or so it seemed, I noticed the piece on the right-hand side. It was called "Perfectly Contented." I tried to play this one as well. It had a lighter melody but the same flowing rhythm and turned out to be quite easy. "Pleading Child" was shorter but slower; "Perfectly Contented" was longer, but faster. And after I played them both a few times, I realized they were two halves of the same song.

When she was a child, **Amy Tan** (1952–) wanted to be an artist. In her introduction to Belle Yang's *Baba: A Return to China on My Father's Shoulders,* she explains, "Even though I swept my brush boldly across the page, even though I dabbed at details with blind patience, the right line, colors and shapes always eluded me. And so I eventually turned to my tools of second choice: I tried to use words to paint pictures."

Tan's second choice has proven quite successful. "Two Kinds" was taken from *The Joy Luck Club,* her first novel. The book was on the bestseller list for seventy-seven weeks and was also made into a feature film.

Respond

- Do you think it would be exciting to be a prodigy? Why or why not?
- Imagine you're a friend of the daughter's and she tells you about her mother's hopes for her. What advice would you give your friend?

Explore Your Reading

Look Back (Recall)

1. Name three talents the mother tries to develop in her daughter.

Think It Over (Interpret)

2. Why does the narrator react against her mother's efforts to change her?
3. How does the narrator's attitude toward her mother change at the talent show?
4. What new meaning does the piano take on when the narrator is older?
5. How do the last paragraph and the title of this story illustrate what the narrator learns?

Go Beyond (Apply)

6. How might the daughter's experience help her when she has children of her own?

Develop Reading and Literary Skills

Recognize Dynamic and Static Characters

Filling in your diagram helped you identify the daughter's moment of growth. As she looks into a mirror, she decides that she "won't be what [she's] not." When characters in stories change how they think or act, we call them **dynamic characters.** This means that they can surprise you by growing, just as real people can.

The opposite of a dynamic character is a **static character** who is completely predictable. In "Two Kinds," Auntie Lindo is a static character because all she does is boast about her daughter. She never surprises you with an unexpected change.

1. Is the mother in this story a static or a dynamic character? Explain.
2. After the daughter's moment of growth, how does her relationship with her mother change?

Ideas for Writing

This story describes the struggle that occurs when a mother and her daughter have very different expectations about the daughter's future.

Job Description Write a job description that shows what qualities the mother's ideal daughter might possess. Include the responsibilities her daughter would have as well as the rewards.

Scene From a Story What might happen if the daughter told her mother how she felt? Write a scene to include in the story.

Ideas for Projects

Class Exhibit When the narrator was younger, she didn't think the piano expressed her true self. Bring to school an item that does represent "the real you"—for instance, a hockey mitt, a paintbrush, or a cookbook. Without including your name, attach a brief explanation of how this object conveys "the real you." Display all the items in class, and work with your classmates to match individuals with objects.

Soundtrack Imagine you are the chief recording engineer at a studio that is recording the soundtrack for a TV production of "Two Kinds." Choose contrasting musical themes for the mother and the daughter. Share your choices with the class by singing or recording samples of your selections. [Music Link]

How Am I Doing?

Share your thoughts about these questions with a partner:

What did my diagram help me understand about character development? How could a diagram like this help me read other works?

Which part of the narrator's experience can I relate to my own life?

Who Is the Real Me?

Think Critically About the Selections

The selections you have read in this section explore the question "Who is the real me?" With a partner or a small group, complete one or two of the following activities to show your understanding of the question. You can present your responses orally or in writing.

1. Some of the characters and speakers in this section tried out a new identity. Choose two who did so. Compare and contrast their experiences and the results. (**Compare and Contrast**)

2. Look at the art on this page. It also appears on page F9. How do you think the artist would answer the question "Who is the real me?" Refer to the details of the art as you answer your question. (**Make Inferences; Provide Evidence**)

3. Which character from these selections would you like to be friends with? Why? What do you have in common? What differences between you and the character could you learn from? (**Compare and Contrast**)

4. Which character's experience led you to learn something about yourself? Explain how. (**Synthesize**)

Student Art *Possibilities* Jennifer Vota St. John's, Holmdel, New Jersey

Projects

Personal Profile Plan and create a personal profile, complete with a self-portrait, for a class book of student profiles. Brainstorm to gather personal details that you will include. Then use your details to write about yourself, describing who you are. Attach a photograph, drawing, or silhouette, and add your profile to a class book entitled *Who Is the Real Me?*

Mural Work with a group of classmates to plan and create a mural (picture on a wall) that expresses the personality of your class. Include collages or montages that you may have already made, and create new ones. Decide on an organization for the mural, and make a small-scale sketch of it before creating the larger one. Give it a title and display it on paper on a wall. [Art Link]

Monologue Write a monologue that tells about "the real you." Draw upon the journal entries, poems, artwork, or home videos you've made that say something important about you. Write your monologue, trying to make it sound natural when spoken. Practice it several times, and present it to the class. Make an audio or video recording to help you evaluate your performance.

Looking at The Short

Marie G. Lee

Terms to know

Plot is the sequence of events in a literary work. In most short stories, the plot involves a central **conflict**, or struggle between opposing sides.

Characters are the fictional people in stories.

The **narrator** is the person telling the story. Sometimes the narrator is a character. At other times, the narrator stands outside the action.

Setting is the time and place of the action.

A **theme** is the central message of a literary work. A theme can usually be expressed as a general statement about people or life.

Characters in Short Stories "What a character!" is what we say when we meet someone who is unique, interesting, and unforgettable. As a writer of short stories, brief works of fiction, I try to keep this in mind as I write. I want my stories' characters to be people *like no other.*

Sometimes, I will begin by modeling story characters on real people. For instance, my sister Michelle and I spent a summer living in an apartment. We parked our tiny "bug" car in our apartment's designated space, but soon we were getting notes from the lady next door. She kept telling us we were too close and were going to hit her new car.

We had such a tiny car, it was easy to park between the lines, which we did. But to make her happy, we scooted the car as far over to the other side as possible. Boy, were we surprised when we still got those notes!

This experience inspired me to write a story about a lady whose car is her only friend. While I was writing it, I decided to try to see the situation as she might experience it. I made the characters of my sister and me into two teenage boys with a big, noisy souped-up car. As I wrote the story, I began to understand why the woman might be worried about her car.

"The Lie" In the same way, in Kurt Vonnegut's story, "The Lie," at first you see a boy who does little more than sit there. Later, however, you begin to see how things like his rich parents and his nervousness about going to school make him act the way he does.

Vonnegut increases the suspense by making you wonder about a character for a while. Usually, the writer has to get you to know the character *fast.* I often try to let readers get to know a character by showing what the character is thinking. That way, characters don't have to be flamboyant to be interesting. In fact, many of my characters have more going on inside than outside, just like a lot of real people.

"The Captive Outfielder" Likewise, in Leonard Wibberly's short story, "The Captive Outfielder," the boy and his music teacher are both quiet people, but because the author lets us get to know them, we feel the

Literary Forms Story

drama in the story. We begin to really care about what a character cares about. That's a neat feeling.

Caring About Characters Writers also come to care about their characters. When you sit in someone's head long enough, the character actually seems to become real. This is probably why when you read a story, you may think, "wow, that character seems so real!" even though you know the character was made up by a writer. Many writers I know come to be so attached to their characters that they become sad when they finish a story. One writer even cries because she enjoys the company of her characters so much.

However, it is lucky for readers that writers do finish these stories and share their characters with us. This way, we can sit down, read, and meet people who make us say "what a character!" without even leaving the house.

Marie G. Lee (1964–   ) creates characters for a living. She began sharing her writing at ten when she sold copies of her stories to her parents. She reached a much larger audience at 16 when an essay she had written was published in *Seventeen* magazine.

Her book *If It Hadn't Been for Yoon Jun* features a Korean student who arrives in a typical seventh-grade American class. Lee has also written *Finding My Voice* and *Saying Goodbye*, two popular young adult novels.

The Captive Outfielder
by Leonard Wibberley

What makes a good story?

Reach Into Your Background

Whether it's gossip you hear from the grapevine or a thriller you see on TV, good stories have something in common. They show people facing and solving problems.

Work with a group on one or both of the following activities:

- Brainstorm to list your favorite books and movies. Show how each is about someone trying to solve a problem.
- Imagine a situation in which a person is facing a problem. Pass the story around your group, with each person adding details, until the problem is solved.

Read Actively
Recognize Plot Development

The stories you discussed contain a sequence of events, or **plot,** that describes how a problem is solved. The problem, or **conflict,** grows more intense until it reaches a **climax,** the point at which the struggle is greatest. After the climax you learn the **resolution,** or outcome, of the conflict.

This pattern, shown in the diagram, will help you understand many stories. Keep this diagram in mind as you read "The Captive Outfielder," and identify the conflict, the climax, and the resolution.

Climax

Conflict Increases

Resolution

Conflict Introduced

The Captive Outfielder

Leonard Wibberley

The boy was filled with anxiety which seemed to concentrate in his stomach, giving him a sense of tightness there, as if his stomach were all knotted up into a ball and would never come undone again. He had his violin under his chin and before him was the music stand and on the walls of the studio the pictures of the great musicians were frowning upon him in massive disapproval. Right behind him on the wall was a portrait of Paganini, and he positively glowered down at the boy, full of malevolence and impatience.

That, said the boy to himself, *is because he could really play the violin and I can't and never will be able to. And he knows it and thinks I'm a fool.*

Below Paganini was a portrait of Mozart, in profile. He had a white wig tied neatly at the back with a bow of black ribbon. Mozart should have been looking straight ahead, but his left eye, which was the only one visible, seemed to be turned a little watching the boy. The look was one of disapproval. When Mozart was the boy's age— that is, ten—he had already composed several pieces and could

Johann Sebastian Bach

play the violin and the organ. Mozart didn't like the boy either.

On the other side of the Paganini portrait was the blocky face of Johann Sebastian Bach. It was a grim face, bleak with disappointment.

Ludwig von Beethoven

Whenever the boy was playing it seemed to him that Johann Sebastian Bach was shaking his head in resigned disapproval of his efforts. There were other portraits around the studio—Beethoven, Brahms, Chopin. Not one of them was smiling. They were all in agreement that this boy was certainly the poorest kind of musician and never would learn his instrument, and it was painful to them to have to listen to him while he had his lesson.

Of all these great men of music who surrounded him the boy hated Johann Sebastian Bach the most. This was because his teacher, Mr. Olinsky, kept talking about Bach as if without Bach there never would have been any music. Bach was like a god to Mr. Olinsky, and he was a god the boy could never hope to please.

"All right," said Mr. Olinsky, who was at the grand piano. "The 'Arioso.' And you will kindly remember the time. Without time no one can play the music of Johann Sebastian Bach." Mr. Olinsky exchanged glances with the portrait of Bach, and the two seemed in

Words to Know

glowered (GLOW uhrd) *v.*: Scowled; stared angrily
malevolence (muh LEV uh luhns) *n.*: Spite or ill-will

perfect agreement with each other. The boy was quite sure that the two of them carried on disheartened conversations about him after his lesson.

There was a chord from the piano. The boy put the bow to the string and started. But it was no good. At the end of the second bar Mr. Olinsky took his hands from the piano and covered his face with them and shook his head, bending over the keyboard. Bach shook his head too. In the awful silence all the portraits around the studio expressed their disapproval, and the boy felt more wretched than ever and not too far removed from tears.

"The *time*," said Mr. Olinsky eventually. "The time. Take that first bar. What is the value of the first note?"

"A quarter note,"[1] said the boy.

"And the next note?"

"A sixteenth."[2]

"Good. So you have one quarter note and four sixteenth notes making a bar of two quarters. Not so?"

"Yes."

"But the first quarter note is tied to the first sixteenth note. They are the same note. So the first note, which is C sharp, is held for five sixteenths, and then the other three sixteenths follow. Not so?"

"Yes," said the boy.

"THEN WHY DON'T YOU PLAY IT THAT WAY?"

---

1. **quarter note** *n.*: A note in music that is held one fourth as long as a whole note.

2. **sixteenth** *n.*: A note in music that is held one sixteenth as long as a whole note.

To this the boy made no reply. The reason he didn't play it that way was that he couldn't play it that way. It wasn't fair to have a quarter note and then tie it to a sixteenth note. It was just a dirty trick like Grasshopper Smith pulled when he was pitching in the Little League. Grasshopper Smith was on the Giants, and the boy was on the Yankees. The Grasshopper always retained the ball for just a second after he seemed to have thrown it and struck the boy out. Every time. Every single time. The boy got a hit every now and again from other pitchers. Once he got a two-base hit. The ball went joyously through the air, bounced and went over the center-field fence. A clear, good two-base hit. But it was a relief pitcher. And whenever Grasshopper Smith was in the box, the boy struck out. Him and Johann Sebastian Bach. They were full of dirty tricks. They were pretty stuck-up too. He hated them both.

Meanwhile he had not replied to Mr. Olinsky's question, and Mr. Olinsky got up from the piano and stood beside him, looking at him, and saw that the boy's eyes were bright with frustration and disappointment because he was no good at baseball and no good at music either.

"Come and sit down a minute, boy," said Mr. Olinsky, and led him over to a little wickerwork sofa.

Mr. Olinsky was in his sixties, and from the time he was this boy's age he had given all his life to music. He loved the boy, though he had known him for only a year. He was a good boy, and he had a good ear. He wanted him to get excited about music, and the boy was not excited about it. He didn't practice properly.

Early European Composers of Classical Music

This story names several European composers of classical music.
How many names do you recognize?

Nicolo Paganini (nee koh LOH pag gah NEE nee): 1782–1840; Italian composer and violinist

Wolfgang Amadeus Mozart (VAWLF gahng ah ma DAY oos MOH tsahrt): 1756–1791; Austrian composer known for his precocious talent

Johann Sebastian Bach (YOH hahn si BAS chuhn BAHK): 1685–1750; German composer

Ludwig van Beethoven (LOOT vik vahn BAY toh vuhn): 1770–1827; German composer

Johannes Brahms (yoh HAHN uhs BRAHMZ): 1833–1897; German composer

Frederick Chopin (FRED uh rik SHOH pan): 1810–1849; Polish composer and pianist

He didn't apply himself. There was something lacking, and it was up to him, Mr. Olinsky, to supply whatever it was that was lacking so that the boy would really enter into the magic world of music.

How to get to him then? How to make a real contact with this American boy when he himself was, though a citizen, foreign-born?

He started to talk about his own youth. It had been a very grim youth in Petrograd.[3] His parents were poor. His father had died when he was young, and his mother had, by a very great struggle, got him into the conservatory. She had enough money for his tuition only. Eating was a great problem. He could afford only one good meal a day at the conservatory cafeteria so that he was almost always hungry and cold. But he remembered how the great Glazunov had come to the cafeteria one day and had seen him with a bowl of soup and a piece of bread.

"This boy is thin," Glazunov had said. "From now on he is to have two bowls of soup, and they are to be big bowls. I will pay the cost."

There had been help like that for him—occasional help coming quite unexpectedly—in those long, grinding, lonely years at the conservatory. But there were other terrible times. There was the time when he had reached such an age that he could no longer be boarded at the conservatory. He had to give up his bed to a smaller boy and find lodgings somewhere in the city.

He had enough money for lodgings, but not enough for food. Always food. That was the great problem. To get money for food he had taken a room in a house where the family had consumption.[4] They rented him a room cheaply because nobody wanted to board with them. He would listen to the members of the family coughing at nighttime—the thin, shallow, persistent cough of the consumptive. He was terribly afraid—afraid that he would contract consumption himself, which was incurable in those days, and die. The thought of death frightened him. But he was equally frightened of disappointing his mother, for if he died he would not graduate and all her efforts to make him a musician would be wasted.

Then there was the time he had had to leave Russia after the Revolution. And the awful months of standing in line to get a visa and then to get assigned to a train. It had taken seven months. And the train to Riga[5]—what an ordeal that had been. Normally it took eighteen hours. But this train took three weeks. Three weeks in cattle cars in midwinter, jammed up against his fellow passengers, desperately trying to save his violin from being crushed. A baby had died in the cattle car, and the mother kept pretending it was only asleep. They had had to take it from her by force eventually and bury it beside the tracks out in the howling loneliness of the countryside.

And out of all this he had got music. He had become a musician. Not a concert violinist, but a great orchestral violinist, devoted to his art.

He told the boy about this, hoping to get him to understand what he himself had gone through in order to become a musician. But when he was finished, he knew he had not reached the boy.

That is because he is an American boy, Mr. Olinsky thought. *He thinks all these things*

Words to Know

disheartened (dis HAHRT end) *adj.*: Disappointed; discouraged

conservatory (kuhn SER vuh taw ree) *n.*: A school of music

tuition (too ISH uhn) *n.*: Money paid by someone to attend a private school

ordeal (or DEEL) *n.*: A difficult or painful experience

---

3. Petrograd: The capital of Russia during the time of the Russian Revolution; now called St. Petersburg.

4. consumption (kuhn SUMP shuhn) *n.*: Tuberculosis, a disease that affects the lungs.

---

5. Riga (REE guh): The capital of Latvia.

happened to me because I am a foreigner, and these things don't happen in America. And maybe they don't. But can't he understand that if I made all these efforts to achieve music—to be able to play the works of Johann Sebastian Bach as Bach wrote them—it is surely worth a little effort on his part?

But it was no good. The boy, he knew, sympathized with him. But he had not made a real contact with him. He hadn't found the missing something that separated this boy from him and the boy from music. He tried again. "Tell me," he said, "what do you do with your day?"

"I go to school," said the boy flatly.

"But after that? Life is not all school."

"I play ball."

"What kind of ball?" asked Mr. Olinsky. "Bouncing a ball against a wall?"

"No," said the boy. "Baseball."

"Ah," said Mr. Olinsky. "Baseball." And he sighed. He had been more than thirty years in the United States and he didn't know anything about baseball. It was an activity beneath his notice. When he had any spare time, he went to a concert. Or sometimes he played chess. "And how do you do at baseball?" he said.

"Oh—not very good. That Grasshopper Smith. He always strikes me out."

"You have a big match coming up soon perhaps?"

"A game. Yes. Tomorrow. The Giants against the Yankees. I'm on the Yankees. It's the play-off. We are both tied for first place." For a moment he seemed excited, and then he caught a glimpse of the great musicians around the wall and the bleak stare of Johann Sebastian Bach, and his voice went dull again. "It doesn't matter," he said. "I'll be struck out."

"But that is not the way to think about it," said Mr. Olinsky. "Is it inevitable that you be struck out? Surely that cannot be so. When I was a boy—" Then he stopped, because when he was a boy he had never played anything remotely approaching baseball, and so he had nothing to offer the boy to encourage him.

Here was the missing part then—the thing that was missing between him and the boy and the thing that was missing between the boy and Johann Sebastian Bach. Baseball. It was just something they didn't have in common, and so they couldn't communicate with each other.

"When is this game?" said Mr. Olinsky.

"Three in the afternoon," said the boy.

"And this Grasshopper Smith is your *bête noire*—your black beast, huh?"

"Yeah," said the boy. "And he'll be pitching. They've been saving him for this game."

Mr. Olinsky sighed. This was a long way from the "Arioso." "Well," he said, "we will consider the lesson over. Do your practice and we will try again next week."

The boy left, conscious that all the musicians were watching him. When he had gone, Mr. Olinsky stood before the portrait of Johann Sebastian Bach.

"Baseball, maestro," he said. "Baseball. That is what stands between him and you and him and me. You had twenty children and I had none. But I am positive that neither of us knows anything about baseball."

He thought about this for a moment. Then he said, "Twenty children—many of them boys. Is it possible, maestro—is it just possible that with twenty children and many of them boys? . . . You will forgive the thought, but is it just possible that you may have played something like baseball with them sometimes? And perhaps one of those boys always being—what did he say?—struck out?"

He looked hard at the blocky features of Johann Sebastian Bach, and it seemed to him that in one corner of the grim mouth there was a touch of a smile.

Mr. Olinsky was late getting to the Clark Stadium Recreation Park in Hermosa Beach for the play-off between the Giants and the Yankees because he had spent the morning transposing the "Arioso" from A major into C major to make it simpler for the boy. Indeed, when he got there the game was in the sixth

Words to Know

conscious (KAHN shuhs) *adj.*: Aware; alert
fervent (FER vuhnt) *adj.*: Showing intense or strong feeling

and last inning and the score was three to nothing in favor of the Giants.

The Yankees were at bat, and it seemed that a moment of crisis had been reached.

"What's happening?" Mr. Olinsky asked a man seated next to him who was eating a hot dog in ferocious bites.

"You blind or something?" asked the man. "Bases loaded, two away and if they don't get a hitter to bring those three home, it's goodbye for the Yankees. And look who's coming up to bat. That dodo!"

Mr. Olinsky looked and saw the boy walking to the plate.

Outside the studio and in his baseball uniform he looked very small. He also looked frightened, and Mr. Olinsky looked savagely at the man who had called the boy a dodo and was eating the hot dog, and he said the only American expression of contempt he had learned in all his years in the United States. "You don't know nothing from nothing," Mr. Olinsky snapped.

"That so?" said the hot-dog man. "Well, you watch. Three straight pitches and the Grasshopper will have him out. I think I'll go home. I got a pain."

But he didn't go home. He stayed there while the Grasshopper looked carefully around the bases and then, leaning forward with the ball clasped before him, glared intently at the boy. Then he pumped twice and threw the ball, and the boy swung at it and missed, and the umpire yelled, "Strike one."

"Two more like that, Grasshopper," yelled somebody. "Just two more and it's in the bag."

The boy turned around to look at the crowd and passed his tongue over his lips. He looked directly at where Mr. Olinsky was sitting, but the music teacher was sure the boy had not seen him. His face was white and his eyes glazed so that he didn't seem to be seeing anybody.

Mr. Olinsky knew that look. He had seen it often enough in the studio when the boy had made an error and knew that however much he tried he would make the same error over and over again. It was a look of pure misery—a fervent desire to get an ordeal over with.

The boy turned again, and the Grasshopper threw suddenly and savagely to third base. But the runner got back on the sack in time, and there was a sigh of relief from the crowd.

Again came the cool examination of the bases and the calculated stare at the boy at the plate. And again the pitch with the curious whip of the arm and the release of the ball one second later. Once more the boy swung and missed, and the umpire called, "Strike two." There was a groan from the crowd.

"Oh and two the count," said the score-keeper, but Mr. Olinsky got up from the bench and, pushing his way between the people on the bleachers before him, he went to the backstop fence.

"You," he shouted to the umpire. "I want to talk to that boy there."

The boy heard his voice and turned and looked at him aghast. "Please, Mr. Olinsky," he said. "I can't talk to you now."

"Get away from the back fence," snapped the umpire.

"I insist on talking to that boy," said Mr. Olinsky. "It is very important. It is about Johann Sebastian Bach."

"Please go away," said the boy, and he was very close to tears. The umpire called for time out while he got rid of this madman, and the boy went to the netting of the backstop.

"You are forgetting about the 'Arioso'!" said Mr. Olinsky urgently. "Now you listen to me, because I know what I am talking about. You are thinking of a quarter note, and it should be five sixteenths. It is a quarter note—C sharp—held for one sixteenth more. *Then* strike. You are too early. It must be exactly on time."

"What the heck's he talking about?" asked the coach, who had just come up.

The boy didn't answer right away. He was looking at Mr. Olinsky as if he had realized for the first time something very important which he had been told over and over again, but had not grasped previously.

"He's talking about Johann Sebastian Bach," he said to the coach. "Five sixteenths. Not a quarter note."

"Bach had twenty children," said Mr. Olinsky to the coach. "Many of them were boys. He would know about these things."

"Let's get on with the game," said the coach.

Mr. Olinsky did not go back to the bleachers. He remained behind the backstop and waited for the ceremony of the base inspection and the hard stare by the pitcher. He saw the Grasshopper pump twice, saw his hand go back behind his head, saw the curiously delayed flick of the ball, watched it speed to the boy and then he heard a sound which afterward he thought was among the most beautiful and satisfying he had heard in all music.

It was a clean, sharp "click," sweet as birdsong.

The ball soared higher and higher into the air in a graceful parabola.[6] It was fifteen feet over the center fielder's head, and it cleared the fence by a good four feet.

Then pandemonium broke loose. People were running all over the field, and the boy was chased around the bases by half his teammates, and when he got to home plate he was thumped upon the back and his hair ruffled, and in all this Mr. Olinsky caught one glimpse of the boy's face, laughing and yet with tears pouring down his cheeks.

A week later the boy turned up at Mr. Olinsky's studio for his violin lesson. He

6. **parabola** (pa RA buh luh) *n.*: A high curve.

looked around at all the great musicians on the wall, and they no longer seemed to be disapproving and disappointed in him.

Paganini was almost kindly. There was a suggestion of a chuckle on the noble profile of Mozart, and Beethoven no longer looked so forbidding. The boy looked at the portrait of Johann Sebastian Bach last.

He looked for a long time at the picture, and then he said two words out loud—words that brought lasting happiness to Mr. Olinsky. The words were: "Thanks, coach."

The "Arioso" went excellently from then on.

Respond

- Would you like to have a teacher like Mr. Olinsky? Why or why not?
- With a partner, list activities in which success depends on exact timing.

Leonard Wibberley (1915–1983):

Q: What was a challenge Wibberley had to face?
A: He was born in Dublin, Ireland, and educated in Irish Gaelic, the language widely spoken in ancient Ireland and studied today in Irish schools. However, he had to learn English at the age of nine, when his family moved to England.

Q: Were his attempts at learning a new language successful?
A: Yes! He eventually learned English so well that he became a reporter for an English newspaper.

Q: How did his reporting job help him with his fiction writing?
A: As a reporter, Wibberley observed people and places that he could write about in his stories.

Activities
MAKE MEANING

Explore Your Reading
Look Back (Recall)

1. What are the various ways in which Mr. Olinsky tries to connect with the boy?

Think It Over (Interpret)

2. Why can't Mr. Olinsky connect his experiences at the conservatory with his student's life?
3. Why does Mr. Olinsky go to the baseball game?
4. Explain how two things Mr. Olinsky does lead to a better performance of the "Arioso."

Go Beyond (Apply)

5. How do you think the boy will use what he has learned in the future?

Develop Reading and Literary Skills
Understand Plot

The plot diagram may have helped you identify the central struggle or problem **(conflict)** of the story, the point at which this problem is greatest **(climax)**, and the solution to the problem **(resolution).**

Because short stories are brief, they usually focus on one conflict and they introduce this conflict quickly. In this story, for example, we learn right away that the boy is having a problem playing the violin.

The writer then builds toward the climax by showing everything that prevents the conflict from being solved. One difficulty is the boy's fear of music, indicated by his reactions to the portraits.

1. How does the teacher's foreign background make it more difficult to solve the conflict?
2. Which moment is the climax, the point of greatest tension? Explain.
3. How does Mr. Olinsky contribute to the resolution?

Ideas for Writing

As in this story, many things in life depend on precise timing.

How-To Manual Think of a skill you do that requires an attention to timing. Consider sewing, skiing, or even telling a joke. Write an instruction manual that would teach someone else your special skill.

Science-Fiction Story What would happen if time moved backward instead of forward? How would life change if every year of your life were only a month? Choose one of these ideas or make up one yourself and write a story about a world where time works differently.

Ideas for Projects

Activities Survey The boy in this story was able to link two apparently unrelated activities, music and baseball. With a group, list activities you pursue outside of class. Look for hidden connections among them, considering practice requirements, timing, and other factors. Share your results with the class.

Report on Timing in Music This selection mentions the system of timing used in music. Research this subject and report your findings to the class. If possible, support your points by playing musical pieces on CDs or audiocassettes. [Math Link; Music Link]

How Am I Doing?

Answer these questions and then compare responses with a partner:

How did the plot diagram help me understand this story?

In what other subjects do I have to find hidden connections between things? How can I improve that skill?

What can we learn from a character's experience?

Reach Into Your Background

Like people in life, characters in fiction say and do a variety of things—things that are brave, stupid, mean, helpful, careless, or clever. Their words and actions can get you thinking about important ideas. To show how this happens, try one or both of the following activities:

- Answer the following questions: *Which character in fiction do I most or least admire? Why? Has a character changed my mind about something? Explain.* Then compare answers with a partner.
- With a group, act out a scene from a story that will prompt people to think about a problem—for instance, what happens when a character doesn't tell the truth?

Read Actively

Make Judgments About Characters

You can judge, or evaluate, people in fiction by the same standards you use to judge real people. Often a character's behavior is a key to the central message the author is trying to communicate. By making **judgments about characters,** you can better understand that message.

Try imagining you had to confide an embarrassing secret to one of the characters in this story. As you read, note the positive and negative traits of each character. Then decide which one you'd trust.

The Lie

KURT VONNEGUT

It was early springtime. Weak sunshine lay cold on old gray frost. Willow twigs against the sky showed the golden haze of fat catkins about to bloom. A black Rolls-Royce streaked up the Connecticut Turnpike from New York City. At the wheel was Ben Barkley, a black chauffeur.

"Keep it under the speed limit, Ben," said Doctor Remenzel. "I don't care how ridiculous any speed limit seems; stay under it. No reason to rush—we have plenty of time."

Ben eased off on the throttle. "Seems like in the springtime she wants to get up and go," he said.

"Do what you can to keep her down—OK?" said the doctor.

"Yes, sir!" said Ben. He spoke in a lower voice to the thirteen-year-old boy who was riding beside him, to Eli Remenzel, the doctor's son. "Ain't just people and animals feel good in the springtime," he said to Eli. "Motors feel good too."

"Um," said Eli.

"Everything feel good," said Ben. "Don't you feel good?"

"Sure, sure I feel good," said Eli emptily.

"Should feel good—going to that wonderful school," said Ben.

The wonderful school was the Whitehill School for Boys, a private preparatory school in North Marston, Massachusetts. That was where the Rolls-Royce was bound. The plan was that Eli would enroll for the fall semester, while his father, a member of the class of 1939, attended a meeting of the Board of Overseers of the school.

"Don't believe this boy's feeling so good, doctor," said Ben. He wasn't particularly seri-ous about it. It was more a genial[1] springtime blather.

"What's the matter, Eli?" said the doctor absently. He was studying blueprints, plans for a thirty-room addition to the Eli Remenzel Memorial Dormitory—a building named in honor of his great-great-grandfather. Doctor Remenzel had the plans draped over a walnut table that folded out of the back of the front seat. He was a massive, dignified man, a physician, a healer for healing's sake, since he had been born as rich as the Shah of Iran. "Worried about something?" he asked Eli without looking up from the plans.

---

1. **genial** (JEE nee uhl) *adj.*: Cheerful, pleasant.

"Nope," said Eli.

Eli's lovely mother, Sylvia, sat next to the doctor, reading the catalog of the Whitehill School. "If I were you," she said to Eli, "I'd be so excited I could hardly stand it. The best four years of your whole life are just about to begin."

"Sure," said Eli. He didn't show her his face. He gave her only the back of his head, a pinwheel of coarse brown hair above a stiff white collar, to talk to.

"I wonder how many Remenzels have gone to Whitehill," said Sylvia.

"That's like asking how many people are dead in a cemetery," said the doctor. He gave the answer to the old joke, and to Sylvia's question too. "All of 'em."

"If all the Remenzels who went to Whitehill were numbered, what number would Eli be?" said Sylvia. "That's what I'm getting at."

The question annoyed Doctor Remenzel a little. It didn't seem in very good taste. "It isn't the sort of thing you keep score on," he said.

"Guess," said his wife.

"Oh," he said, "you'd have to go back through all the records, all the way back to the end of the eighteenth century, even, to make any kind of a guess. And you'd have to decide whether to count the Schofields and the Haleys and the MacLellans as Remenzels."

"Please make a guess—" said Sylvia, "just people whose last names were Remenzel."

"Oh—" The doctor shrugged, rattled the plans. "Thirty maybe."

"So Eli is number thirty-one!" said Sylvia, delighted with the number. "You're number

thirty-one, dear," she said to the back of Eli's head.

Doctor Remenzel rattled the plans again. "I don't want him going around saying something asinine, like he's number thirty-one," he said.

"Eli knows better than that," said Sylvia. She was a game, ambitious woman, with no money of her own at all. She had been married for sixteen years but was still openly curious and enthusiastic about the ways of families that had been rich for many generations.

"Just for my own curiosity—not so Eli can go around saying what number he is," said Sylvia, "I'm going to go wherever they keep the records and find out what number he is. That's what I'll do while you're at the meeting and Eli's doing whatever he has to do at the Admissions Office."

"All right," said Doctor Remenzel, "you go ahead and do that."

"I will," said Sylvia. "I think things like that are interesting, even if you don't." She waited for a rise on that but didn't get one. Sylvia enjoyed arguing with her husband about her lack of reserve and his excess of it, enjoyed saying, toward the end of arguments like that, "Well, I guess I'm just a simple-minded country girl at heart, and that's all I'll ever be; and I'm afraid you're going to have to get used to it."

But Doctor Remenzel didn't want to play that game. He found the dormitory plans more interesting.

"Will the new rooms have fireplaces?" said Sylvia. In the oldest part of the dormitory, several of the rooms had handsome fireplaces.

"That would practically double the cost of construction," said the doctor.

"I want Eli to have a room with a fireplace, if that's possible," said Sylvia.

"Those rooms are for seniors."

"I thought maybe through some fluke—" said Sylvia.

The Lie   F·63

"What kind of fluke do you have in mind?" said the doctor. "You mean I should demand that Eli be given a room with a fireplace?"

"Not *demand*—" said Sylvia.

"Request firmly?" said the doctor.

"Maybe I'm just a simple-minded country girl at heart," said Sylvia, "but I look through this catalog, and I see all the buildings named after Remenzels, look through the back and see all the hundreds of thousands of dollars given by Remenzels for scholarships, and I just can't help thinking people named Remenzel are entitled to ask for a little something extra."

"Let me tell you in no uncertain terms," said Doctor Remenzel, "that you are not to ask for anything special for Eli—not anything."

"Of course I won't," said Sylvia. "Why do you always think I'm going to embarrass you?"

"I don't," he said.

"But I can still think what I think, can't I?" she said.

"If you have to," he said.

"I have to," she said cheerfully, utterly unrepentant. She leaned over the plans. "You think those people will like those rooms?"

"What people?" he said.

"The Africans," she said. She was talking about thirty Africans who, at the request of the State Department, were being admitted to Whitehill in the coming semester. It was because of them that the dormitory was being expanded.

"The rooms aren't for them," he said. "They aren't going to be segregated."

"Oh," said Sylvia. She thought about this awhile, and then she said, "Is there a chance Eli will have to have one of them for a roommate?"

"Freshmen draw lots for roommates," said the doctor. "That piece of information's in the catalog too."

"Eli?" said Sylvia.

"H'm?" said Eli.

"How would you feel about it if you had to room with one of those Africans?"

Eli shrugged listlessly.

"That's all right?" said Sylvia.

Eli shrugged again.

"I guess it's all right," said Sylvia.

Words to Know

unrepentant (un re PENT int) *adj.*: Without feeling sorry for having done wrong

segregated (SEG ruh gayt ed) *adj.*: Separated; isolated by race

listlessly (LIST luhs lee) *adv.*: Without interest or energy

assumption (uh SUMP shuhn) *n.*: Idea accepted as a fact

deterred (dee TERD) *v.*: Stopped; discouraged

"It had better be," said the doctor.

The Rolls-Royce pulled abreast of an old Chevrolet, a car in such bad repair that its back door was lashed shut with clothesline. Doctor Remenzel glanced casually at the driver, and then, with sudden excitement and pleasure, he told Ben Barkley to stay abreast of the car.

The doctor leaned across Sylvia, rolled down his window, yelled to the driver of the old Chevrolet, "Tom! Tom!"

The man was a Whitehill classmate of the doctor. He wore a Whitehill necktie, which he waved at Doctor Remenzel in gay recognition. And then he pointed to the fine young son who sat beside him, conveyed with proud smiles and nods that the boy was bound for Whitehill.

Doctor Remenzel pointed to the chaos of the back of Eli's head, beamed that his news was the same. In the wind blustering between the two cars they made a lunch date at the Holly House in North Marston, at the inn whose principal business was serving visitors to Whitehill.

"All right," said Doctor Remenzel to Ben Barkley, "drive on."

"You know," said Sylvia, "somebody really ought to write an article—" And she turned to look through the back window at the old car now shuddering far behind. "Somebody really ought to."

"What about?" said the doctor. He noticed that Eli had slumped way down in the front seat. "Eli!" he said sharply. "Sit up straight!" He turned his attention to Sylvia.

"Most people think prep schools are such snobbish things, just for people with money," said Sylvia, "but that isn't true." She leafed through the catalog and found the quotation she was after.

"The Whitehill School operates on the assumption," she read, "that no boy should be deterred from applying for admission because his family is unable to pay the full cost of a Whitehill education. With this in mind, the Admissions Committee selects each year from approximately 3,000 candidates the 150 most promising and deserving boys, regardless of their parents' ability to pay the full $2,200 tuition. And those in need of financial aid are given it to the full extent of their need. In certain instances, the school will even pay for the clothing and transportation of a boy."

Sylvia shook her head. "I think that's perfectly amazing. It's something most people don't realize at all. A truck driver's son can come to Whitehill."

"If he's smart enough," he said.

"Thanks to the Remenzels," said Sylvia with pride.

"And a lot of other people too," said the doctor.

Sylvia read out loud again: *"In 1799, Eli Remenzel laid the foundation for the present Scholarship Fund by donating to the school forty acres in Boston. The school still owns twelve of those acres, their current evaluation being $3,000,000."*

"Eli!" said the doctor. "Sit up! What's the matter with you?"

Eli sat up again, but began to slump almost immediately, like a snowman in the sun. Eli had good reason for slumping, for actually hoping to die or disappear. He could not bring himself to say what the reason was. He slumped because he knew he had been denied admission to Whitehill. He had failed the entrance examinations. Eli's parents did not know this, because Eli had found the awful notice in the mail and had torn it up.

Doctor Remenzel and his wife had no doubts whatsoever about their son's getting into Whitehill. It was inconceivable to them that Eli could not go there, so they had no curiosity as to how Eli had done on the examinations, were not puzzled when no report ever came.

"What all will Eli have to do to enroll?" said Sylvia, as the black Rolls-Royce crossed the Rhode Island border.

"I don't know," said the doctor. "I suppose they've got it all complicated now with forms to be filled out in quadruplicate,[2] and punch-card machines and bureaucrats.[3] This business of entrance examinations is all new, too. In my day a boy simply had an interview with the headmaster. The headmaster would look him over, ask him a few questions, and then say, 'There's a Whitehill boy.'"

"Did he ever say, 'There isn't a Whitehill boy'?" said Sylvia.

"Oh sure," said Doctor Remenzel, "if a boy was impossibly stupid or something. There have to be standards. There have always been standards. The African boys have to meet the standards, just like anybody else. They aren't getting in just because the State Department wants to make friends. We made that clear. Those boys had to meet the standards."

"And they did?" said Sylvia.

"I suppose," said Doctor Remenzel. "I heard they're all in, and they all took the same examination Eli did."

"Was it a hard examination, dear?" Sylvia asked Eli. It was the first time she'd thought to ask.

"Um," said Eli.

"What?" she said.

"Yes," said Eli.

"I'm glad they've got high standards," she said, and then she realized that this was a fairly silly statement. "Of course they've got high standards," she said. "That's why it's such a famous school. That's why people who go there do so well in later life."

Sylvia resumed her reading of the catalog again, opened out a folding map of "The Sward," as the campus of Whitehill was traditionally called. She read off the names of features that memorialized Remenzels—the Sanford Remenzel Bird Sanctuary, the George

---

2. quadruplicate (kwa DROO pli kit) *n.*: Four copies.
3. bureaucrats (BYOO roh kratz) *n.*: Office workers who strictly follow rules and procedures.

MacLellan Remenzel Skating Rink, the Eli Remenzel Memorial Dormitory, and then she read out loud a quatrain printed on one corner of the map:

"When night falleth gently
Upon the green Sward,
It's Whitehill, dear Whitehill,
Our thoughts all turn toward."

"You know," said Sylvia, "school songs are so corny when you just read them. But when I hear the Glee Club sing those words, they sound like the most beautiful words ever written, and I want to cry."

"Um," said Doctor Remenzel.

"Did a Remenzel write them?"

"I don't think so," said Doctor Remenzel. And then he said, "No—Wait. That's the *new* song. A Remenzel didn't write it. Tom Hilyer wrote it."

"The man in that old car we passed?"

"Sure," said Doctor Remenzel. "Tom wrote it. I remember when he wrote it."

"A scholarship boy wrote it?" said Sylvia. "I think that's awfully nice. He *was* a scholarship boy, wasn't he?"

"His father was an ordinary automobile mechanic in North Marston."

"You hear what a democratic school you're going to, Eli?" said Sylvia.

Half an hour later Ben Barkley brought the limousine to a stop before the Holly House, a rambling country inn twenty years older than the Republic. The inn was on the edge of the Whitehill Sward, glimpsing the school's rooftops and spires over the innocent wilderness of the Sanford Remenzel Bird Sanctuary.

Ben Barkley was sent away with the car for an hour and a half. Doctor Remenzel shepherded Sylvia and Eli into a familiar, low-ceilinged world of pewter, clocks, lovely old woods, agreeable servants, elegant food and drink.

Eli, clumsy with horror of what was surely to come, banged a grandmother clock with his elbow as he passed, made the clock cry.

Sylvia excused herself. Doctor Remenzel and Eli went to the threshold of the dining room, where a hostess welcomed them both by name. They were given a table beneath an oil portrait of one of the three Whitehill boys who had gone on to become President of the United States.

The dining room was filling quickly with families. What every family had was at least one boy about Eli's age. Most of the boys wore Whitehill blazers—black, with pale-blue piping, with Whitehill seals on the breast pockets. A few, like Eli, were not yet entitled to wear blazers, were simply hoping to get in.

The doctor ordered a drink, then turned to his son and said, "Your mother has the idea that you're entitled to special privileges around here. I hope you don't have that idea too."

"No, sir," said Eli.

"It would be a source of greatest embarrassment to me," said Doctor Remenzel with considerable grandeur, "if I were ever to hear that you had used the name Remenzel as though you thought Remenzels were something special."

"I know," said Eli wretchedly.

"That settles it," said the doctor. He had nothing more to say about it. He gave abbreviated salutes to several people he knew in the dining room, speculated as to what sort of party had reserved a long banquet table that was set up along one wall. He decided that it was for a visiting athletic team. Sylvia arrived, and Eli had to be told in a sharp whisper to stand when a woman came to a table.

Words to Know

inconceivable (in kuhn SEEV uh buhl) *adj.*: Unthinkable; unimaginable

wretchedly (RECH id lee) *adv.*: Miserably; very unhappily

think everything's exciting here. I only wish Eli had a blazer on."

Doctor Remenzel reddened. "He isn't entitled to one," he said.

"I know that," said Sylvia.

"I thought you were going to ask somebody for permission to put a blazer on Eli right away," said the doctor.

"I wouldn't do that," said Sylvia, a little offended now. "Why are you always afraid I'll embarrass you?"

"Never mind. Excuse me. Forget it," said Doctor Remenzel.

Sylvia brightened again, put her hand on Eli's arm, and looked radiantly at a man in the dining-room doorway. "There's my favorite person in all the world, next to my son and husband," she said. She meant Dr. Donald Warren, headmaster of the Whitehill school. A thin gentleman in his early sixties, Doctor Warren was in the doorway with the manager of the inn, looking over the arrangements for the Africans.

Sylvia was full of news. The long table, she related, was for the thirty boys from Africa. "I'll bet that's more black people than have eaten here since this place was founded," she said softly. "How fast things change these days!"

"You're right about how fast things change," said Doctor Remenzel. "You're wrong about the black people who've eaten here. This used to be a busy part of the Underground Railroad."[4]

"Really?" said Sylvia. "How exciting." She looked all about herself in a birdlike way. "I

It was then that Eli got up abruptly, fled the dining room, fled as much of the nightmare as he could possibly leave behind. He brushed past Doctor Warren rudely, though he knew him well, though Doctor Warren spoke his name. Doctor Warren looked after him sadly.

"I'll be darned," said Doctor Remenzel. "What brought that on?"

"Maybe he really *is* sick," said Sylvia.

The Remenzels had no time to react more elaborately, because Doctor Warren spotted them and crossed quickly to their table. He greeted them, some of his perplexity about Eli showing in his greeting. He asked if he might sit down.

---

4. Underground Railroad: A system set up to help fugitive slaves escape to the North and to Canada before the Civil War.

"Certainly, of course," said Doctor Remenzel expansively. "We'd be honored if you did. Heavens."

"Not to eat," said Doctor Warren. "I'll be eating at the long table with the new boys. I would like to talk, though." He saw that there were five places set at the table. "You're expecting someone?"

"We passed Tom Hilyer and his boy on the way," said Doctor Remenzel. "They'll be along in a minute."

"Good, good," said Doctor Warren absent-ly. He fidgeted, looked again in the direction in which Eli had disappeared.

"Tom's boy will be going to Whitehill in the fall?" said Doctor Remenzel.

"H'm?" said Doctor Warren. "Oh—yes, yes. Yes, he will."

"Is he a scholarship boy, like his father?" said Sylvia.

"That's not a polite question," said Doctor Remenzel severely.

"I beg your pardon," said Sylvia.

"No, no—that's a perfectly proper question these days," said Doctor Warren. "We don't keep that sort of information very secret any more. We're proud of our scholarship boys, and they have every reason to be proud of themselves. Tom's boy got the highest score anyone's ever got on the entrance examinations. We feel privileged to have him."

"We never *did* find out Eli's score," said Doctor Remenzel. He said it with good-humored resignation, without expectation that Eli had done especially well.

"A good strong medium, I imagine," said Sylvia. She said this on the basis of Eli's grades in primary school, which had ranged from medium to terrible.

The headmaster looked surprised. "I didn't tell you his scores?" he said.

"We haven't seen you since he took the examinations," said Doctor Remenzel.

"The letter I wrote you—" said Doctor Warren.

"What letter?" said Doctor Remenzel. "Did we get a letter?"

"A letter from me," said Doctor Warren, with growing incredulity. "The hardest letter I ever had to write."

Sylvia shook her head. "We never got any letter from you."

Doctor Warren sat back, looking very ill. "I mailed it myself," he said. "It was definitely mailed—two weeks ago."

Doctor Remenzel shrugged. "The U.S. mails don't lose much," he said, "but I guess that now and then something gets misplaced."

Doctor Warren cradled his head in his hands. "Oh, dear—oh, my, oh, Lord," he said. "I was surprised to see Eli here. I wondered that he would want to come along with you."

"He didn't come along just to see the scenery," said Doctor Remenzel. "He came to enroll."

"I want to know what was in the letter," said Sylvia.

Doctor Warren raised his head, folded his hands. "What the letter said was this, and no other words could be more difficult for me to say: *'On the basis of his work in primary school and his scores on the entrance examinations, I must tell you that your son and my good friend Eli cannot possibly do the work required of boys at Whitehill.'"* Doctor Warren's voice steadied, and so did his gaze. *"To admit Eli to Whitehill, to expect him to do Whitehill work,'"* he said, *"'would be both unrealistic and cruel.'"*

Thirty African boys, escorted by several faculty members, State Department men, and

diplomats from their own countries, filed into the dining room.

And Tom Hilyer and his boy, having no idea that something had just gone awfully wrong for the Remenzels, came in, too, and said hello to the Remenzels and Doctor Warren gaily, as though life couldn't possibly be better.

"I'll talk to you more about this later, if you like," Doctor Warren said to the Remenzels, rising. "I have to go now, but later on—" He left quickly.

"My mind's a blank," said Sylvia. "My mind's a perfect blank."

Tom Hilyer and his boy sat down. Hilyer looked at the menu before him, clapped his hands and said, "What's good? I'm hungry." And then he said, "Say—where's your boy?"

"He stepped out for a moment," said Doctor Remenzel evenly.

"We've got to find him," said Sylvia to her husband.

"In time, in due time," said Doctor Remenzel.

"That letter," said Sylvia; "Eli knew about it. He found it and tore it up. Of course he did!" She started to cry, thinking of the hideous trap Eli had caught himself in.

"I'm not interested right now in what Eli's done," said Doctor Remenzel. "Right now I'm a lot more interested in what some other people are going to do."

"What do you mean?" said Sylvia.

Doctor Remenzel stood impressively, angry and determined. "I mean," he said, "I'm going to see how quickly people can change their minds around here."

"Please," said Sylvia, trying to hold him, trying to calm him, "we've got to find Eli. That's the first thing."

"The first thing," said Doctor Remenzel quite loudly, "is to get Eli admitted to Whitehill. After that we'll find him, and we'll bring him back."

"But darling—" said Sylvia.

"No 'but' about it," said Doctor Remenzel. "There's a majority of the Board of Overseers in this room at this very moment. Every one of them is a close friend of mine, or a close friend of my father. If they tell Doctor Warren Eli's in, that's it—Eli's in. If there's room for all these other people," he said, "there's darn well room for Eli too."

He strode quickly to a table nearby, sat down heavily, and began to talk to a fierce-looking and splendid old gentleman who was eating there. The old gentleman was chairman of the board.

Sylvia apologized to the baffled Hilyers and then went in search of Eli.

Asking this person and that person, Sylvia found him. He was outside—all alone on a bench in a bower of lilacs that had just begun to bud.

Eli heard his mother's coming on the gravel path, stayed where he was, resigned. "Did you find out," he said, "or do I still have to tell you?"

"About you?" she said gently.

"About not getting in? Doctor Warren told us."

"I tore his letter up," said Eli.

"I can understand that," she said. "Your father and I have always made you feel that you had to go to Whitehill, that nothing else would do."

"I feel better," said Eli. He tried to smile, found he could do it easily. "I feel so much better now that it's over. I tried to tell you a couple of times—but I just couldn't. I didn't know how."

"That's my fault, not yours," she said.

"What's father doing?" said Eli.

Sylvia was so intent on comforting Eli that she'd put out of her mind what her husband was up to. Now she realized that Doctor Remenzel was making a ghastly mistake. She didn't want Eli admitted to Whitehill, could see what a cruel thing that would be.

She couldn't bring herself to tell the boy what his father was doing, so she said, "He'll be along in a minute, dear. He understands." And then she said, "You wait here, and I'll go get him and come right back."

But she didn't have to go to Doctor Remenzel. At that moment, the big man came out of the inn and caught sight of his wife and son. He came to her and to Eli. He looked dazed.

"Well?" she said.

"They—they all said no," said Doctor Remenzel, very subdued.

"That's for the best," said Sylvia. "I'm relieved. I really am."

"Who said no?" said Eli. "Who said no to what?"

"The members of the board," said Doctor Remenzel, not looking anyone in the eye. "I asked them to make an exception in your case—to reverse their decision and let you in."

Eli stood, his face filled with incredulity and shame that were instant. "You what?" he said, and there was no childishness in the way he said it. Next came anger. "You shouldn't have done that!" he said to his father.

Doctor Remenzel nodded. "So I've already been told."

"That isn't done!" said Eli. "How awful! You shouldn't have!"

"You're right," said Doctor Remenzel, accepting the scolding lamely.

"Now I *am* ashamed," said Eli, and he showed that he was.

Doctor Remenzel, in his wretchedness, could find no strong words to say. "I apologize to you both," he said at last. "It was a very bad thing to try."

"Now a Remenzel *has* asked for something," said Eli.

"I don't suppose Ben's back yet with the car?" said Doctor Remenzel. It was obvious that Ben wasn't. "We'll wait out here for him," he said. "I don't want to go back in there now."

"A Remenzel asked for something—as though a Remenzel were something special," said Eli.

"I don't suppose—" said Doctor Remenzel, and he left the sentence unfinished, dangling in the air.

"You don't suppose what?" said his wife, her face puzzled.

"I don't suppose," said Doctor Remenzel, "that we'll ever be coming here any more."

In this story, **Kurt Vonnegut** (1922–   ) writes about the relationships among family members. However, Vonnegut is probably best known for his science fiction, which sometimes describes relationships between humans and machines! Two of Vonnegut's novels, *Cat's Cradle* and *Slaughterhouse Five,* include elements of science fiction.

 **Respond**

- Which character seemed most dishonest to you? Why?
- Share your evaluations of characters with a small group of classmates. Compare notes and discuss your reactions to each member of the Remenzel family.

Activities

MAKE MEANING

Explore Your Reading

Look Back (Recall)

1. How do Eli's parents react differently to the truth?

Think It Over (Interpret)

2. At the beginning of the story, how does Mrs. Remenzel's attitude toward the school differ from her husband's? What does her view tell you about her?
3. Why didn't Eli tell his parents about the letter?
4. What do you learn about Eli's parents from their different responses to his lie?
5. The title of this story is "The Lie." How are different ways of lying shown in the story?

Go Beyond (Apply)

6. How do you think family life for the Remenzels will change in the future?

Develop Reading and Literary Skills

Discover Theme Through Character

Judgments you make about characters can lead you to a story's **theme,** its central message about life. By completing the sentences that follow you can begin to turn your judgments into a statement of theme. You may want to refer to the notes you made while reading.

- I would trust ____ more than ____ or _____.
- Why? The lie that ___ tells is less serious than the deceptions of ___ and ___ .
- What does this comparison of lies suggest about the author's message?

Using your judgments of the characters, together with your responses to the questions, write a statement of the author's theme. Use the following statement as a model:

The theme of the story is that _____ is the worst kind of lying. It is worse than _____ or _____ because _____.

Ideas for Writing

Often short stories show you a limited part of the action, leaving you to imagine the rest. You can learn a great deal about "The Lie" by imagining what its author did *not* write.

Diary Entries As one of the characters, write three diary entries. Date the first entry the night before the trip, the second at the end of the story, and the third a year later.

Story Sequel Extend the story by writing a short account of the Remenzels' trip home.

Ideas for Projects

Dramatic Scene Work with a group of classmates to stage a drama in which Dr. Remenzel meets with the Whitehall's Board of Directors. Present his arguments for Eli's admission to the school and the board's reaction.

Bar Graph Use a graph showing bars of different lengths to indicate which lies in this story were the worst. After drawing your graph, present it to the class and explain your conclusions. [Math Link]

How Am I Doing?

Answer the following questions in your journal:

What did I learn from the story by focusing my reading on characters?

In group work, was I better at listening or sharing my own views? What do I need to work on next time I'm in a group?

Who Gives Me Inspiration?

Student Art *Celebration* Rudy Torres
Lakewood, California

Student Writing Dyan Watson, *Jefferson High School, Portland, Oregon*

My Father Was a Musician

In the basement they played.
"Jam session" he called it,
halting only to mend a chord or two.

The house swayed from side to side
dancing freely, carelessly
while neighbors shut doors and windows.

Sometimes I would sneak into his bedroom
just to see it, touch it,
pluck a string or two.

At night, I dreamed
of concerts and demos.

I want to be just like him.

What do older and younger people have to offer each other?

Reach Into Your Background

You probably know older people who have shared their experiences with you. Now imagine that you have lived a long time and choose one piece of advice to offer a young person.

• Role-play the scene with a partner, first being the one who gives advice and then the one who receives it.

• Talk with classmates about the advice you give and receive.

Read Actively
Visualize Characters in Drama

Drama comes to life when it is performed. When you read a play, you'll enjoy it more and understand it better if you create a theater in your mind. **Visualize,** or picture, the characters as they move and speak their lines.

"Snow Flowers" is about a friendship between a younger and an older woman. Imagine you must select actors for the play. While reading, picture the characters in your mind and think of friends or well-known actors who could play these roles.

Snow Flowers

Amanda Gross

Characters **Estelle** Elderly woman
Young Samantha
Adult Samantha

Place Empty stage with chair (stage 1), board and care home (stage 2), and museum (stage 3)

Time Present and 10 years ago

Scene 1

[*As lights come up on "stage 1," a woman in her twenties is sitting in a chair.*]

ADULT SAMANTHA. Sometimes when I got there you'd be waiting for me. The nurses said you would walk out of art class and go to the bench to wait. They said you always left at 3:25 because I came at 3:30 and you didn't want me to have to come inside to get you.

[*Lights gradually rise on "stage 2."*]

I could see you as I rounded the corner, swaddled in layers of outdated clothing. Floral print top and red and pink striped pants. Your hair was up in that crazy beehive that made it so

hard for you to keep your neck straight.

[*Lights simultaneously fade out on "stage 1" and come up on "stage 2."*

As lights come up, ESTELLE sits with a mug and a dixie cup on the bench. A little girl comes running onto stage. On her shirt she has a paper cut-out imitation of a medal ribbon that says "Citizen of the Day." She is carrying a bookbag and a lunch box.

As YOUNG SAMANTHA nears, ESTELLE rises to hug her.]

ESTELLE. [*As they embrace*] Hi, Sweetie!

YOUNG SAMANTHA. [*Enthusiastic*] Hi, Estelle! I made you something!

ESTELLE. I made you something too!

[*ESTELLE and SAMANTHA exchange gifts. SAMANTHA gives ESTELLE a ceramic flower and ESTELLE gives*

Words to Know

swaddled (SWAHD uhld) *adj.*: Wrapped

SAMANTHA *a paper crown, eloquently colored.*

SAMANTHA *puts on crown after looking at it and smiles.* ESTELLE *still holds the flower.*]

ESTELLE. Samantha! This is beautiful! When did you make it?

SAMANTHA. In art class last week. It's been baking in the kilt, though.

ESTELLE. You mean kiln[1]—a kilt is a skirt that Scottish men wear.

SAMANTHA. Scottish men wear skirts?

ESTELLE. Some do. [SAMANTHA *ponders this over a while.*] I made yours in art class today. [*Noticing "Citizen of the Day" pin*] Hey! Samantha, you got "citizen of the day" again!

SAMANTHA. Yeah! It's from Mrs. Kay, the one who reminds me of the good witch from the Wizard of Oz.

[ESTELLE *smiles, then remembers.*]

ESTELLE. Oh! I almost forgot I bribed Pinky into making you some hot cocoa so you wouldn't freeze on me out here! And . . . [*Smiling*] I saved you one of those lemon creme cookies from the snack cart.

SAMANTHA. You got Pinky to make *me* hot cocoa! Wow! [*Starts to eat cookies*] These are really good! Want some? [*Takes crown off and puts it beside her*]

ESTELLE. No, that's okay. I don't really care for them. [*Pause*] Did you have Brownies Thursday?

SAMANTHA. No, chocolate chip.

ESTELLE. Silly, I meant like Girl Scouts, Brownies.

SAMANTHA. Oh. [SAMANTHA *is quiet and puts her head down.*]

ESTELLE. Samantha, what happened?

SAMANTHA. It's nothing . . . Well, it's just . . . Lindsay Ellis is so mean to me!

ESTELLE. How is she mean to you?

SAMANTHA. Well, lots of ways. Let's see . . . Oh! I know! She always steps on the toe I broke last year. She steps on it real hard and then laughs and says "Sorry." AND! She told everyone I wear Miss Piggy underwear.

ESTELLE. Do you?

SAMANTHA. What?

ESTELLE. Wear Miss Piggy underwear?

SAMANTHA. Estelle!!

ESTELLE. [*Laughing*] Sorry! Is there anything else this Lindsay is doing to you, because if she's hurting you, you have to tell a teacher.

SAMANTHA. Well, it's not exactly doing, I mean it's sorta, well . . . making fun.

ESTELLE. Making fun of what, Samantha?

SAMANTHA. Well, making fun of you.

ESTELLE. [*Half-laughing, half-concerned*] Making fun of me?

SAMANTHA. Yeah.

ESTELLE. Samantha, how was she making fun of me?

[SAMANTHA *is annoyed now; this is obviously an inner conflict which she has problems expressing.*]

SAMANTHA. [*Mildly*] Well, um, she was making fun of your hair and the way you dressed.

ESTELLE. [*Mildly outraged/slightly hurried*] What about my hair and my clothing?

---

1. **kiln** (KILN) *n.*: An oven for drying or baking pottery.

SAMANTHA. I don't know.

ESTELLE. [*Pressing*] What about my hair?

SAMANTHA. [*Harshly/rushed*] She said your hair looked like a bird could live in it and that your clothes were so old they didn't even use that kind of material anymore. She said you looked as if you were stuck in a time warp and not coming out any time soon. And it wasn't only Lindsay; it was Brooke and Melissa, too, and then they all laughed and agreed.

📖 **Read Actively**

Visualize the young Samantha.

OKAY? [*Pause*] It doesn't matter.

ESTELLE. [*Firmly*] No, Samantha, obviously it does, it is apparent that what she said bothered you. [*Pause*] You don't have to come visit me anymore. That adopt a grandparent thingy is way over.

SAMANTHA. I know, but I like to come visit.

Words to Know

apparent (uh PAR uhnt) *adj.*: Obvious; clearly seen

ESTELLE. Well then, if you like visiting, then it doesn't matter what Lindsay Whosybody says, does it?

SAMANTHA. [*Not very convincingly*] No, I guess not. [*She takes a bite of cookie and puts crown back on her head. She sips from the mug, smiling cautiously at ESTELLE.*]

[*Lights fade off "stage 2" and come up on "stage 1."*]

ADULT SAMANTHA. I didn't go back to visit you the next week. Instead, I walked home, sat on my bed, and watched my pink radio clock: 3:29, 3:30.

📖 **Read Actively**

Ask yourself how much time has passed.

I watched until 4:00, when I imagined you would've gotten up from our bench to go inside. I tried to picture what it would be like when you got into your room. But I couldn't. I didn't know what your room looked like, because you'd never invited me to it. I imagined it the same as the ones I had seen when I came to visit the first time and had to go to the bathroom. I imagined it all white with a yellow curtain on the window and a chair by your bed. You never told me why you didn't want me to come in, but I guessed it was because you didn't want me to see the people in their wheel chairs, sitting facing the walls. I couldn't blame you. [*Pause*] When I went back the next week to visit, you didn't mention anything about how I hadn't come.

[*Lights cross fade to "stage 2."*]

ESTELLE. Hi, sweetie! What, no "citizen of the day" ribbon?

YOUNG SAMANTHA. No, today we had Mrs. Archer, the wicked witch. She doesn't give them out. [*Pause*] Close your

eyes. I have a surprise for you. [*She pulls out a real ribbon that is bright blue—in red magic marker it says "VERY SPECIAL PERSON."*] I know it's not "citizen of the day" or anything, but I thought you might like it. [ESTELLE *pins on the ribbon.*]

SAMANTHA. [*Bowing head*] Look, I'm sorry about last week.

ESTELLE. [*Smiling*] Last week?

SAMANTHA. That I didn't, um, you know, come to visit last week.

ESTELLE. Oh gosh, Samantha, you know how bad my memory is and all, I hadn't even remembered . . . you didn't visit?

SAMANTHA. No.

ESTELLE. Well, don't worry, it doesn't matter! [*Smiling*] Hey, little lady, do you feel like seeing some dinosaurs on Sunday?

SAMANTHA. Dinosaurs?

ESTELLE. There's an exhibit at the museum on Sunday, whadda ya think?

SAMANTHA. [*Excited*] Did you get a pass from Mrs. Ackerby?

ESTELLE. Would you think I couldn't? [*Waves pass at SAMANTHA*]

[*Lights cross fade to "stage 1."*]

ADULT SAMANTHA. Sunday came and I met you and we walked holding hands, like me and my mom did when I was younger, to the bus stop. It started to snow as we went in to see the dinosaurs.

[*Lights cross fade to "stage 3."*]

SAMANTHA. How old are the dinosaurs?

ESTELLE. Very, very old.

SAMANTHA. Yeah, but how old?

ESTELLE. They are so old that when

that covers everything. It stings my eyes.

[*Lights cross fade to "stage 3."*]

ESTELLE. You see all that white, Samantha? That's what it was like when the dinosaurs lived—untouched, pure. If you look real hard, Samantha, all that white snow is dozens and dozens of white flowers covering the land. White flowers that no one will pick. [SAMANTHA *reaches for the ground/snow;* ESTELLE *stops her.*] No . . . There's our bus. [SAMANTHA *goes to cross the snow to get to the bus.*] No, we'll walk around.

SAMANTHA. But we'll miss it . . . ?

ESTELLE. There'll be another.

Untitled Susi Kilgore, Courtesy of the artist

they lived, there were no buildings, no museums, in fact, there were no people. Just lots of land.

SAMANTHA. No people?

ESTELLE. No people.

SAMANTHA. Wow! There must've been lots of flowers if there were no people or buildings. If there was all that land like you said, lots and lots of flowers and no one would pick them. I wish we could've seen it. The purple, the yellow, the red, the white. I bet it looked pretty.

[*Lights cross fade to "stage 1."*]

YOUNG SAMANTHA. The ground is covered with snow. A complete white blanket

> 📖 **Read Actively**
>
> **Ask yourself** what this shows you about Estelle's character.

[*Lights cross fade to "stage 1."*]

ADULT SAMANTHA. As we stood there watching, our bus drove away. If we would've walked through the snow, or flowers, we could've caught it. But there *would* be another and we could wait.

[*Lights cross fade to "stage 2."* SAMANTHA *enters with her head down, dragging her bookbag.*]

ESTELLE. Sweetie, what's wrong?

SAMANTHA. [*In tears*] I wanted to get my ears pierced, but my parents won't let me.

ESTELLE. Oh! Samantha, what do you need earrings for? You're beautiful with or without holes in your ears.

SAMANTHA. It's just that everyone else has theirs pierced. I'm the only one who doesn't. And we take class pictures Friday! All the girls will have earrings except for me! They'll make fun of me, all of them, even the boys.

ESTELLE. I know what'll cheer you up! They've done another part for the dinosaur exhibit at the museum. They found the bones of Tyrannosaurus Rex. He's enormous. Probably will be pretty scary!

[SAMANTHA *is sulking; she leans over and hugs* ESTELLE.]

SAMANTHA. Do you want to take the 1:00 bus on Sunday?

[*Lights cross fade to "stage 1."*]

ADULT SAMANTHA. I sulked about my ears and picture day the whole week. I looked forward to Thursday though.

[*Lights cross fade to "stage 2."*]

ESTELLE. I have something for you. [*No response*] C'mon, cheer up! [ESTELLE *takes out a box with a bow on it and hands it to* SAMANTHA.] Now, don't tell me your little heart isn't beating fast, and you aren't wondering what's in that box!

[SAMANTHA *stops sulking and smirks. She opens the box and finds a pair of earrings and two loops made from gold baker box tying string.*]

ESTELLE. You see. [*Demonstrating*] You put these over your ears and dangle a pair of earrings from 'em.

[*Lights cross fade to "stage 1."*]

ADULT SAMANTHA. I didn't wear the earrings for picture day. It would've been one thing to be laughed at for not having pierced ears, but to wear the earrings you made, would've been too much to bear.

[*Lights cross fade to "stage 1" as they embrace.*]

ADULT SAMANTHA. It was cold the next Thursday when I went to visit. I was putting on my gloves, as I rounded the corner I knew I'd soon see you with your silly hairdo sticking up, sitting on our bench.

YOUNG and ADULT SAMANTHA. Estelle!

ADULT SAMANTHA. There she lay, swaddled in layers of outdated clothing, her floral print shirt and red and pink striped pants.

YOUNG and ADULT SAMANTHA. Estelle!

ADULT SAMANTHA. It was too late . . . I stared in amazement as the ambulance drove away . . . Wondering why they hadn't put the siren on.

Respond

- Would you have enjoyed knowing Estelle? Why?
- With a group of classmates, compare the ideas you had for casting this play.

"When I was seven or eight, both my brother and sister were doing volunteer work in a nursing home. I'd go with them, taking along my violin to entertain the people there. Finally, the residents told me my playing was terrible, but they liked me. And I kept going back."

Amanda Gross (1976–) used this experience to create "Snow Flowers." She was still in high school when "Snow Flowers" was performed at the New Jersey Young Playwright's Festival.

Activities

MAKE MEANING

Explore Your Reading

Look Back (Recall)

1. Summarize what goes on between Estelle and Samantha during their friendship.

Think It Over (Interpret)

2. What is special about their continued friendship?
3. Of the things Estelle hears from Samantha, which probably give her the most pleasure? Which might be painful? Why?
4. How does the friendship help Samantha feel better about herself?
5. How does the title of the play relate to the friendship?

Go Beyond (Apply)

6. How will Samantha continue to be influenced by her childhood friendship with Estelle?

Develop Reading and Literary Skills

Analyze Characters in Drama

Visualizing, or picturing, the characters in this drama helped you see a challenge that playwrights face. They must present **characters,** or made-up people, through actions, words, and the stage directions in brackets that go with the words. Unlike story writers, they cannot explain in detail how a character is happy or sad, kind or cruel.

Remember how each character's words and the stage directions suggested something about her. For instance, Samantha's first words to Estelle—"[Enthusiastic] Hi, Estelle! I made you something!"—suggest that Samantha is a warm person and that she likes Estelle very much.

Explain what the following words and stage directions tell you about each character.

SAMANTHA [Mildly] Well, um, she was making fun of your hair and the way you dressed.

ESTELLE [Mildly outraged/slightly hurried] What about my hair and my clothing?

Ideas for Writing

Imagine you are a director planning to stage this play.

How-to Memorandum Write a memo to the actor who will play Estelle. Give her instructions on what to wear and how to move and speak.

Dramatic Monologue Extend the play by writing a brief speech for an adult Samantha ten years older than the one in the play. Have her think back on her friendship with Estelle. Make sure her words give a clear picture of what she is thinking and feeling.

Ideas for Projects

Field Trip Visit a local senior center and talk with some of the people who spend time there. After the visit, create a work of art or a piece of writing that conveys what the experience meant to you. [Social Studies Link]

Pen Pal Work with the administration of a nursing home to provide pen pals for your class. Share both the letters you write and the ones you receive. [Social Studies Link]

How Am I Doing?

Consider the following questions in a small group:

How did visualizing the characters help me understand the play better? How can I use this skill when reading other types of writing?

Which writing assignment or project helped me think about older people in a new way? How?

What childhood memories will stay with you as you grow?

Reach Into Your Background

As you grow older, certain experiences you've shared with adults will stand out in your memory. Years from now, you may remember a family camping trip or a time when an adult shared an afternoon with you. Think of a moment like this from your own experience or from a movie you've seen. Then try one or both of these activities:

• Write about the moment in a journal.
• Describe the experience to a partner.

Read Actively
Gather Evidence About Theme

Each of these selections describes a moment shared by a child and an adult. What message, or **theme**, are the writers trying to give you? You can answer that question by **gathering evidence**, or important facts and details, about the relationships that are described. Gathering evidence as you read will help you understand the ideas that writers want to communicate.

To gather evidence, imagine that you're writing a thank-you card that each boy might give his father. While reading, jot down specific things for which the boys might thank their fathers.

Back-to-Back

Ken Burns and Geoffrey C. Ward

SEPTEMBER 14, 1990. The Seattle Mariners were playing the California Angels. It was the top of the first when 40-year-old Ken Griffey Sr. came to bat. Watching from the on-deck circle was his son, Ken Griffey Jr. The younger Griffey was just 20, but he was already a star.

A year earlier, Ken Sr. had been playing for the Reds, and Ken Jr. was a Mariner rookie. It was the first time a father and son had ever played in the same major league season. They were proud of each other—baseball was a family tradition. Someday, they dreamed, they might play the outfield together. Then, in August, Ken Sr. joined the Mariners, and the dream came true.

Now the Griffeys were the first father and son to be on the same major league team. Ken Sr. waited for the pitch. There was a man on first with no one out. Down two strikes, Ken saw the change-up[1] coming. He lined the ball hard, 402 feet to center. Home run!

Ken Jr. stepped into the batter's box. The pitcher threw him three straight balls.[2] But he smacked the fourth pitch 388 feet to left-center. Home run!

The Griffeys had achieved yet another first—back-to-back homers by father and son. The California crowd had unexpectedly seen baseball history. "What a moment," the Seattle manager said later. "You're never going to see this happen again."

Ken Sr. retired in 1991. In 1992, Ken Jr. was named the All-Star Game's Most Valuable Player. His dad had won the same award twelve years earlier. They're the only father and son in baseball history to accomplish that feat.

By 1993, Ken Jr. was a superstar slugger. Ken Sr. watched him proudly from the stands. As in many baseball-loving families, a father had taught his son to love—and play—the game.

Ken Griffey Sr. (left) and his son

---

1. change-up n.: A pitch slower than a fastball used to surprise a batter expecting a faster pitch.

2. balls n.: Pitches judged by the umpire to be out of the strike zone between a batter's knees and shoulders. If a pitcher throws a batter four balls, the batter is advanced to first base.

Words to Know

rookie (ROO kee) n.: A first-year player

feat (FEET) n.: A remarkable accomplishment

The Gift
Li-Young Lee

To pull the metal splinter from my palm
my father recited a story in a low voice.
I watched his lovely face and not the blade.
Before the story ended, he'd removed
5   the iron sliver I thought I'd die from.

I can't remember the tale,
but hear his voice still, a well
of dark water, a prayer.
And I recall his hands,
10 two measures of tenderness
he laid against my face,
the flames of discipline
he raised above my head.

Had you entered that afternoon
15 you would have thought you saw a man
planting something in a boy's palm,
a silver tear, a tiny flame.
Had you followed that boy
you would have arrived here,
20 where I bend over my wife's right hand.

Look how I shave her thumbnail down
so carefully she feels no pain.
Watch as I lift the splinter out.
I was seven when my father
25 took my hand like this,
and I did not hold that shard
between my fingers and think,
Metal that will bury me,
christen it Little Assassin,
30 Ore Going Deep for My Heart.

And I did not lift up my wound and cry,
Death visited here!
I did what a child does
when he's given something to keep.
35 I kissed my father.

Hand and collage Fred Otnes, Courtesy of the artist

Words to Know

shard (SHAHRD) *n.*: A fragment or broken
piece, especially glass or pottery (line 26)

Dawn Discovery

Jim Sanderson

One day when I was a small boy during the lean days of the Depression, my father got me up before dawn to go duck hunting. He had been a car salesman but nobody was buying De Sotos that year, so he finally found a job in a gas station. That morning he carried a shotgun he had borrowed from a friend "to shoot a little something for our table."

It was first light when we settled ourselves into the reeds at the edge of the lake. Almost immediately a wave of thirty of the big birds passed high overhead, filling the air with their haunting, unforgettable honking. I can still hear it now, when I set my memory on it. I had never seen before such majestic, purposeful birds, formed into a perfect aerial V.

I looked at my father as he uttered a little groan of awe. He stood transfixed as the flock flew across the sunrise. "Canadian snow geese," he finally said, the shotgun still at his feet.

We never saw another bird the entire morning. But driving home, Dad appeared strangely unconcerned that we were coming home empty-handed without fifty cents in our pockets. "Weren't they something?" he exulted.

Words to Know

transfixed (trans FIKSD) *adj.*: Unable to move, as if pierced through

exulted (eg ZULT id) *v.*: Rejoiced; said happily

As a boy, **Ken Burns** (1953–   ) played baseball all the time. When he was a college student, he and his father protested at antiwar demonstrations. Later, Burns would combine his interests in sports and social awareness to make acclaimed films. Burns and historian **Geoffrey C. Ward** (1940–   ) achieved fame with *The Civil War,* a documentary made for the Public Broadcasting Company. This was followed by another excellent documentary film on the national pastime, *Baseball.*

Li-Young Lee (1957–   ) often writes about his father. Born in Indonesia of Chinese parents, Li-Young Lee lived in Hong Kong, Macao, and Japan before settling in the United States. His father, a minister, was arrested in Indonesia as a political prisoner and later led a congregation in Pennsylvania. Much of Li-Young Lee's memoir, *The Winged Seed* (1995), is about his father.

After working for years as a foreign correspondent, **Jim Sanderson** (1925–   ) wrote a syndicated column, *Liberated Male,* which appeared during the 1970's and early 1980's. Sanderson found that when men began to look at themselves as something other than tough guys and wage earners, they often came face-to-face with memories of their fathers. This column is one of several pieces he wrote about his own dad.

Respond

- Which father did you like the best? Why?
- Picture another day in the life of these families. Compare ideas with a partner and together imagine another situation that reveals the family relationships.

Activities
MAKE MEANING

Explore Your Reading

Look Back (Recall)

1. Briefly summarize each selection.

Think It Over (Interpret)

2. How did his father's career in major league baseball help inspire Ken Griffey Jr.?
3. Why does the narrator of "Dawn Discovery" remember this event as an adult?
4. Why do you think the poem by Li-Young Lee is titled "The Gift"?
5. What have these fathers contributed to their sons' identities?

Go Beyond (Apply)

6. How do adults help shape children's values and personalities? Explain.

Develop Reading and Literary Skills

Use Evidence to Identify Implied Theme

Gathering important facts and details in a piece of reading will help you identify a selection's **theme,** its central message. Sometimes the theme is stated directly. More often, it is **implied,** or suggested, and you must figure it out from the evidence you've gathered.

For instance, you know these facts about "The Gift": The title suggests the poem is about giving and in the poem, a father helps his son overcome a fear. Putting these facts together, you can figure out what the father is giving his son.

1. Use the titles and facts from the two other selections to state their implied themes.
2. Choose the statement that best expresses the theme of all three selections and explain your choice:

     Fathers are human beings just like everybody else.

     Fathers contribute to their children's identities in many ways.

Ideas for Writing

Many different people help you grow and give you inspiration. Think of someone who has been especially helpful to you recently.

Letter Write a letter of appreciation to this person. If you prefer, choose a character from any selection in this group and write the letter he might write.

Poem Imagine that the local mall is sponsoring a contest in which teenagers are invited to submit artwork, essays, or poems in honor of their adult heroes. Write a poem that you would submit to honor an adult who has helped you.

Ideas for Projects

Advertisement As a character in one of these pieces, write a job description for a good father. List the duties the job requires and describe the qualities the candidate must have.

Inspirations Album Collect evidence of adults helping children. You may want to include pictures from magazines, video footage, or popular songs. Also include an explanation for each item you choose, and present your album to the class.
[Social Studies Link]

How Am I Doing?

Take a few minutes to write the answers to these questions in your journal:

What did these selections help me understand about people who inspire me?

What information did I use to discover the theme? What did I learn that will help me find the theme in future readings?

Activities PREVIEW
The Bear Boy   by Joseph Bruchac

What can humans learn from animals?

Reach Into Your Background

It's more usual to think of humans teaching animals than animals teaching humans. However, many Native American groups stress what they can learn from animals. Often their folk tales, stories passed down over many years, have animal characters who teach important lessons. With a partner, do one or both of the following:

• List some lessons that we might learn from animals.

• Imagine what animals could tell us if they could talk.

Read Actively
Identify Cultural Details

Beyond telling a story, folk tales also tell you about the **culture**, or group of people, that created them. They may tell you such cultural details as what people eat and wear, the customs they follow, and the beliefs they share. For instance, the Pueblo tale "The Bear Boy" reflects the belief that animals can teach important lessons.

As you read, keep a list of animals in the story and note how each is helpful. You might even create a card for each type of animal, with its picture on the front and what it teaches on the back.

Mimbres bowl from Swarts Ruin
Mimbres Valley, New Mex. Peabody
Museum of Archaeology & Ethnology
Cambridge, Mass.

The Bear Boy

Joseph Bruchac

Long ago, in a Pueblo village, a boy named Kuo-Haya lived with his father. But his father did not treat him well. In his heart he still mourned the death of his wife, Kuo-Haya's mother, and did not enjoy doing things with his son. He did not teach his boy how to run. He did not show him how to wrestle. He was always too busy.

As a result, Kuo-Haya was a timid boy and walked about stooped over all of the time. When the other boys raced or wrestled, Kuo-Haya slipped away. He spent much of his time alone.

Time passed, and the boy reached the age when his father should have been helping him get ready for his initiation into manhood. Still Kuo-Haya's father paid no attention at all to his son.

One day Kuo-Haya was out walking far from the village, toward the cliffs where the bears lived.

Words to Know

timid (TIM id) *adj.*: Showing fear or shyness

initiation (i nish ee AY shuhn) *n.*: The ceremony by which a boy is accepted as a man; a beginning

Now the people of the village always knew they must stay away from these cliffs, for the bear was a very powerful animal. It was said that if someone saw a bear's tracks and followed them, he might never come back. But Kuo-Haya had never been told about this. When he came upon the tracks of a bear, Kuo-Haya followed them along an arroyo, a small canyon cut by a winding stream, up into the mesas.[1] The tracks led into a little box canyon below some caves. There, he came upon some bear cubs.

When they saw Kuo-Haya, the little bears ran away. But Kuo-Haya sat down and called to them in a friendly voice.

"I will not hurt you," he said to the bear cubs. "Come and play with me."

---

1. **mesas** (MAY suhs) *n.*: Large, high rocks with steep sides and flat tops.

The bears walked back out of the bushes. Soon the boy and the bears were playing together. As they played, however, a shadow came over them. Kuo-Haya looked up and saw the mother bear standing above him.

"Where is Kuo-Haya?" the people asked his father.

"I do not know," the father said.

"Then you must find him!"

So the father and other people of the pueblo began to search for the missing boy. They went through the canyons calling his name. But they found no sign of the boy there. Finally, when they reached the cliffs, the best trackers found his footsteps and the path of the bears. They followed the tracks along the arroyo and up into the mesas to the box canyon. In front of a cave, they saw the boy playing with the bear cubs as the mother bear watched them approvingly, nudging Kuo-Haya now and then to encourage him.

The trackers crept close, hoping to grab the boy and run. But as soon as the mother bear caught their scent, she growled and pushed her cubs and the boy back into the cave.

"The boy is with the bears," the trackers said when they returned to the village.

"What shall we do?" the people asked.

"It is the responsibility of the boy's father," said the medicine man. Then he called Kuo-Haya's father to him.

"You have not done well," said the medicine man. "You are the one who must guide your boy to manhood, but you have neglected him. Now the mother bear is caring for your boy as you should have done all along. She is teaching him to be strong as a young man must be strong. If you love your son, only you can get him back."

Every one of the medicine man's words went into the father's heart like an arrow. He began to realize that he had been blind to his son's needs because of his own sorrow.

"You are right," he said. "I will go and bring back my son."

Kuo-Haya's father went along the arroyo and climbed the cliffs. When he came to the bears' cave, he found Kuo-Haya wrestling with the little bears. As the father watched, he saw that his son seemed more sure of himself than ever before.

"Kuo-Haya," he shouted. "Come to me."

Bear Storyteller, 1981
Louis Naranjo (Cochiti)

The boy looked at him and then just walked into the cave. Although the father tried to follow, the big mother bear stood up on her hind legs and growled. She would not allow the father to come any closer.

So Kuo-Haya's father went back to his home. He was angry now. He began to gather together his weapons, and brought out his bow and his arrows and his lance.[2] But the medicine man came to his lodge and showed him the bear claw that he wore around his neck.

"Those bears are my relatives!" the medicine man said. "You must not harm them. They are teaching your boy how we should care for each other, so you must not be cruel to them. You must get your son back with love, not violence."

Kuo-Haya's father prayed for guidance. He went outside and sat on the ground. As he sat there, a bee flew up to him, right by his face. Then it flew away. The father stood up. Now he knew what to do!

"Thank you, Little Brother," he said. He began to make his preparations. The medicine man watched what he was doing and smiled.

Kuo-Haya's father went to the place where the bees had their hives. He made a fire and put green branches on it so that it made smoke. Then he blew the smoke into the tree

2. **lance** (lans) *n.*: A long pole used as a weapon.

Words to Know

neglected (ni GLEKT id) *v.*: Failed to take care of; failed to give enough attention

where the bees were. The bees soon went to sleep.

Carefully Kuo-Haya's father took out some honey from their hive. When he was done, he placed pollen and some small pieces of turquoise at the foot of the tree to thank the bees for their gift. The medicine man, who was watching all this, smiled again. Truly the father was beginning to learn.

Kuo-Haya's father traveled again to the cliffs where the bears lived. He hid behind a tree and saw how the mother bear treated Kuo-Haya and the cubs with love. He saw that Kuo-Haya was able to hold his own as he wrestled with the bears.

He came out from his hiding place, put the honey on the ground, and stepped back. "My friends," he said, "I have brought you some-thing sweet."

The mother bear and her cubs came over and began to eat the honey. While they ate, Kuo-Haya's father went to the boy. He saw that his little boy was now a young man.

"Kuo-Haya," he said, putting his hands on his son's shoulders, "I have come to take you home. The bears have taught me a lesson. I shall treat you as a father should treat his son."

"I will go with you, Father," said the boy. "But I, too, have learned things from the bears. They have shown me how we must care for one another. I will come with you only if you promise you will always be friends with the bears."

The father promised, and that promise was kept. Not only was he friends with the bears, but he showed his boy the love a son deserves. And he taught him all the things a son should be taught.

Everyone in the village soon saw that Kuo-Haya, the bear boy, was no longer the timid little boy he had been. Because of what the bears had taught him, he was the best wrestler among the boys. With his father's help, Kuo-Haya quickly became the greatest runner of all. To this day, his story is told to remind all parents that they must always

Joseph Bruchac (1942 –) has roots that are both Native American (Abenaki) and Czechoslovakian. Here's what he says about the value of reading folk tales:

"We learn about ourselves by understanding others. Our own traditions can be made stronger only when we pay attention to and respect the traditions of people who are different from ourselves. Hearing or reading the stories of the native peoples of North America will not make any of us Native Americans, but it may help make all of us more human."

Mimbres bowl from Swarts Ruin Mimbres Valley, New Mex. Peabody Museum of Archaeology & Ethnology Cambridge, Mass.

Respond

- Do you think the boy should return to his father or remain with the bears? Explain.
- How will the relationship between the boy and his father change? Role-play a conversation between them that takes place after the boy returns.

Activities
MAKE MEANING

Explore Your Reading

Look Back (Recall)

1. Why does Kuo-Haya go off to live with bears?
2. In what ways has Kuo-Haya changed during his time with the bear family?

Think It Over (Interpret)

3. Why doesn't Kuo-Haya's father spend time with him at the beginning of the folk tale?
4. Why do you think the father acts as he does when he sees the boy's decision to stay with the bears?
5. What does the father learn from the experience of almost losing his son?

Go Beyond (Apply)

6. Is this story more educational for parents or for young people? Explain.
7. Will the boy continue to have a relationship with the bears? Why?

Develop Reading and Literary Skills

Interpret Cultural Details in a Folk Tale

As stories told by a group for many years, **folk tales** help you understand a group's beliefs and customs. Your notes on animals in this tale show that Pueblos believed animals can be teachers. As the medicine man says, the bear helps the boy "when his father should have been helping him."

What else do details in this story show about Pueblo beliefs and customs? Think about the details listed below. Then tell what each detail suggests about the Pueblo way of life.

1. The community helps the father search for the missing boy.
2. The trackers will not try to rescue the boy from the bears.
3. The father leaves turquoise at the bee hive.

Ideas for Writing

An African proverb says, "It takes a whole village to raise a child." In this story, animals help when a father shirks his responsibility.

Persuasive Dialogue Imagine you are a member of the Pueblo community. Write a dialogue in which you urge the father to take more interest in his child. Give reasons why he should do so.

Folk Tale How would the bears tell this story? Write the folk tale from the animals' point of view.

Ideas for Projects

Animal Kingdom Report Animals have different styles of raising their young. Choose one type of animal that interests you and report on how its young are raised. Present your findings to the class, using illustrations if possible. [Science Link]

Model Make a scale-model stage set or diorama of a key scene in this folk tale. As you plan, reread the story and list important details of the setting that you should include. [Art Link]

How Am I Doing?

Discuss these questions with a partner:

How did recognizing cultural details help me understand the Pueblo way of life?

How could I apply this skill to other types of reading?

What aspects of nature have given me inspiration?

Activities
PREVIEW
Mother to Son by Langston Hughes
basketball by Nikki Giovanni

When others look at you, what side of your personality do they see?

A teacher who taught others in your family may see you as "Cory's baby sister." The crowd at a basketball game may know you as number 46, the center with the highest-scoring average on the team. People who know you in different ways have different ideas about who you are.

- Choose one person in your life and imagine how they see you. Deliver a short monologue, or speech, that shows how they might describe you.
- In a journal entry called *How ____ Sees Me*, describe yourself as that person might.

Read Actively
Identify the Traits of Speakers

You probably had fun describing yourself from someone else's point of view. Sometimes poets write as if they're someone else, and this made-up person is called a **speaker.** By asking yourself who is speaking in a poem, you will understand it better.

Describe the speakers in these poems by using cluster diagrams like the one at left. Note the **traits** (qualities and feelings) that each speaker displays. Make a new cluster diagram for Junior, the speaker of "basketball."

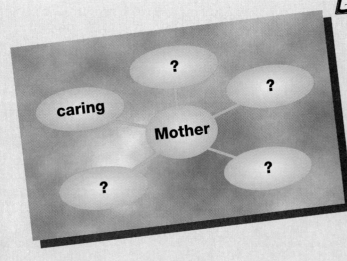

Mother to Son
Langston Hughes

Well, son, I'll tell you:
Life for me ain't been no crystal stair.
It's had tacks in it,
And splinters,
5 And boards torn up,
And places with no carpet on the floor—
Bare.
But all the time
I'se been a-climbin' on,
10 And reachin' landin's,

And turnin' corners,
And sometimes goin' in the dark
Where there ain't been no light.
So boy, don't you turn back.
15 Don't you set down on the steps
'Cause you finds it's kinder hard.
Don't you fall now—
For I'se still goin', honey,
I'se still climbin',
20 And life for me ain't been no crystal stair.

Respond

Do you think the mother's advice to her son is inspirational? Why?

basketball
Nikki Giovanni

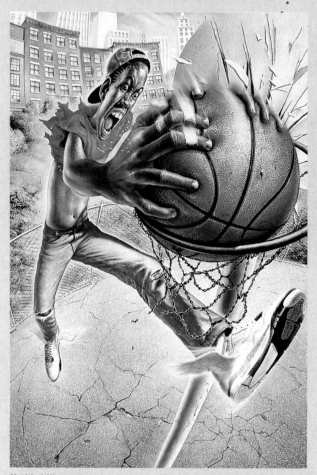

when spanky goes
to the playground all the big boys say
  hey big time—what's happenin'
'cause his big brother plays basketball
  for their high school
and he gives them the power sign and says
  you got it
5 but when i go and say
  what's the word
they just say
  your nose is running junior

one day i'll be seven feet tall
10 even if i never get a big brother
and i'll stuff that sweaty ball down
their laughing throats

Untitled Illustration Mark Fredrickson, Courtesy of Levi Strauss & Co.

Respond
What advice would you give
the speaker of this poem?

Langston Hughes, 1939 Carl Van
Vechten, *Photograph copyright ©
Estate of Carl Van Vechten Gravure
and compilation copyright ©
Eakins Press Foundation*

In the 1920's, **Langston Hughes** (1902–1967)
was part of a group of artists and writers who
celebrated their African American heritage.
This group of poets, novelists, painters, and
musicians was called the Harlem Renaissance
because they lived in the New York City community of Harlem. Hughes continued to write
about his heritage and, like the caring mother
in his poem, gave help to younger writers.

"I write
about my own
experiences—
which also hap-
pen to be the experiences
of my people. But if I had to
choose between my people's
experiences and mine, I'd
choose mine because that's
what I know best," explains
Nikki Giovanni (1943–   ).

MAKE MEANING

Explore Your Reading

Look Back (Recall)

1. Summarize the advice the mother gives her son.
2. According to the speaker in "basketball," why do the boys greet "spanky" on the playground?

Think It Over (Interpret)

3. What is the most important thing the speaker in "Mother to Son" tells her son? Why?
4. Why is the mother telling her son these things?
5. In "basketball," why is the person telling the story jealous of spanky?
6. In each poem, how does the boy's family affect the way he sees himself?

Go Beyond (Apply)

7. Imagine each of the boys as adults. What kind of men do you think they'll be?

Develop Reading and Literary Skills

Understand the Speaker

Your cluster diagrams helped you understand the **speaker** in each poem, the person who says the words of the poem. Sometimes the poet and the speaker are the same. At other times, a writer chooses a character to speak the poem's words.

When poets use speakers, they give you details that help you understand who the speaker is and what he or she is like. For example, you don't know the real name of the speaker in "basketball," but you do know what the older kids call him and how he feels about not having a big brother. Use details from your cluster diagrams to help answer these questions.

1. Describe the speaker of each poem.
2. What advice would the mother in Hughes's poem give to the boy in Giovanni's poem?

Ideas for Writing

Is your life a crystal stair, a highway, or a bowl of cherries? People often try to draw comparisons to make poetic connections between life and other things.

Character Sketch Imagine a person who thought life *was* like a crystal stair. What qualities would that person have? Write a sketch that describes him or her.

Poem Respond to the "Mother to Son" poem by writing a poem that features the son as the speaker. Include a comparison that he would use to describe his life.

Ideas for Projects

Survey Ask adults in your community to tell you one piece of advice they would give younger people. Design a questionnaire, tabulate the results on a chart or graph, and see whether you can draw any conclusions from these responses. Share your findings with the class. [Math Link]

Song Imagine that you are the speaker in "basketball." Write a song in which you explain the importance of brothers and sisters to a person's identity.

How Am I Doing?

Take a moment to think about these questions. Write your responses in your journal:

How did the art accompanying these poems help me understand the speakers better? How can I use art or illustration to understand what I read?

What did I learn when I described myself from someone else's point of view?

Have you ever thought somebody else had it better and then decided you were wrong?

Reach Into Your Background

It's easy to think that other people have life better than you or to take what you have for granted. Imagine yourself going through a typical day, from the time the alarm rings in the morning to the time you drift off to sleep. In your journal, jot down some of the little things that give you pleasure, even if you don't usually think about them. Also note some of the family members, friends, or teachers who mean a lot to you just by being there.

Read Actively

*Make Inferences
About the Narrator*

Bonnie, the narrator of this story, thinks someone else has it better. You can learn more about Bonnie, or any narrator, by noticing what she says, thinks, and does. Then you can use your observations to make guesses about her based on the facts you've gathered. Such guesses are called **inferences.**

As you read, jot down what Bonnie says, thinks, and does. What can you figure out about her from your notes? How do you think her feelings influence the way she tells the story?

Take My Mom—
Please!

Ellen Conford

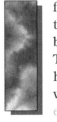

I felt sorry for Tamara Cherp the first time I saw her. Even before I knew her name was Tamara Cherp I felt sorry for her. Oh, there's nothing wrong with "Tamara"—it's a sort of exotic-sounding, romantic name. But Tamara *Cherp?*

It was the first day of our first year in high school, so all us freshmen were kind of floundering around in a state of general confusion. The school seemed huge, and there were a lot of sadistic sophomores who seemed to enjoy misdirecting us when we asked how to get to our rooms.

I got to my last class of the day, which was Spanish, feeling generally frazzled and practically friendless. The high school takes kids from four different areas, and though I knew there were kids from my old school in there somewhere, I hadn't seen a friend all day.

A girl stood in front of the door to 412 looking up at the room number and down at her schedule card. She kept shaking her head.

She looked as confused as I'd felt most of the day, but that wasn't why I felt sorry for her. It was the way she was dressed.

She wore a yellow T-shirt with a picture of Mozart on the front—I only knew it was a picture of Mozart because underneath the head it said MOZART—a shapeless black skirt that drooped halfway down her calves, and a black leotard. A red scarf wound around her forehead like an Indian headband. The ends hung down over one ear.

I couldn't imagine why she was dressed like that, unless she'd just arrived here from another planet. No one dresses like that in our school. She

Words to Know

exotic (eg ZAHT ik) *adj.*: Strange; different; foreign in a fascinating way

looked bizarre, and I was sure she'd had an even more miserable day than I did. I may have been a timid, floundering freshman, but at least I looked like all the other timid, floundering freshmen. No one pointed or stared or snickered as I walked down the hall; I was sure they must have at this girl.

"It *says* 412," she said. I didn't know if she was talking to me, because she was still looking back and forth from her schedule card to the door.

📖 **Read Actively**

Visualize what Tamara looks like.

"Then this must be the place," I said. "Spanish One?"

"Yes, but this boy told me I had to go downstairs, past the main office, through the gym—"

"One of their little jokes," I said wearily. "It's happened to me twice today. I think this'll be the only class I'm not late to. And that's only because I had English in 410 last period."

"Oh."

We went into the classroom and sat down at adjoining desks. The room was only about one-third full. I knew that people would be straggling in for a good ten minutes after the bell rang.

"Are you new?" I asked, trying to be friendly because I felt so sorry for her.

"Aren't we all?"

"I meant new in the neighborhood."

"No," she said, puzzled. "I went to Parkside."

"Oh, well, that's why I don't know you." I felt a little embarrassed. I hoped she hadn't guessed that I thought she was new to the area—the state, the *planet!*—because she looked so weird.

"I'm Tamara Cherp," she said.

I felt myself on the verge of giggling, of repeating, "Tamara *Cherp?*" and really hurting her feelings. Then I saw two girls poke each other and bite their lips to keep from laughing as they looked sideways at her, and my heart went out to Tamara Cherp.

"I'm Bonnie Snyder," I said. "How do you like the place so far?"

Tamara Cherp shrugged. "Whether I like it or not, the law says I have to be here till I'm sixteen. So what difference does it make?"

"I never thought about it that way." And I didn't think I was going to like this girl very much, either. She seemed sort of sullen and antisocial.

So I was surprised—to say the least—when Spanish was over and Tamara invited me to come home with her.

"Well, I don't know. See, I have to take the bus, and it's the first day and all, and I'm not sure—"

"Okay." Tamara shrugged. "No big deal."

I wondered if it was hard for her to make friends, and how many times she'd tried and been rejected. Maybe it had happened so often she *expected* me to say no. Saying "no big deal" was just a cover-up, so I wouldn't see how hurt she was by this newest rejection.

Words to Know

bizarre (bi ZAHR) *adj.:* Very odd or unusual; weird

adjoining (uh JOYN ing) *adj.:* Next to, or side by side

antisocial (an ti SOH shuhl) *adj.:* Not liking to be with other people

"No, hey, listen, I *want* to, I just thought I'd better take my own bus the first day, so I know how to get home. I could come tomorrow if you want."

"Okay. I walk. It's only a few blocks from here. My mother can drive you home."

"Fine. See you tomorrow."

y the next afternoon, I was sorry I'd ever felt sorry for Tamara Cherp. A whole bunch of my old friends were going to the mall and they'd asked me to meet them. Now I couldn't. Not only that, I was beginning to talk to people in my classes, beginning to realize I would make new friends in high school. I didn't even *like* Tamara Cherp. I didn't particularly want to be friends with her. Why should I feel guilty because she'd been rejected by other people?

But there was nothing I could do about it without feeling more guilty. I'd agreed to go to her house, and I'd go—just this once. That didn't mean I'd have to be bosom buddies with her. It might be a little uncomfortable sitting next to her in Spanish all year if she kept hitting me with invitations, but I couldn't help that.

📖 **Read Actively**

Predict whether Bonnie and Tamara will become friends.

On the four-block walk to Tamara's house, we hardly exchanged four words. I didn't think I'd have to worry about her getting too friendly. We didn't seem to have anything to say to each other.

Tamara opened the door to her house, which was unlocked—a foolish thing, I thought, even in our quiet neighborhood—and we walked into the living room.

In the middle of the floor, someone dressed in a purple leotard and lots of bead necklaces was standing on her head. I couldn't see her face, because the beads dangled down over it and covered it almost completely.

"Hi, Cerise. This is Bonnie."

Cerise must be her sister. She lowered her knees to the floor slowly and came up out of her headstand.

"This is my mother, Cerise," Tamara said.

I was surprised that Tamara called her mother by her first name—not to mention surprised at the name—but then Cerise pulled on a long red-and-yellow skirt and threw a fringed shawl over her purple shoulders, and all I could think of was: So this is where Tamara gets her taste in clothes!

"Hi, Bonnie," Cerise said. She walked over to me and held out her hand. I shook it. "Welcome to our house."

"Thank you. That was a terrific headstand. I've been trying for years, but I always fall over."

"It takes preparation and practice," Cerise said. "But it's worth the effort. It gets the blood rushing to the brain, starts the creative juices flowing, gives you mental energy, and it's super for sinus trouble."

"Have you got sinus trouble?"

"No, but I can use all the creative juices I can stir up. I'm going nuts trying to come up with new slogans."

"New slogans? For what? Are you in advertising?"

Cerise grinned broadly. Her whole face lit up when she smiled, and I realized she looked young enough to actually be Tamara's sister.

"Not exactly. Not the kind you mean. Come on in the kitchen, I'll show you."

I heard Tamara give a deep sigh. I glanced over at her. She looked bored.

We followed Cerise into the kitchen. There were picket signs everywhere. The materials for picket signs littered the floor and the kitchen table. The signs were stacked in corners, against the side of the refrigerator, leaning against the walls.

"Did you do all these yourself?" I asked.

"No, we've been working on them for a week. A whole committee of us. But the demonstration[1] is this Saturday, and we don't have enough yet, and everyone had something else to do today, so I got stuck finishing up. And I'm sick of painting 'No Nukes'[2] and 'Save Our Land' over and over again."

"How about 'No Nukes Is Good Nukes'?" I blurted out, without even thinking.

Cerise gave a little shriek of delight. "That's fan*tastic*! Tamara, where did you find this *pearl*?"

Tamara looked as if she'd like to toss this pearl back to the oyster.

"Spanish," she said.

" 'No Nukes Is Good Nukes,' " Cerise mused. "I *love* it!"

"If you need some help," I said tentatively, "we could do some signs for you. I'm not great at lettering, but—"

"Oh, no," Cerise protested. "You didn't come here to paint picket[3] signs. I can't impose on you like that. Even if everybody *did* fink out on me, I'm sure you and Tamara—"

"I don't mind," I said. "Really. It'd be fun. Wouldn't it, Tamara?"

Tamara scowled. I didn't think she thought it would be fun. But I did. A lot more

---

1. **demonstration:** A gathering or parade of many people to show publicly how they feel about something.
2. **nukes** *slang*: Nuclear power plants or nuclear weapons.
3. **picket** *n*.: A sign used in a demonstration.

fun than talking to—or not talking to—Tamara. Except for the clothes, it was hard to believe she was Cerise's daughter. Cerise was so lively and cheerful, so involved and friendly. Tamara acted sulky and aloof.

"I suppose," Tamara said sourly, "this means the Colonel is cooking dinner again tonight?"

"Now, Tamara, it's only a couple of days till the demonstration, and then we'll be able to get to the stove again. By Monday everything will be back to normal."

Tamara snorted. She muttered something under her breath. It sounded like, "Till next month."

> **Read Actively**
> **Ask yourself** how Tamara relates with her mother.

It was a great afternoon. Cerise told us about the hideous things that could happen if there was an accident at a nuclear power plant and read us excerpts from secret hearings held after a near disaster at the site they were going to picket.

Tamara yawned a lot. I guess she must have heard all this stuff before but I hadn't, and I was fascinated. It was as scary as a good horror movie. And Cerise was so enthusiastic about my sign-painting and my slogan, she made me feel like the demonstration couldn't take place without my help.

Cerise drove me home. Tamara sat in the backseat of the Volkswagen and didn't say a word except "good-bye" as I got out in my driveway.

"You must come again," Cerise said warmly. "It was a joy meeting you. And thanks for all your help."

"It was fun." I glanced at Tamara. I didn't think she'd be too eager to have me come again. But then, that was okay. I hadn't

Words to Know

tentatively (TENT uh tive lee) *adv*.: Hesitantly; not decisively

aloof (ah LOOF) *adj*.: Keeping oneself apart or at a distance

excerpts (EK suhrpts) *n*.: Extracts; parts of a longer piece of writing

planned on visiting her again. I just went today because I'd promised. I didn't want to be friends with Tamara.

But what a shame I couldn't be friends with Cerise.

I went into my house. My mother was sitting in the living room working on a needlepoint picture of a country church.

"Hi, Janet," I said experimentally.

📖 **Read Actively**

Ask yourself how Bonnie gets along with her mother.

She looked up, startled. "Hi *Janet?* What happened to Mom?"

"You don't mind if I call you Janet, do you?"

"Actually, I do. I waited a long time to be called Mom, and you're the only person who can call me that."

"Oh, *Mother*."

"Of course, when you say it like that, I have second thoughts."

"It's just that if I call you Janet we're more like equals. We can relate to each other on a person-to-person basis, instead of—"

"What makes you think we're equals?" my mother asked, dropping her needlepoint.

"Wouldn't it be nice if we were more like friends than mother and daughter?"

"I *have* friends," my mother said. "I want a daughter."

"You know, you're awfully old-fashioned," I said in exasperation.

"I know," she replied comfortably, and picked up her needlepoint.

urprisingly enough, a couple of weeks later Tamara invited me to her house again. I got the definite impression that she only asked me because Cerise pushed her into it. Although Tamara and I still didn't have very much to say to each other, and I still didn't want to be friends with her, I couldn't help but feel flattered that Cerise liked me enough to want me to come over.

I couldn't tell whether Tamara was pleased or resentful when I said I would. I think Tamara guessed it was Cerise I really wanted to visit.

When we got to the house, Cerise was in the kitchen. She heard the door open and called out to us. "Tamara? Did Bonnie come?"

Hearing the eagerness in Cerise's voice, I felt a warm glow. Even Tamara's almost sarcastic, "Yes, Bonnie came," didn't diminish my pleasure.

"Come say hello," Cerise yelled. "I can't move. I'm up to my elbows in tofu."[4]

Tamara rolled her eyes toward the ceiling. She trudged into the kitchen. I followed, wondering what tofu was, and how someone up to their elbows in it would look.

Cerise was standing next to the sink, working at a wooden chopping block. The kitchen table was littered with papers, books, a typewriter, pencils, and a sketch pad. The kitchen counter was chaos—bottles, jars, cans, utensils. It looked like an earthquake in a supermarket.

"Bonnie!" Cerise cried. "It's good to see you again. Can you stay for dinner?"

"Think twice before you answer that," Tamara said.

"Oh, Tamara, don't be so negative. Tonight I think I've really outdone myself. This is going to be my *pièce de résistance*."[5]

"What are you making?" I asked curiously. It must be something pretty spectacular, I thought, considering the mess in the kitchen.

"Something with tofu in it," Tamara said.

"Well, of course, dear. I still have twenty recipes to go."

"Recipes for what?" I asked.

"My cookbook. *One Hundred and One Things To Do with Tofu*."

"I can think of a hundred and second," Tamara said grimly.

"You're writing a cookbook?" I said. "Hey, that's great. But what's tofu?"

"Bean curd. And it's fantastic. It has tons of protein! I mean, you wouldn't believe, ounce for ounce, the nourishment you can get out of tofu compared to meat. And the cost is so much less."

---

4. tofu (TOH foo) *n*.: A bland food similar to cheese and rich in protein; it is made from soybeans.

5. *pièce de résistance* (pee ES duh RAY zee stahns) *n*.: Masterpiece.

She was cutting some white stuff into cubes.

"Is that it?" I asked.

"Yes. Want to try some?"

"I don't know. It looks kind of—"

"I know. Bland. It is, really. That's why you have to be ingenious using it. But it's incredibly versatile. I've come up with some marvelous dishes. This is going to be a tofu and broccoli casserole *gratinée*."[6]

For a second Tamara looked almost faint. She actually turned pale.

Cerise finished up the casserole and popped it into the oven. I offered to help her clean the kitchen, and the next thing I knew, Tamara and I were standing over the sink and Cerise was sitting at the table, sipping a cup of Red Zinger tea and reading us excerpts from her cookbook.

Tamara's face was like a thundercloud.

Well, what did she expect? I wondered. She didn't invite me because she wanted to. She invited me because Cerise asked her to.

I didn't stay for dinner. It wasn't the tofu. I tasted it, and I could see how you could do an awful lot with it to make it interesting. Plain, it tasted like custard without any sugar in it, but I was sure Cerise had wonderful ways to cook it. I just have this thing about broccoli. I told Cerise I was allergic.

When I got home, my mother was in the kitchen.

"What's for dinner?" I asked.

"Roast beef, Yorkshire pudding, spinach and bacon salad, and broiled tomatoes."

---

6. **gratinée** (grah ti NAY) *adj.*: Served with grated cheese.

"Boring," I muttered. "Boring."

She stared at me as if I were crazy.

"Do you realize that for the price of that roast beef you could have bought ten pounds of tofu?"

"No, I didn't realize that. And I don't think I care for tofu all that much. Oh, it's nice to find a little piece of it in my soup at a Japanese restaurant, but that's about it. I can't conceive of ten pounds of tofu."

"You're not very adventurous, you know that?" I said.

"You've forgotten my asparagus and squid salad," she said sweetly.

very few weeks Tamara would ask me over to her house, and I would go. We talked a little more now, but not about anything personal, except Cerise. Tamara really didn't appreciate her mother.

Cerise was always involved in something interesting. One time it was organizing a crafts fair to raise funds for an American Indian museum. (Only Cerise called them Native Americans, not Indians.)

Tamara said the reason Cerise wanted to have a crafts fair was because she had just gotten a potter's wheel and was now into pottery, and she thought it would be a good way to display her own crafts. I thought that was pretty nasty of Tamara, but I wasn't surprised. Tamara just didn't have any sense of perspective where her mother was concerned.

Another time Cerise was taking a course in Chinese and was totally immersed, not only in the language, but also in the history and culture of China. She was hoping to take a trip to China within a year, and she wanted to be prepared to get the most out of it when she went.

"I don't want to be just another tourist snapping pictures of everything," Cerise said scornfully. "When I go, I want to *feel* Chinese, *think* Chinese, *understand* Chinese, *live* Chinese. You have to prepare for that kind of experience."

I hoped that part of the preparation would be *eating* Chinese, but unfortunately, Cerise wasn't into *cooking* Chinese. She just didn't have the time. She got some stuff from McDonald's.

Tamara would visit her father when Cerise went to China. Tamara's father lived in California, and she saw him summers. I wondered, being divorced and all, why Cerise didn't have to work. Unless Tamara's father was very rich and sent them piles of money, how did they manage?

I sort of hinted around the subject one day, saying something like, with all Cerise's projects, it was a good thing she didn't have to work, or she'd never have time for the really important things in life.

Tamara almost smiled. "Even without working," she said, "she doesn't have time for them."

I didn't know what she meant. Tamara saw my puzzled look and then really did smile. But it was a strange smile.

"You know, I've never met *your* mother, Bonnie."

"Hey, that's right," I said, trying to sound as if I just realized it. I hadn't, of course, just realized it, but I'd been avoiding inviting Tamara to my house. The only reason I went to *her* house was to visit with Cerise; if I invited Tamara to my house, she might take it as a sign I wanted to be friendlier.

But I couldn't be rude forever. Or pretend not to be aware that I'd been at Tamara's eight times, and she'd been at my house zero.

"How about tomorrow?" I asked.

ice," Tamara said, coming into the living room. "Comfortable."

"I guess," I said, sort of startled. "I never thought about it. It's boring, though. Not like your house. There's always something interesting—"

My mother called out hello from the kitchen.

We went in and I introduced Tamara.

📖 **Read Actively**

Predict how Tamara will react to Bonnie's mother.

Tamara just stood there and stared at my mother. My mother stared back. Tamara looked particularly

bizarre today in purple harem pants, a bright green shirt, and a rope of beads that hung down to her waist.

My mother was clipping coupons out of the newspaper, making separate little piles of them on the table.

I looked at one of the coupons. It was for dog food.

"We don't have a dog," I said.

"The Jarmans do."

"You just like cutting out things," I said.

"Everybody needs a hobby."

I was mortified. Tamara gazed at my mother, the mad coupon-clipper, and I knew she must be comparing her to Cerise, who had more important, more interesting, more intelligent things to do with her time than to cut out coupons for things she didn't need.

Words to Know

ingenious (in JEEN yuhs) *adj.:* Clever; skillful; creative

mortified (MORT uh fīd) *adj.:* Ashamed; very embarrassed

Right now Cerise was probably saving the whale, or standing on her head, or studying arc welding by mail.

It was hard to believe that up to two years ago my mother had had a responsible job. When she decided to quit, she said she'd worked for fifteen years, and she'd probably work again in a couple of years, but right then she wanted to *rest*. My father was making enough money so we wouldn't starve, and if she found she was going crazy just sitting home, she'd go back to work.

But she hadn't gone crazy.

She enjoyed it. All she did was read, do needlepoint, shop, cook, clean the house, and work in the garden. And, of course, clip coupons.

I didn't understand it at all.

"That's not really her hobby," I said. "She just does it to save money."

"What's wrong with that?" my mother asked. "Stop apologizing for me and take something to eat. You must be hungry."

We got some potato chips and Cokes. I figured I'd have to ask Tamara up to my room, and we'd have to try to make some conversation for a while, but just then my mother glanced up at the clock.

"Three-thirty! I'm missing *Doctor's Hospital*!"

This was really embarrassing. Why did the only soap opera she watched have to be on now, when Tamara could see her practi-cally leaping out of her chair and sprinting into the family room to turn the TV on? She'd think my mother spent her whole day watching those dumb shows.

"You like that, too?" Tamara said. "Hey, would it be all right if I watched with you? I hate to miss it. I can't wait to see what happens when Brick finds out Blake is his real father."

"You watch that drivel?" I said incredulously. But I said it to Tamara's back. She was already headed for the family room with her Coke.

"Sure, come on. It's just starting." My mother patted the couch next to her, and Tamara sat down.

"Come on, Bonnie," my mother said. "It won't kill you to watch it just this once."

I couldn't believe it. I trudged into the family room, plopped down on a chair with my Coke and the potato chips, and sat there for an hour, bored out of my mind.

But what else could I do? All those times I'd been at Tamara's house, she'd stayed with me, no matter what Cerise and I were doing. I couldn't just walk out of the room, bored or not. Maybe all the afternoons I'd spent at her house painting signs, cleaning up tofu, and learning to say *cloud* in Mandarin Chinese, Tamara had really wanted to be watching her soap opera but felt she had to stay with her guest.

Words to Know

incredulously (in KRE dyoo luhs lee) *adv.*: In a disbelieving way

Maybe, I thought, remembering the look of impatience I'd seen so often on her face, maybe Tamara was just as bored with all those things as I was sitting there watching *Doctor's Hospital.*

During the commercials, they compared their favorite characters on the show and argued amiably about whether Noelle really had amnesia or was faking it to get out of testifying at Buck's trial.

I couldn't believe it. How could Tamara, daughter of the most fascinating, active, youthful mother I'd ever seen, be sitting here with *my* mother, staring at the boob tube as if it were as important as, say, nuclear disaster?

When the program was over, Tamara and I went up to my room.

"She's really nice, your mother," Tamara said.

"Well, yeah. But she must seem awfully . . . ordinary . . . compared to Cerise."

"Sometimes ordinariness is a relief," Tamara said softly.

"Want to trade?" I joked.

"Would you want to?" Tamara asked. "I mean, think about it. Would you really?"

 thought about it. Long after Tamara left, I was still thinking about it. Would I want Cerise for my mother, instead of my own mother? It was exciting to visit Tamara's house: There was always something interesting going on. Cerise was always on a new kick, busy, involved, full of vitality.

But, I realized, none of those things had anything to do with Tamara. Cerise didn't seem to be all that involved in Tamara's activities—whatever they were—and Tamara wasn't interested in Cerise's projects.

But *I* would be, I told myself. I'd enjoyed painting picket signs, helping Cerise with her cookbook, learning how to say *cloud* in Chinese.

But that was as a visitor. Maybe living with Cerise was different than dropping in once a month.

She's like New York, I thought suddenly. Cerise is like that cliché about New York. "It's a great place to visit, but I wouldn't want to live there."

How strange. I hadn't thought about my mother like this before. In fact, I hadn't given all that much thought to my mother for years.

I walked downstairs into the kitchen. My mother was stir-frying something at the stove.

"You know what, Mom? You're a lot like Bent Fork, Tennessee."

She looked up from her wok. "*What?*"

I put my arm around her. "It's a compliment. Believe me. I hope you never change."

"Oh, honey, what a nice thing to say." She positively beamed.

"What's for dinner? Smells delicious."

"I hope you like it. You inspired me. It's tofu and bean sprouts. Bonnie! Bonnie, what's the matter? You look so pale."

 **Respond**

- Did you predict the end of this story? Why?
- With a partner, choose a symbol for each of the mothers in this story—a place or thing that expresses who each is.

"It's hard to describe how an idea for a book comes to me. Some books 'just happen,' and I never know how I thought them up. Some books were inspired by hearing an interesting name and then imagining what a character with that name would be like," explains **Ellen Conford** (1945–). Maybe the seed of this story was planted when Conford found the name Tamara Cherp.

Activities

MAKE MEANING

Explore Your Reading

Look Back (Recall)

1. How does Tamara's mother spend her time?
2. Describe how Bonnie's mother spends hers.

Think It Over (Interpret)

3. Compare the interests of each mother.
4. Does Bonnie's attitude toward Cerise change in the course of the story? Explain.
5. What does Bonnie come to realize about her mother at the end of the story?

Go Beyond (Apply)

6. What lesson about life does this story teach?

Develop Reading and Literary Skills

Understand a First-Person Narrator

The inferences, or guesses based on facts, you made about Bonnie can help you understand how she tells the story. Bonnie is a **first-person narrator,** a character in the story who tells what happens as she sees it and refers to herself as "I." She can tell you what she observes and thinks, but she can't see into the minds of others.

Bonnie's feelings affect the way she describes the events and characters in this story. For instance, she is critical of her mother through most of the story but then changes her mind at the end.

1. Choose two pieces of evidence you gathered about Bonnie and explain how they influence the way she tells the story.
2. How do you think Tamara's feelings about the events and characters differ from Bonnie's?
3. How would the story be different if Tamara told it?

Ideas for Writing

Bonnie and Tamara are starting to become friends. The beginning of a friendship is a time to learn about someone, develop routines together, and decide if you will continue the relationship.

Epilogue Will this friendship last? What do Tamara and Bonnie have in common? What makes them different? In a brief follow-up to the story, tell what you think will happen to the girls' friendship.

Poem Write a poem that captures the spirit of a new friendship. Base your poem on your own experience or on friendships you have observed in films, television, or stories. You might try writing a poetic recipe for friendship or a poem using only verbs.

Ideas for Projects

Family Scrapbooks Create two family scrapbooks, one for Tamara and one for Bonnie. Include things mentioned in the story as well as anything else that suits their families. [Art Link]

Family Drama Write a scene in which these two families get together for dinner. Choose the setting and try to maintain the humorous tone set in the story. Perform your scene for classmates.

How Am I Doing?

Answer these questions in your journal:

What have I learned about first-person narrators from considering a different character's perspective? How can what I've learned help me understand other stories I read?

What has Tamara's experience taught me about who gives me inspiration?

Who Gives Me Inspiration?

Think Critically About the Selections

All of the selections you have read in this section focus on the question "Who Gives Me Inspiration?" With a partner or a small group, complete one or two of the following activities to show what you've learned. You can write your responses in a journal or share them in discussion.

1. Imagine you could interview a character from one of the selections about the question "Who Gives Me Inspiration?" Which character would you choose? Why? How would you expect him or her to respond? **(Apply/Hypothesize)**

2. Many of these selections deal with adults who help young people grow. Choose two such adults and compare how they teach and guide young people. **(Compare and Contrast)**

3. Which young people in these selections learn the most about who gives them inspiration? Choose two young people and explain what they have learned. **(Draw Conclusions)**

4. Which story taught you something about yourself and the people who give you inspiration? Explain. **(Synthesize)**

Student Art Celebration Rudy Torres Lakewood, California

Projects

Panel of Guest Speakers Invite adults from your community to give you inspirational advice about careers. Choose role models from careers involving science, mathematics, and social studies. Have classmates prepare questions for the panel in advance. [Social Studies Link; Science Link; Math Link]

Multimedia Album of Celebrity Inspirations Collect pictures of famous people your classmates admire—world leaders, movie stars, sports heroes, and others. Explain how each celebrity is an inspiration. If possible, include slides, videotape footage, and audio-cassettes. [Social Studies Link]

Inspiration Pageant Design a parade with signs and displays to honor those who inspire you and your classmates. Record or perform music to accompany your pageant and then stage it for an audience. [Art Link]

Looking at Biography and

Barbara A. Lewis

Terms to know

Autobiography is a form of non-fiction in which a person tells his or her own life story. The best autobiographies contain many elements of short stories, including plot, setting and characters.

Biography is a form of nonfiction in which a writer tells the life story of another person. Biographies deal with true stories of real people and real events.

Biography When I was chatting with a writing friend, he told me of a newspaper article about a teenaged boy who had helped a stranger on a crowded bus. I bolted upright in my chair. I knew right then I wanted to write his biography, a story of his life. I found out more about Frank Daily and wrote that biography, and I called it "Reaching Out to a Stranger."

Frank Daily wasn't a sports hero like Babe Ruth or a scientist like Albert Einstein. Their biographies can inform you of history and inspire you. But Frank was an ordinary kid— not rich or famous— who had acted in a heroic way. Here was a hero you could touch. Here was someone like you.

If you think about it, history is just a series of stories about people who have invented, destroyed, led, or discovered. But by the time you read their biographies, these heroes' images are cast in bronze statues in museums.

That's why I decided to write biographies about ordinary kids. I wanted to give you a yardstick to hold up next to yourself so that you could say, "I'm as tall as they are. I could do that too."

Getting the Stories Researching these stories presented a problem. Since my subjects weren't famous, how would I find them? I snooped through newspapers, contacted national groups that have given awards to kids, and called friends around the country to ask them if they knew about any amazing kids. Stories poured in.

Then I called these young people on the phone, spoke with their parents and teachers, and talked with the kids themselves. It took weeks of interviewing, writing, and rewriting for each short biography and the job resulted in a *huge* phone bill.

After I wrote each biography, I mailed or read it to the kids, and they corrected any mistakes. I was surprised how often they said, "How did you know that was the way I felt?" After you have crawled around in someone else's head for a while, you sometimes begin to think and feel as they do.

Autobiography An autobiography, the story of *your* life, involves an even more intense excavating in your own mind. It

Literary Forms
Autobiography

means being truthful with yourself. You choose important episodes in your life, just as in a biography. You can interview people who know you to get their memories and reactions to you. But, in contrast to writing a biography, when you create an autobiography you are the expert on what happened.

You write about your experiences, other people in your life, details of your surroundings, and most important, how you felt or reacted to all of these things. You include what made you happy, fearful, or angry and what you believe in.

Writing about yourself can become a way of getting to know who you are. Who knows? Maybe some day you will write a biography of a special hero of yours. You may even write an autobiography. In writing about yourself, you might find a hero down inside, someone that other people will want to read about, too.

Barbara Lewis has written *Kids With Courage*, a collection of young people's biographies. The book includes stories about kids who have faced extraordinary challenges, including two young men who saved a busload of children when the driver had a heart attack.

As a teacher in Salt Lake City, Utah, Lewis encourages her students to get involved in their community. She has used her experience in the classroom to publish two books about student activism, *The Kid's Guide to Service Projects* and *The Kid's Guide to Social Action*.

Why do we like to read about other people's lives?

Reach Into Your Background

Believe it or not, you're an expert on other people's lives. You've seen movies and read books in which people tell their own or someone else's story. With a partner, do one or both of these activities and surprise yourself with how much you know:

- Choose a celebrity or historic figure. Imagine this person is writing his or her life story and wants to know what would interest readers. Give this person your advice.
- Imagine you have been asked to write about yourself for your class book. Have your partner interview you and help you select details to include.

Read Actively
Contrast Characters in Autobiography

In telling their life story (autobiography), writers sometimes present themselves side by side with someone who is different. By pointing out differences between, or contrasting, characters in autobiography you will learn more about the writer.

In this autobiography, look for differences between Russell and his sister, Doris. They are in the photograph opposite this page. Try making a word cluster like the one that follows for each of them. As you read, fill in each cluster with words that show contrasts between them.

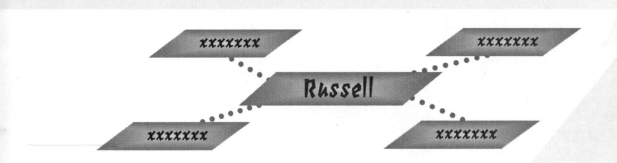

No Gumption

Russell Baker

I began working in journalism when I was eight years old. It was my mother's idea. She wanted me to "make something" of myself and, after a levelheaded appraisal of my strengths, decided I had better start young if I was to have any chance of keeping up with the competition.

The flaw in my character which she had already spotted was lack of "gumption." My idea of a perfect afternoon was lying in front of the radio rereading my favorite Big Little Book, *Dick Tracy Meets Stooge Viller*. My mother despised inactivity. Seeing me having a good time in repose, she was powerless to hide her disgust. "You've got no more gumption than a bump on a log," she said. "Get out in the kitchen and help Doris do those dirty dishes."

My sister Doris, though two years younger than I, had enough gumption for a dozen people. She positively enjoyed washing dishes, making beds, and cleaning the house. When she was only seven she could carry a piece of short-weighted cheese back to the A&P, threaten the manager with legal action, and come back triumphantly with the full quarter-pound we'd paid for and a few ounces extra thrown in for forgiveness. Doris could

Words to Know

appraisal (uh PRAY zuhl) *n.*: Evaluation; decision about the value of an item
flaw (FLAW) *n.*: Problem; imperfection
gumption (GUMP shun) *n.*: Courage; enterprise

have made something of herself if she hadn't been a girl. Because of this defect, however, the best she could hope for was a career as a nurse or schoolteacher, the only work that capable females were considered up to in those days.

This must have saddened my mother, this twist of fate that had allocated all the gumption to the daughter and left her with a son who was content with Dick Tracy and Stooge Viller. If disappointed, though, she wasted no energy on self-pity. She would make me make something of myself whether I wanted to or not. "The Lord helps those who help themselves," she said. That was the way her mind worked.

She was realistic about the difficulty. Having sized up the material the Lord had given her to mold, she didn't overestimate what she could do with it. She didn't insist that I grow up to be President of the United States.

Fifty years ago parents still asked boys if they wanted to grow up to be President, and asked it not jokingly but seriously. Many parents who were hardly more than paupers still believed their sons could do it. Abraham Lincoln had done it. We were only sixty-five years from Lincoln. Many a grandfather who walked among us could remember Lincoln's time. Men of grandfatherly age were the worst for asking if you wanted to grow up to be President. A surprising number of little boys said yes and meant it.

I was asked many times myself. No, I would say, I didn't want to grow up to be President. My mother was present during one of those interrogations. An elderly uncle, having posed the usual question and exposed my lack of interest in the Presidency, asked, "Well, what *do* you want to be when you grow up?"

I loved to pick through trash piles and collect empty bottles, tin cans with pretty labels, and discarded magazines. The most desirable job on earth sprang instantly to mind. "I want to be a garbage man," I said.

My uncle smiled, but my mother had seen the first distressing evidence of a bump budding on a log. "Have a little gumption, Russell," she said. Her calling me Russell was a signal of unhappiness. When she approved of me I was always "Buddy."

When I turned eight years old she decided that the job of starting me on the road toward making something of myself could no longer be safely delayed. "Buddy," she said one day, "I want you to come home right after school this afternoon. Somebody's coming and I want you to meet him."

When I burst in that afternoon she was in conference in the parlor with an executive of the Curtis Publishing Company. She introduced me. He bent low from the waist and shook my hand. Was it true as my mother had told him, he asked, that I longed for the opportunity to conquer the world of business?

> "Well, what *do* you want to be when you grow up?"

My mother replied that I was blessed with a rare determination to make something of myself.

"That's right," I whispered.

"But have you got the grit, the character, the never-say-quit spirit it takes to succeed in business?"

My mother said I certainly did.

"That's right," I said.

He eyed me silently for a long pause, as though weighing whether I could be trusted to keep his confidence, then spoke man-to-man. Before taking a crucial step, he said, he wanted to advise me that working for the Curtis Publishing Company placed enormous responsibility on a young man. It was one of the great companies of America. Perhaps the greatest publishing house in the world. I had

Words to Know

allocated (ALL uh kay tid) *v.*: Given; set aside
interrogations (in teh ruh GAY shunz) *n.*: Formal questioning sessions

heard, no doubt, of the *Saturday Evening Post?*

Heard of it? My mother said that everyone in our house had heard of the *Saturday Evening Post* and that I, in fact, read it with religious devotion.

Then doubtless, he said, we were also familiar with those two monthly pillars of the magazine world, the *Ladies Home Journal* and the *Country Gentleman.*

Indeed we were familiar with them, said my mother.

Representing the *Saturday Evening Post* was one of the weightiest honors that could be bestowed in the world of business, he said. He was personally proud of being a part of that great corporation.

My mother said he had every right to be.

Again he studied me as though debating whether I was worthy of a knighthood. Finally: "Are you trustworthy?"

My mother said I was the soul of honesty. "That's right," I said.

he caller smiled for the first time. He told me I was a lucky young man. He admired my spunk. Too many young men thought life was all play. Those young men would not go far in this world. Only a young man willing to work and save and keep his face washed and his hair neatly combed could hope to come out on top in a world such as ours. Did I truly and sincerely believe that I was such a young man?

"He certainly does," said my mother. "That's right," I said.

He said he had been so impressed by what he had seen of me that he was going to make me a representative of the Curtis Publishing Company. On the following Tuesday, he said, thirty freshly printed copies of the *Saturday Evening Post* would be delivered at our door. I would place these magazines, still damp with the ink of the presses, in a handsome canvas bag, sling it over my shoulder, and set forth through the streets to bring the best in journalism, fiction, and cartoons to the American public.

He had brought the canvas bag with him. He presented it with reverence fit for a chasuble.[1] He showed me how to drape the sling over my

> Again he studied me as though debating whether I was worthy of a knighthood.

left shoulder and across the chest so that the pouch lay easily accessible to my right hand, allowing the best in journalism, fiction, and cartoons to be swiftly extracted and sold to a citizenry whose happiness and security depended upon us soldiers of the free press.

The following Tuesday I raced home from school, put the canvas bag over my shoulder, dumped the magazines in, and, tilting to the left to balance their weight on my right hip, embarked on the highway of journalism.

We lived in Belleville, New Jersey, a commuter town at the northern fringe of Newark. It was 1932, the bleakest year of the Depression. My father had died two years before, leaving us with a few pieces of Sears, Roebuck furniture and not much else, and my mother had taken Doris and me to live with one of her younger brothers. This was my Uncle Allen. Uncle Allen had made something of himself by 1932. As salesman for a soft-drink bottler in Newark, he had an income of $30 a week; wore pearl-gray spats,[2] detachable collars, and a three-piece suit; was happily married; and took in threadbare relatives.

With my load of magazines I headed toward Belleville Avenue. That's where the

---

1. chasuble (CHAZ uh bul) *n.*: A sleeveless outer garment worn by priests during mass.

2. spats (SPATS) *n.*: Heavy cloth coverings worn over shoes to keep the instep and ankle clean.

Words to Know

reverence (REV uh ruhns) *n.*: Respect; awe; honor

embarked (im BAHRKD) *v.*: Began a journey

people were. There were two filling stations at the intersection with Union Avenue, as well as an A&P, a fruit stand, a bakery, a barber shop, Zuccarelli's drugstore, and a diner shaped like a railroad car. For several hours I made myself highly visible, shifting position now and then from corner to corner, from shop window to shop window, to make sure everyone could see the heavy black lettering on the canvas bag that said *The Saturday Evening Post.* When the angle of the light indicated it was suppertime, I walked back to the house.

"How many did you sell, Buddy?" my mother asked.

"None."

"Where did you go?"

"The corner of Belleville and Union Avenues."

"What did you do?"

"Stood on the corner waiting for somebody to buy a *Saturday Evening Post.*"

"You just stood there?"

> My mother and I had fought this battle almost as long as I could remember.

"Didn't sell a single one."

"For God's sake, Russell!"

Uncle Allen intervened. "I've been thinking about it for some time," he said, "and I've about decided to take the *Post* regularly. Put me down as a regular customer." I handed him a magazine and he paid me a nickel. It was the first nickel I earned.

Afterwards my mother instructed me in salesmanship. I would have to ring doorbells, address adults with charming self-confidence, and break down resistance with a sales talk pointing out that no one, no matter how poor, could afford to be without the *Saturday Evening Post* in the home.

I told my mother I'd changed my mind about wanting to succeed in the magazine business.

"If you think I'm going to raise a good-for-nothing," she replied, "you've got another think coming." She told me to hit the streets with the canvas bag and start ringing doorbells the instant school was out next day. When I objected that I didn't feel any aptitude for salesmanship, she asked how I'd like to lend her my leather belt so she could whack some sense into me. I bowed to superior will and entered journalism with a heavy heart.

My mother and I had fought this battle almost as long as I could remember. It probably started even before memory began, when I was a country child in northern Virginia and my mother, dissatisfied with my father's plain workman's life, determined that I would not grow up like him and his people, with calluses on their hands, overalls on their backs, and fourth-grade educations in their heads. She had fancier ideas of life's possibilities. Introducing me to the *Saturday Evening Post,* she was trying to wean[3] me as early as possible from my father's world where men left with their lunch pails at sunup, worked with their hands until the grime ate into the pores, and died with a few sticks of mail-order furniture as their legacy. In my mother's vision of the better life there were desks and white collars, well-pressed suits, evenings of reading and lively talk, and perhaps—if a man were very, very lucky and hit the jackpot, really made something important of himself—perhaps there might be a fantastic salary of $5,000 a year to support a big house and a Buick with a rumble seat and a vacation in Atlantic City.

And so I set forth with my sack of magazines. I was afraid of the dogs that snarled behind the doors of potential buyers. I was timid about ringing the doorbells of strangers,

---

3. wean (WEEN) *v.*: To draw away gradually from a habit or belief.

Words to Know

aptitude (AP tuh tood) *n.*: Natural skill; talent; ability

canvassed (KAN vust) *v.*: Tried to sell

Russell Baker's mother

"Better get out there and sell the rest of those magazines tonight," my mother would say.

I usually posted myself then at a busy intersection where a traffic light controlled commuter flow from Newark. When the light turned red I stood on the curb and shouted my sales pitch at the motorists.

"Want to buy a *Saturday Evening Post?*"

One rainy night when car windows were sealed against me I came back soaked and with not a single sale to report. My mother beckoned to Doris.

"Go back down there with Buddy and show him how to sell these magazines," she said.

Brimming with zest, Doris, who was then seven years old, returned with me to the corner. She took a magazine from the bag, and when the light turned red she strode to the nearest car and banged her small fist against the closed window. The driver, probably startled at what he took to be a midget assaulting his car, lowered the window to stare, and Doris thrust a *Saturday Evening Post* at him.

"You need this magazine," she piped, "and it only costs a nickel."

er salesmanship was irresistible. Before the light had changed half a dozen times she disposed of the entire batch. I didn't feel humiliated. To the contrary. I was so happy I decided to give her a treat. Leading her to the vegetable store on Belleville Avenue, I bought three apples, which cost a nickel, and gave her one.

"You shouldn't waste money," she said.

"Eat your apple." I bit into mine.

relieved when no one came to the door, and scared when someone did. Despite my mother's instructions, I could not deliver an engaging sales pitch. When a door opened I simply asked, "Want to buy a *Saturday Evening Post?*" In Belleville few persons did. It was a town of 30,000 people, and most weeks I rang a fair majority of its doorbells. But I rarely sold my thirty copies. Some weeks I canvassed the entire town for six days and still had four or five unsold magazines on Monday evening; then I dreaded the coming of Tuesday morning, when a batch of thirty fresh *Saturday Evening Post*s was due at the front door.

"You shouldn't eat before supper," she said. "It'll spoil your appetite."

Back at the house that evening, she dutifully reported me for wasting a nickel. Instead of a scolding, I was rewarded with a pat on the back for having the good sense to buy fruit instead of candy. My mother reached into her bottomless supply of maxims[4] and told Doris, "An apple a day keeps the doctor away."

By the time I was ten I had learned all my mother's maxims by heart. Asking to stay up past normal bedtime, I knew that a refusal would be explained with, "Early to bed and early to rise, makes a man healthy, wealthy, and wise." If I whimpered about having to get up early in the morning, I could depend on her to say, "The early bird gets the worm."

The one I most despised was, "If at first you don't succeed, try, try again." This was the battle cry with which she constantly sent me back into the hopeless struggle whenever I moaned that I had rung every doorbell in town and knew there wasn't a single potential buyer left in Belleville that week. After listening to my explanation, she handed me the canvas bag and said, "If at first you don't succeed . . ."

Three years in that job, which I would gladly have quit after the first day except for her insistence, produced at least one valuable result. My mother finally concluded that I would never make something of myself by pursuing a life in business and started considering careers that demanded less competitive zeal.

One evening when I was eleven I brought home a short "composition" on my summer vacation which the teacher had graded with an A. Reading it with her own schoolteacher's eye, my mother agreed that it was top-drawer seventh grade prose and complimented me.

Nothing more was said about it immediately, but a new idea had taken life in her mind. Halfway through supper she suddenly interrupted the conversation.

"Buddy," she said, "maybe you could be a writer."

I clasped the idea to my heart. I had never met a writer, had shown no previous urge to write, and hadn't a notion how to become a writer, but I loved stories and thought that making up stories must surely be almost as much fun as reading them. Best of all, though, and what really gladdened my heart, was the ease of the writer's life. Writers did not have to trudge through the town peddling from canvas bags, defending themselves against angry dogs, being rejected by surly strangers. Writers did not have to ring doorbells. So far as I could make out, what writers did couldn't even be classified as work.

I was enchanted. Writers didn't have to have any gumption at all. I did not dare tell anybody for fear of being laughed at in the schoolyard, but secretly I decided that what I'd like to be when I grew up was a writer.

> . . . I decided that what I'd like to be when I grew up was a writer.

---

4. maxims (MAKS ims) *n.*: Short sayings that express rules of life or behavior.

Respond

- Are you more like Doris or Russell? Explain.
- Role-play a scene from the essay, focusing on differences between Doris and Russell. For example, pretend you are Doris returning cheese to the market; then act out the scene as Russell.

Russell Baker (1925–   ) grew up in Virginia and New Jersey. As "No Gumption" indicates, he decided to become a writer when he was in the seventh grade. He stuck to this decision and became a reporter, eventually winning the Pulitzer Prize for his newspaper column.

Activities
MAKE MEANING

Explore Your Reading
Look Back (Recall)

1. Which of Russell's activities demonstrate a lack of gumption?
2. What does Doris do in contrast that shows her gumption?

Think It Over (Interpret)

3. Was Russell serious when he said he'd like to be a garbage man? How do you know?
4. Why is Russell unsuccessful in his job with the *Saturday Evening Post*?
5. Which of Russell's traits suggest that he might be a good writer?

Go Beyond (Apply)

6. What interests of yours could help you find a career?

Develop Reading and Literary Skills
Understand Autobiography

In an **autobiography,** a writer tells the story of his or her life. Sometimes people tell their story by contrasting themselves with someone close to them. For instance, Russell Baker contrasts himself to his sister, Doris. Your word clusters for Russell and Doris probably showed you important differences between them.

Think about these differences. Then imagine what Doris's autobiography would be like.

1. Using details from your word clusters, write three sentences that contrast Russell and Doris.
2. Rewrite one of the episodes as Doris might have written it in *her* autobiography. Have her contrast herself with Russell.

Ideas for Writing

You probably noticed that Baker focuses on a word, *gumption,* to tell about himself. Other autobiographical sketches focus on specific events, like a political campaign or a baseball season.

Extended Definition How would you define the word *gumption*? Give a dictionary definition of the word and then extend that definition by including stories, anecdotes, and examples to further explain its meaning.

Autobiographical Sketch Write about an important event in your life for your class book. If you prefer, imagine you are a celebrity and recall an event that shaped your life. Contrast yourself with a person close to you.

Ideas for Projects

Comparison of Self-Portraits In addition to writing an autobiography, an artist can paint a self-portrait. Find self-portraits in art books from the library. In an oral presentation, explain what these self-portraits reveal about the artists. [Art Link]

Career Cards Baker tells how he became interested in writing as a career. With a few classmates, research careers related to math, science, and social studies by interviewing teachers and career counselors. Then, for each career, make a card describing the skills required and the opportunities available. [Social Studies Link; Math Link; Science Link]

How Am I Doing?

Write your responses to these questions in your journal:

How did contrasting characters help me understand this autobiography better? How could I use contrasting to understand other types of writing?

What did I learn from this selection about my own career interests?

Activities PREVIEW
Susan Butcher by Bill Littlefield

Would you endure weeks of freezing temperatures, hunger, thirst, and exhaustion to reach a goal?

Reach Into Your Background

When you read the stories of people's lives, you often learn about the challenges they faced to achieve their goals. Called **biographies** when written by someone other than the subject, these true-life stories can tell about challenges that are mental or physical. With a group, do one or both of the following activities:

- Note the most difficult challenges that people have to face. Without using words, act out some of these challenges.
- List the people whose biographies you would like to read.

Read Actively
Set a Purpose for Reading Biography

You will learn much more by setting a **purpose,** or goal, for reading a biography. In doing this, consider what you already know about the person and what you'd like to know.

This biography is about Susan Butcher, a star of a famous Alaskan sled-dog race called the Iditarod (ī DIT uh rod). Use the map and the photographs on the following pages to imagine some of the challenges she faces. Then set up a three-column KWL chart to guide your reading. In the *What I Know* column, list what you already know about Susan Butcher. In the *What I Want to Know* column, list what you hope to learn in the form of questions. Fill in the *What I Learned* column as you read.

SUSAN BUTCHER

❄ ❄ ❄ ❄ **Bill Littlefield** ❄ ❄ ❄ ❄

For Susan Butcher, it was a day like any other: brutally cold, windy, and snowing hard enough so that it was impossible to see more than a few feet in front of the heavy four-wheel vehicle her sled dogs were dragging for practice. In short, as far as she was concerned, everything was perfect.

Then suddenly Butcher's lead dog went "gee" (right) when Butcher shouted "Haw!" (left), and the four-wheeler, the dogs, and Butcher plunged off a twelve-foot cliff and into a clump of alder trees.

There was, of course, no path out. The trail Butcher and the dogs had fallen from was little traveled, and she figured it might be several days before somebody happened by. She had no saw and no ax. It was only supposed to be a little training run. With pliers, a wrench, and a broken screwdriver, she chopped at the alders. She got the dogs working together, and they pulled the four-wheeler up the hill. Sometimes they'd make as little as twelve inches of progress before Butcher would have to begin hacking away with her pliers and wrench again, but five hours after they'd fallen, Butcher and her dogs were on the road back to her cabin. Butcher had learned not to leave home,

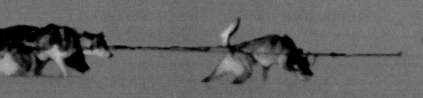

Susan Butcher

even for practice, without all her tools. And she hoped her lead dog had learned that "Haw!" meant "Haw!"

On that day when she and her team fell off the trail, Susan Butcher was training herself and her dogs for the Iditarod,[1] the annual sled dog race that covers the eleven hundred miles between Anchorage and Nome, Alaska. Over the years, Butcher's consistently excellent finishes in this most grueling of athletic events have become the stuff of legend, and some of the tales of her training runs are no less dramatic than the races them-

selves. In a funny way, Butcher's preparation for the Iditarod began before the race ever existed. When she finally entered it for the first time in 1978, Butcher must have felt like she'd finally discovered where she belonged.

As a little girl growing up in Cambridge, Massachusetts, Susan Butcher only knew where she did *not* belong. She hated the congestion of the busy streets, the constant noise of the traffic, and the pollution all around her. She begged her parents to move to the country, or at least to let her live in a tent in the backyard. Her best friends were the dogs she kept. In first grade she wrote an essay entitled "I Hate Cities." That was the first, last, and only sentence in the paper.

When she was finally old enough to leave home, she put Cambridge behind her in favor of Colorado. When the Rockies no longer seemed sufficiently remote, she headed for Alaska. She finally settled in a town called Eureka, which you will not find on many maps. There she cobbled together four one-room cabins, a doorless outhouse, and 120 doghouses. Butcher's dogs have outnumbered the two-legged citizens of Eureka by as many as 150 to 13.

---

1. Iditarod (ī DIT uh rod)

Words to Know

grueling (GROO ling) *adj.*: Very tiring; exhausting
congestion (kuhn JES chuhn) *n.*: Crowds; traffic
remote (ruh MOHT) *adj.*: Isolated; removed; far from people

Eureka is a fine place [...] them or kick the Iditarod, since a chief [...] then the other. is isolation. A pitcher who [...] veling downhill, count on the batter with t[...] their lives and in the ninth inning of a [...] freeze their eyes feel lonely. A marathone[...] rom their hands, beyond whatever certain[...] en the company can provide and still h[...] ng as they can might feel that way, too. [...] er frozen rivers, exists primarily as a [...] mps of burned- conviction[2] that everybo[...] nely inadequate able to take care of himsel[...] dlight, and hope the help of a dozen or so [...] h headlong into is perhaps no loneliness [...] he dog team of ness of someone lost and snow-blind in the middle of Alaska. some poor fool who has become completely confused and started racing backward on the trail.

A very fast and disciplined dog team with an experienced and fortunate musher can complete the race in a little over eleven days. Some competitors take as long as three weeks, and a lot of starters, as high as 30 or 40 percent some years, quit. Leaders and losers alike spend hours and hours alone and cold in a blasted white landscape. When their dog teams are traveling up a hill, the

All these obstacles appeal to Susan Butcher, who's felt since early childhood that taking heat, light, and shelter for granted was missing the point. Only when she has felt close to nature's essentials has she felt challenged. And only when

2. conviction (kuhn VIK shun) *n.*: Belief.

IDITAROD TRAIL

SLED DOG RACE

only from a great distance. He called the race the Iditarod after an Alaskan ghost town bearing the name, which is an old Indian word meaning distant place.

As an incentive to take up this crazy challenge, Redington offered $50,000 to the winner of the first Iditarod, though when the race started he didn't have the money. Twenty days later, when that first race ended, Joe had the dough. He'd hustled it from various individual and corporate[3] donors. But over the years the payoff for winning the Iditarod continued to be a little on the shaky side. Winners have sometimes had to settle for their prizes in installments, unlike all the professional baseball, basketball, and football players who are secure in their guaranteed contracts.

Joe Redington first met Susan Butcher a few years after he'd come up with the Iditarod, and right away he was sure she'd win it one day. Or he was almost sure. He proposed a sled dog trek to the summit of Alaska's Denali, also known as Mount McKinley, perhaps partly to test the mettle[4] of this remarkable young woman who'd come to the far north in search of escape from cars, buildings, and too many people. Together with seven dogs and a sled, Butcher and Redington made the 20,320-foot climb through hundred-mile-an-hour winds and over 2,000-foot-deep crevasses.[5] It took

she has felt challenged has she felt entirely alive.

Joe Redington invented the Iditarod in 1973. He'd always loved the wilderness, particularly the Alaskan wilderness, and he was worried that what he loved was falling into the hands of snowmobilers and settlers with satellite dishes. He scratched his head and wondered how to remind everybody of the toughness and independence that Alaska had always demanded of its residents, and he came up with a race that would require sled drivers and their dogs to brave screaming winds, blinding blizzards, hunger, lack of sleep, and a dozen other hardships that most athletes would just as soon consider

---

3. corporate (KOR puh rit) *adj.*: Business.

4. mettle (MET l) *n.*: Spirit or courage.

5. crevasses (kruh VAS is) *n.*: Deep narrow openings caused by a crack or split.

Words to Know

incentive (in SEN tiv) *n.*: Something that makes a person want or try

them forty-four days. Nobody'd mushed that route before. Nobody's done it since. When they were finished, Redington was *absolutely* sure Susan Butcher would one day win the Iditarod.

But the extent to which Ms. Butcher fulfilled his prophecy must have surprised even Redington himself. Perhaps it shouldn't have. By the time she began to pile up first-place finishes in the Iditarod and other races in the late eighties, Susan Butcher had paid her dues. She'd learned from her limping pups to line up several friends year-round to help her knit booties for race days. Run out of booties on the trail, and the ice would cut the best team's paws to hamburger. She'd learned how to recognize a potential lead dog in a litter and how to raise all the dogs in her team to have confidence in her. And perhaps most important, she'd learned that her loyalty and attention to the needs of her canine partners would sometimes be rewarded by the special gifts the dogs had to give.

Eight years before she ever won an Iditarod, Butcher was mushing perhaps her best lead dog ever, Tekla, and fourteen other huskies across a frozen river in a practice run when suddenly Tekla began pulling hard to the right. Butcher kept tugging on the team to follow the trail, but Tekla wouldn't respond. Though she'd never balked[6] before, the dog insisted on pulling the sled off the trail to the right.

Butcher finally shrugged and decided to follow Tekla's lead. A moment after she'd made that decision and left the track, the whole trail itself sank into the river. "She [Tekla] had a sixth sense that saved our lives," Butcher told Sonja Steptoe of *Sports Illustrated* years later. "That day I learned that the wilderness is their domain. The dogs know more about it than I do, and I'm better off trusting their instincts."

Of course instinct is only part of it. Courage, stamina, and a cool head help, too. In 1985, with a superb team and

---

6. **balked** (BAWKD) *v.*: Stubbornly refused.

Words to Know

prophecy (PRAHF uh see) *n.*: A prediction about the future

potential (puh TEN shuhl) *adj.*: Possible; capable of becoming

high expectations, Susan Butcher seemed to be on her way to winning the Iditarod for the first time. But she ran into a problem no measure of preparation or instinct could have forestalled.[7] Veering around a sharp bend in the trail one night, she was startled to find in the beam of her headlight a full-grown female moose. The dog team hit the animal before Butcher knew the moose was there. By the time Butcher could figure out what had happened, the moose was hopelessly entangled in the harnesses that connected the dogs. In the carnage that followed, two of Butcher's dogs were kicked to death and several others were badly injured. While Butcher fought to free the remaining dogs from their harnesses, the moose stomped on her shoulder and might have killed her, too, if another musher hadn't arrived on the scene and shot the moose. Butcher and her team limped to the next checkpoint and resigned from that Iditarod in the low point of her racing career.

And then, beginning in 1986, the high points began coming in quick succession. Between 1986 and 1990, she won the Iditarod four times. The hottest selling T-shirt in the state bore the legend "Alaska: Where Men Are Men and Women Win the Iditarod." After Butcher's third win in a row in 1988, Joe Redington laughed and told a reporter, "It's getting pretty hard for a man to win anything anymore. Maybe we should start a race especially for them."

It has been suggested that the formula for winning the Iditarod involves having good dogs, a good musher, and good luck—in about equal measure. The good musher is the one who can smile into the wrath of an unexpected hundred-mile-per-hour wind, but he or she better make sure the smile is behind several layers of ski mask, because when that wind joins below-zero temperatures, a smile will freeze on the lips for hours, and maybe forever. Susan Butcher proved she could brave the most vicious weather, but by the time she started winning the Iditarod, she'd learned to prepare herself and her dogs so well that all but the most hideous storms seemed routine. She'd also learned that by working closely with her dogs every day from the hour they were born, she could build a level of trust and loyalty that her competitors could only envy. Of course, this relationship demanded a good deal from Butcher, too. In 1991, she passed up the chance to win her fifth Iditarod when she decided that a blizzard raging over the last hundred miles of the course would unreasonably endanger her team. She prolonged a rest stop, waiting for the weather to improve, and finished second that year.

Even when the blizzards hold off and the moose stay out of the way, the Iditarod demands a tremendous amount from a musher. The rules require one mandatory rest period of twenty-four hours during the race, and once having met that requirement, no serious competitor stops for more than four hours at a time. Nearly all of the four hours of each stop are taken up by feeding the dogs, melting snow so they'll have water, checking their paws for cuts or cracks, mending the harnesses, and maybe catching something to eat—hot chocolate if you're fortunate enough to be stopping at a checkpoint where somebody's cooking, melted snow if you're not.

That doesn't leave much time for sleep, so the Iditarod's exhausted com-

---

7. **forestalled** (for STAHLD) *v.*: Prevented; avoided.

Words to Know

carnage (KAR nij) *n.*: A bloody scene; a slaughter
prolonged (proh LAWNGD) *v.*: Extended; made longer
hallucinate (huh LOOS in ayt) *v.*: See or hear things around one that are not there
capable (KAY puh buhl) *adj.*: Able to do things well; powerful; skilled

petitors have been known to hallucinate on the trail. In a book entitled *Woodsong*, a musher named Gary Paulsen wrote of a fellow who appeared on his sled wearing horn-rimmed glasses, clutching a stack of important-looking papers. "He is the most boring human being I have ever met," Paulsen says in his diary-like account. "He speaks in a low voice about federal educational grants and he goes on and on until at last I yell at him to shut up. The dogs stop and look back at me and of course I am alone."

Though Susan Butcher also might well be susceptible[8] to hallucinations,

---

8. **susceptible** (suh SEPT uh buhl) *adj*.: Easily affected; very sensitive.

---

her dogs probably know her too well to be surprised by anything she could say or do. Certainly she knows them well enough to astonish her friends. "Folks ask how I can call one hundred and fifty of them by name," she says, "but it's natural. They're like children. If you had one hundred and fifty kids, you'd know all their names, wouldn't you?"

Becoming the world's most successful musher and one of the very few sled dog drivers capable of making a living at the

sport has never turned Susan Butcher's head, though it has gone some way toward fulfilling her dream. "I never got into this to make a lot of money," she told an interviewer before winning her fourth Iditarod, in 1990. "But to live just the way you want, to do what you love to do. . . . How could you have any complaints?"

Still, success at the Iditarod *has* changed Susan Butcher, if only a little. Before she became a celebrity, at least by Alaskan standards, she used to go off and live alone for six months or so. No people, no running water, no nothing. Now, in deference to the fact that people want to contact her and because raising and training 150 dogs takes the sort of money only sponsors can provide, she has a phone in her cabin. She has a husband there, too. His name is David Monson, and as a matter of fact the phone was probably his idea. He serves as Susan Butcher's business manager, and he probably got pretty tired of hitching up the dogs and mushing more than twenty miles every time he had to make a call.

Which is not to suggest that David Monson is exactly a softy. He got to know his future wife when they were both unknown mushers competing in the 1981 Iditarod. Monson was struggling to climb a hill and lost control of his sled, which wound up off the trail in the brush. It was the same stretch of brush Susan Butcher had already fallen into a few minutes earlier, and while they were both working to straighten out their dog teams, a third musher also skidded off the trail and landed on them. Monson remembers it as chaos: forty-five dogs and three mushers, including a very angry and competitive woman and one guy (Monson) who didn't really have much idea what he was up to. When they all finally got back on the trail, Butcher told Monson he'd better rest his dog team, and that was the last he saw of her in the race. If it wasn't love at first sight, it was close enough for the two mushers, now partners as well as competitors.

Not all the others who tackle the Iditarod have been as comfortable with Susan Butcher's triumphs in the race as David Monson has been. Rick Swenson, the only person to have won the race as often as Butcher has, tried for some years to get the Iditarod's organizers to adopt a handicapping system that would, in effect, penalize Butcher and other women racers for weighing less than the men who mush against them. When that didn't work, Swenson took to intimating that Butcher won only because she had a lead dog of supernatural strength and endurance, an unintentional[9] compliment, since Butcher had raised and trained the dog. Butcher herself tends to shrug off the bitterness of the men who resent a woman's success in a sport they'd like to claim as their own. "Yes, I am a woman," she told writer Carolyn Coman in an interview for the book *Body and Soul.* "Yes, it is a victory for me to win the Iditarod. But it isn't amazing that I, a woman, did it. I did it because I am capable, and women are capable."

Being capable may never before have involved such an effort. Butcher has said on several occasions that training for the Iditarod—which involves raising, feeding, running, and training her dogs as well as

keeping herself in shape—is an eleven-month proposition. Small wonder that sometimes she thinks about turning her attention exclusively to some of Alaska's shorter races—the three-, four-, or five-hundred-mile jaunts. She already knows these races well. She holds the records in most of them, just as she does for the Iditarod. So easing up a little is a pleasant possibility that occupies Susan Butcher sometimes when she thinks about a post-Iditarod future.

Unhappily, there's an unpleasant possibility that concerns her, too. She has adjusted to the modern improvements David Monson has made in their cabin, but other adjustments won't come so easily to the woman who hated the noise and pollution and hustle of Cambridge when she was a little girl. The authorities have begun to improve the roads up Susan Butcher's way, and Butcher has watched "progress" suspiciously. "In ten years we may have ten or fifteen neighbors," she was overheard to say. "If that happens, we'll be gone."

---

9. **unintentional** (un in TEN shun uhl) *adj.:* Not deliberate; chance; random.

Bill Littlefield (1948–   ), a sports commentator for National Public Radio, says this about exceptional athletes:

> Our best athletes fire our imaginations. Within their games they give us images of excellence, which are often hard to find elsewhere. But the most admirable of our athletes do even more. They demonstrate in their work such qualities as perseverance and grace under pressure. . . . The stories of their lives give us patterns, and from these patterns we can learn something about finding a passion and working hard and believing in ourselves.

Respond

- Of the Iditarod's challenges, which would you find the most difficult? Why?
- With a partner, list questions you still have about Susan Butcher.

Activities

MAKE MEANING

Explore Your Reading

Look Back (Recall)

1. What obstacles did Susan Butcher overcome in becoming an Iditarod champion?

Think It Over (Interpret)

2. Why wasn't Joe Redington absolutely sure Susan Butcher would win the Iditarod when he first met her?
3. Describe the relationship between a musher and a dog team.
4. Why is Susan Butcher a successful musher? Rank her qualities in order of importance and explain your ranking system.

Go Beyond (Apply)

5. Explain why men and women should or shouldn't be allowed to participate in the same Iditarod.

Develop Reading and Literary Skills

Understand Biography

There are many reasons for reading a **biography,** a writer's account of someone else's life. Your **purpose,** or goal, for reading may have helped you learn about one or more of the following things:

- What Susan Butcher values
- Challenges she has faced and goals she has achieved
- Her personal life
- The background of the Iditarod
- What Alaska is like

Use your KWL chart to help you answer these questions:

1. For each of these items, describe something you learned from this biography.
2. What information in this biography did you find most interesting? Why? What would you like to learn more about?

Ideas for Writing

Bill Littlefield has written a biography of an Iditarod racer. However, this famous race might inspire other types of writing as well.

Musher's Journal Imagine you are training for the Iditarod. What elements of the Alaskan course would concern you most? Draft the journal entry you would write the night before the race began.

Book Review Imagine you have been assigned to review the Susan Butcher biography for an Alaskan tourism magazine. Tell readers what they can learn about Alaska from this biography and whether they should read the book.

Ideas for Projects

Sports Interview Choose a school athlete or local sports personality to interview. Before the interview, jot down what people would want to know about this person and then write your questions. If possible, videotape your interview. [Social Studies Link]

Media Review Form your own "Thumbs Up–Thumbs Down" media review team. With a partner, determine what makes a good biography. Then make a list of biographical movies and books and evaluate each according to your standards.

Exercise Report The Iditarod is an extremely demanding race. Research and explain the exercises that could increase an athlete's strength and endurance for this contest. Share your findings with the class. If possible, demonstrate some of the exercises. [Science Link]

How Am I Doing?

Spend a moment with a partner to discuss these questions:

How did the map and photographs help me to understand Susan Butcher's experiences? Why?

In what other kinds of assignments could the KWL chart help? How would I modify it?

How Do I Show What I Can Do?

Student Art *Basketball* Luckshimi B. Balasubramanian, Sri Lanka

Scoring High

Student Writing Antoine Mack, Age 11
Boston, Massachusetts

Sometimes I feel like a star,
Scoring high
In the sky.
When I reach the hoop,
I dunk

Sky shatters like glass.

With the sun as my backboard
I shoot
The clouds swish.

Activities
PREVIEW
from **Poetry to Read Out Loud** by James Earl Jones
Lyric 17 by José García Villa
Suppose by Siv Cedering

What achievement would you like your classmates to remember you for?

Reach Into Your Background

You can make your achievements sound even more impressive by using comparisons to describe them. For instance, you may have heard sports announcers say that a quarterback has an arm "like a cannon" or that a tennis player moves "like a cat." Practice using comparisons by doing one or both of the following:

- In your journal, use a comparison to describe something you achieved in sports or any other area.
- With a group, think of comparisons to describe the performances of famous singers, sports figures, or actors.

Read Actively
Recognize Similes

Poets like to show what they can do by writing **similes**, comparisons of things that seem different but are really similar. Using the word *like* or *as* to alert you to a simile, poets make comparisons to give you a fresh way of seeing the world. If you recognize comparisons in poetry, you will be able to enjoy the vivid word pictures that poets create and to understand what the writer is telling you.

In the poems that follow, look for the clue words *like* or *as* to find places where a poet is making a comparison. Try recording the comparison in a chart like the following (the first line is filled in).

Title: Lyric 17

Item Being Described	What Item Is Being Compared To	Quality They Share
poem	seagull	being musical

from Poetry to Read Out Loud

James Earl Jones

Poetry has always been a lifeline for me. When I was a small boy, I began to stutter. From the time I was nearly six until I was about fourteen, I chose silence over speech. I retreated into muteness because my stuttering made speaking too difficult. But because I needed some way to express myself, even to myself, and to track the progress of my mind, I became a "closet" poet. I loved poetry, and began writing it myself.

In one of those fortunate accidents that can change lives, my high school English

James Earl Jones

teacher in Brethren, Michigan, helped me to use poetry to reclaim my ability to speak. When Professor Donald Crouch discovered that I wrote poems, he asked to see some. One seemed to him good enough that he wondered if I might have plagiarized it. To defend myself, I had to read the poem aloud. Since I never spoke at school, this was an ordeal for me, but my honor was at stake. I had no choice but to stand up and read my poem to my teacher and classmates.

To my amazement and theirs, I read it without stumbling. That is how my teacher and I discovered that I did not stutter when I read the rhythmic *written* word aloud. It was no accident, then, that in the comfortable realm of the poetry I had written, expressing my own ideas and feelings, I found that I could speak. Poetry helped me to discover my own voice and to resurrect my powers of speech. At the same time, poetry led me into the hearts and minds of the poets, giving me a more intimate understanding of the universal human experience. This breakthrough gave me an insatiable appetite for the sheer joy of communicating.

Words to Know

fortunate (FAWR chuh nuht) *adj.*: Lucky

plagiarized (PLAY juh rīzd) *v.*: Taken writings of others and presented them as one's own

resurrect (rez uh REKT) *v.*: Bring back to use or life

insatiable (in SAY shuh buhl) *adj.*: Never satisfied; always wanting more

Respond

Why do you think many people are uncomfortable speaking to large groups?

Lyric 17

José García Villa

First, a poem must be magical,
Then musical as a sea-gull.
It must be brightness moving
And hold secret a bird's flowering.
5 It must be slender as a bell,
And it must hold fire as well.
It must have the wisdom of bows
And it must kneel like a rose.
It must be able to hear
10 The luminance of dove and deer.
It must be able to hide
What it seeks, like a bride.
And over all I would like to hover
God, smiling from the poem's cover.

Unfinished Man 1968, Rupert García, Courtesy of the artist and Sammi Madison-García, Rena Bransten Gallery, San Francisco, California

 **Respond**
What do you think a poem "must be"?

Words to Know

luminance (LOO muh nuhns) *n.*: Brightness; brilliance (line 10)
hover (HUV uhr) *v.*: Hang in the air; flutter in one place (line 13)

Suppose
Siv Cedering

Suppose I were as clever as a bird
and the words for what I am
could be contained
in one precise song,
5   repeated, repeated
while each jubilant phrase
spells it all
in variations
too refined for the human ear

10 Or that the song has not yet been found
but waits inside me
like the long note that sounds
when a blade of grass
is placed between the thumbs
15 and blown

It could be
that the place my words are looking for
will turn out to be so small
that there will be room for nothing
20 but silence
—or an ocean so large
some waves will never reach
the sound of the shore

Respond
What kind of song could
express your personality?

Into the Future 1987, Max Papart, Nahan Galleries, New York

Words to Know

precise (pree SĪS) *adj*.: Exact;
accurate (line 4)
jubilant (JOO buh luhnt) *adj*.:
Joyful; proud (line 6)
variations (var ee AY shunz) *n*.:
Changes; differences (line 8)
refined (ree FĪND) *adj*.: Purified;
polished (line 9)

Meet the Authors

After overcoming his childhood stutter, **James Earl Jones** (1931–   ) developed one of the best-known voices in television and film today. You may know it as the powerful deep voice of both the evil Darth Vader in the *Star Wars* film series and the wise King Mufasa in *The Lion King*. Jones has also lent his voice to other projects, including numerous television commercials and the 1993 documentary *Lincoln.* In addition to his off-screen voice work, Jones won two Emmys for his on-screen acting in 1991.

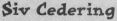

Siv Cedering
(1939–   )

Q: How do you pronounce Cedering's first name?

A: Siv rhymes with Steve.

Q: Where was she born?

A: She was born in Sweden and came to the United States when she was fourteen.

Q: Where has her poetry taken her?

A: Cedering has given poetry readings in Japan, Australia, and France.

Q: What other interests does she have?

A: Cedering's photographs were once exhibited in a New York City gallery.

Q: What does Cedering like about poetry?

A: She says that a poem is "often small, but it can surprise you."

José García Villa (1914–   ) was born in Manila, Philippines, and emigrated to the United States when he was sixteen. One critic's review of García Villa's poetry seems to answer "Lyric 17," declaring that García Villa's poems come "straight from the poet's being, from his blood, his spirit, as a fire breaks from wood, or as a flower grows from its soil."

Activities

MAKE MEANING

 ## Explore Your Reading

Look Back (Recall)

1. With what two sounds does Siv Cedering compare the song that "waits inside" her?
2. What qualities does José García Villa say a poem must have?

Think It Over (Interpret)

3. Why is the speaker in "Suppose" trying to identify "the place my words are looking for"?
4. In "Lyric 17," why do you think the poet uses comparisons to tell what poetry is rather than giving a simple definition?

Go Beyond (Apply)

5. Basing your answer on one or both of these poems, explain why James Earl Jones found his voice through poetry.
6. How can writing stories and poems be a way of saying who you are?

 ## Develop Reading and Literary Skills

Appreciate Similes

As you filled in your chart, you were finding **similes**—comparisons showing how two apparently different things are really alike. For example, the first simile in "Lyric 17" compares a poem to a seagull because they are both "musical."

In everyday speech, you hear similes that are as worn out as old clothes. One simile like this is "tough as nails." Poets try to use similes that are fresher to help you see the world in a new way. When Cedering writes, "Suppose I were as clever as a bird," the simile makes you wonder how a bird is "clever." It also makes you wonder how a person could be clever in the same way.

1. Choose two similes from your chart and tell why you like them.
2. Explain how each helps you to see something in a new way.

 ## Ideas for Writing

Similes add flavor not only to poetry but to many other kinds of writing as well.

Radio Sportscast Describe your favorite athlete in action as a radio commentator would. Use several similes to paint a vivid picture for listeners who can't see the game. Read your description aloud for the class.

Poem Using "Lyric 17" as a model, write a poem that sets standards for quality. For instance, tell what makes a good meal, a good friend, or a good action hero. Use similes to make your point.

Ideas for Projects

Song Write the lyrics for a song that describes what you can accomplish. Use similes to enhance your song, and select music to go with your words. If you are a musician, compose the music yourself and record it.

Comparisons in Science Ask your science teacher how scientists use comparisons. For example, biologists are able to classify animals into groups by comparing their similarities and differences. Prepare a report on comparisons in science and present it to the class. [Science Link]

How Am I Doing?

In a small group, consider these questions:
How did the comparison chart help me find similes in the poetry? How could such a chart help me read other kinds of literature?

What did these selections teach me about how people express their identity?

What would you do if you suddenly discovered a movie star was a relative of yours?

Reach Into Your Background

The ancient Greek gods and goddesses were something like today's celebrities. They lived above it all on Mt. Olympus very much as movie stars live in Hollywood. They were ruled by Zeus, king of the gods, and his wife, Hera. Handsome Apollo, who controlled the sun's movements, was a child of Zeus.

Although the gods lived apart from humans and could not die, they still quarreled, loved, and competed like humans. Also, they took part in human wars and even had children with humans.

With a small group, do one or both of the following activities:

*   Share what you know about Greek gods.
*   Imagine being a teenager in ancient Greece and learning that Apollo is your father. Role-play a scene in which you tell this news to a classmate.

Read Actively

Preview a Myth

You can learn a lot about new movies by watching the "coming attractions." You can also **preview**, or peek ahead at, a book by reading a few passages.

"Phaethon and the Horses of the Sun" is a story about an ancient Greek boy who wants to prove himself. Preview it by reading a few sentences and looking at the pictures. Do you think the boy will be successful? Keep your impressions in mind as you read, and note in your journal whether they change.

PHAETHON
and the
Horses of the Sun

Retold by Anne Terry White

Young Phaethon[1] was in a rage. His schoolmates had been making fun of him, laughing at the idea that he was the son of a god. But he was, he was! His mother, the sea nymph Clymene, had many times told him so.

"There is your glorious father," she had said, pointing to the glistening Sun. "See how skillfully he drives his fiery chariot!"

Flushed with shame and anger, Phaethon stood now before Clymene. "If I am indeed of heavenly birth, mother, give me some proof of it!" he pleaded.

"What proof can I give you?" Clymene answered. Then she stretched her hands upward to the skies. "I call to witness the Sun which looks down upon us, that I have told you the truth," she said solemnly. "If I speak falsely, let this be the last time I behold[2] his light! But," she added, "why don't you go and

Words to Know

solemnly (SAHL uhm lee) *adv*.: Seriously

---

1. **Phaethon** (FAY uh tahn)
2. **behold** *n*.: Look at; see.

ask him yourself? The land where the Sun rises lies next to ours. Go and ask Apollo whether he will own you for his son."

Phaethon's face lit up. Without delay he set off for India, and not long afterwards stood before the glittering palace of the Sun.

His heart beat with pride and hope and wonder as he gazed upon the lofty columns, all ablaze with precious stones, at the ceilings of polished ivory, the doors of silver. Yet he hardly paused to look at the splendid scenes of earth and sky and sea which Hephaestus[3] had cunningly wrought upon the walls. Phaethon was too impatient to behold the god. He ran lightly up the steps and went on into the great hall. There, however, he was forced to halt—the light was so dazzling he could not bear it. At the other end of the hall he could make out the god, clad in purple raiment,[4] seated on a throne glittering with diamonds. And on either side stood his attendants. They were the Day,

📖 **Read Actively**
Visualize the palace.

the Month, the Year, the Hours, and the Seasons—Spring crowned with flowers, Summer decked with sheaves of yellow grain, Autumn stained with wine, and Winter with snowy locks.

The great god saw the youth standing by the door and called out to him, "What brings you here?"

"O light of the boundless world, Phoebus[5] my father—if you will let me use that honored name—" the youth blurted out, "I am Phaethon. Give me, I implore you, some proof by which men may know that I am indeed your son."

Apollo laid aside the blinding rays of light about his head.

"Approach, my son," he said, and embraced Phaethon warmly. "I confirm what your mother has told you. But to put an end to your doubts, ask of me anything in the world that you want. I swear by the river Styx,[6] upon which all gods take their oath, that I will grant you whatever you desire."

"Then, father," Phaethon quickly replied, "let me drive the chariot of the Sun for just one day."

Phoebus Apollo shook his radiant head four times, so taken aback was he by the request.

"I have spoken rashly," he said, and his voice was deep with regret. "This one request I would deny. I beg you, Phaethon—choose something else. What you ask is not suited to your years and strength. None but myself—not even Zeus[7] who hurls the thunderbolts—may drive the flaming car of day, and even for me it is not easy. The road is so steep at the start that the horses can

Words to Know

lofty (LAWF tee) *adj.*: Very high
implore (im PLAWR) *v.*: Plead; beg

3. **Hephaestus** (he FES tuhs): The Greek god of fire; the forge.
4. **raiment** (RAY muhnt) *n.*: Clothing.
5. **Phoebus** (FEE bus)
6. **Styx** (STIKS) *n.*: In Greek mythology, river crossed by dead souls before they enter the underworld.
7. **Zeus** (ZOOS): The chief Greek god; ruler of the other gods.

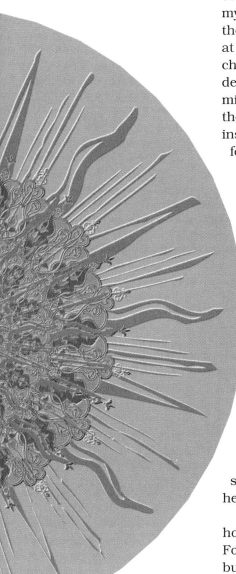

scarcely climb it, fresh though they are at dawn. Midway, the course is so high above the earth that often as I stand upright in my chariot I get dizzy and dare not look down. And the last part of the way drops so sharply that the sea gods waiting to receive me at my journey's end wonder how it is I do not fall. If I lent you my chariot, what would you do? You think the road lies among the delightful dwellings of the gods. But no, it passes through the midst of frightful monsters—the Bull, the Lion, the Scorpion, and the Crab. Nor will you find it easy to control the horses. Do not insist, my son. You ask proof that you are my own. Are not my fears for you proof enough? The oath is sworn and I must keep it, but I beg you—choose more wisely! Look around the world. Choose what you will that is most precious, and it shall be yours. Only do not ask to drive the chariot."

📖 **Read Actively**

Make a **connection.**
What would you do?

Phaethon listened. But his mind was closed, and he would not change his request. So, much against his will, Apollo led him to where the chariot stood.

It, too, was the work of Hephaetus' hands, and dazzling to behold. Axle, pole, and wheels were all of gold, the spokes were of silver, the seat sparkled with rows of chrysolites[8] and diamonds. But there was not time to examine the gleaming chariot, for already Dawn had thrown open the doors of the east. The stars faded, the earth began to glow. The Moon gave the command to harness the horses, and the Hours led the four winged beasts out of their lofty stalls.

Phoebus took out a vial. With his own hands he rubbed his son's face with the protective salve, then set the rays upon his head.

"Spare the whip," were the god's words to Phaethon. "The horses go fast enough of themselves. And hold the reins tight. Follow the marks of the wheels. Do not go too high or you will burn the dwellings of the gods, nor too low lest you set the earth on fire. I leave you now to your fate. Take the reins—we can delay no longer."

Stammering his thanks, Phaethon sprang into the chariot and grasped the reins. If only his schoolmates could see him now!

In a moment, the boundless plain of the universe lay before him. The spirited horses dashed through the clouds, outrunning the morning breeze. But soon they felt that strange hands were

Words to Know

stammering (STAM uh ring) *v*.: Speaking unsurely because of fear or excitement

---

8. **chrysolites** (KRIS uh lītz) *n*.: Green or yellow gems.

guiding them. Snorting, they rushed headlong and left the traveled road. The chariot swung wildly from side to side and up and down, while Phaethon looked toward the earth and grew pale. His knees shook, his head swam, his eyes were dim.

He wished that he had heeded his father and never entered the chariot. But now he had no choice. He had to go on, carried along like a ship that flies before the tempest.

Read Actively
Predict what will happen to Phaethon.

His eyes wide with terror, he looked around him. He wanted to call out to the horses, but he had forgotten their names. His heart pounded like a hammer, while he tried to think of what to do. Should he draw the reins tight, or let them loose? Even as he hesitated, they slipped from his trembling hands. The wild steeds, feeling no restraint, dashed off into the unknown regions of high heaven, then plunged down almost to the earth. The clouds smoked, the mountain tops took fire, the fields were parched with heat. Great cities and whole countries began to burn. The entire world was on fire.

Phaethon saw the flames, and felt the unbearable heat. The air he breathed was like a roaring furnace. The smoke was so thick that down on earth the skins of the Ethiopians turned black. The sea shrank and the fishes sought the lowest depths.

At last Earth could endure no more and cried out to Zeus, "O ruler of the gods, save what yet remains to us from the devouring flame!"

Then mighty Zeus rose to his high tower and filled the air with thunder. Brandishing a lightning bolt, he hurled it at the charioteer and struck him from his seat. Phaethon fell headlong. His hair all on fire, he sped to earth, flaring like a shooting star. . . . And far below, Eridanus, the great river, received his charred and broken body.

The Greek Gods: Some Sons and Daughters of Zeus

Athena (uh THEE nuh): The goddess of wisdom, she sprang from Zeus' head in full armor.
Apollo (uh PAH loh): The god of light and truth, he controlled the sun and was often shown playing the lyre, an ancient stringed instrument.
Artemis (ART uh mis): Apollo's twin sister, she was goddess of hunting.
Aphrodite (a froh DĪ tee): Born from the foam of the sea, she was the goddess of love and beauty.

Respond

- Why does Phaethon insist on driving the chariot of the Sun? What would you have wished for in his place?
- In a group, cast this story for a film by selecting actors for each role and explaining your choices.

Words to Know

devouring (duh VOW ring) *adj.*: Destructive; greedy
brandishing (BRAN dish ing) *v.*: Waving in a threatening way
charred (CHAHRD) *adj.*: Burnt; scorched

Anne Terry White (1896–1980), reteller of this myth, was the author of many history, biography, literature, mythology, and science books for children and young adults.

Activities

MAKE MEANING

Explore Your Reading

Look Back (Recall)

1. What does Phaethon hope to accomplish by driving the chariot of the Sun for one day?

Think It Over (Interpret)

2. Why doesn't Phaethon change his request when his father begs him to do so?
3. Describe the conflict Apollo faces when he gives Phaethon permission to drive the chariot.
4. What qualities in Phaethon lead to his destruction?

Go Beyond (Apply)

5. What lesson might this myth offer to today's teenagers?

Develop Reading and Literary Skills

Analyze a Greek Myth

Your preview probably gave you a hint of the disaster that occurs at the end of this **myth**, or made-up story about gods and heroes. Passed from generation to generation by word of mouth, myths tell a great deal about a group's customs and beliefs.

This myth shows that the ancient Greeks believed gods and humans were similar in many ways. For instance, Phaethon is handsome like his father, the god Apollo. However, the Greeks also believed that humans shouldn't try to act like gods. A human who did this was guilty of hubris (U bris), boastful pride, and would be punished.

1. Using a Venn diagram like the one that follows, show how Apollo and his son Phaethon are alike and different. Record their similarities where the circles overlap and their differences at either end.

Apollo Phaethon

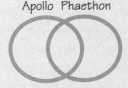

2. At what point in the story does Phaethon show hubris? Explain.
3. Do you know Phaethon will be punished even before the chariot goes out of control? Why?

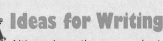

Ideas for Writing

Although myths are ancient stories, they contain messages that still speak to us today.

Gossip Column Imagine that Phaethon is the son of a celebrity and wants to drive his father's sportscar. Tell what happens as a gossip columnist might describe it.

Speech Imagine that following the death of his son, Apollo takes to the road, speaking to students at ancient Greek schools. What advice would he give his young listeners? Write the speech he might make.

Ideas for Projects

Math Cards In addition to creating myths, the ancient Greeks made discoveries in the field of mathematics. Ask your math teacher about these achievements or read about them in an encyclopedia. Make illustrated cards to show some of these discoveries. Share them with your classmates. [Mathematics Link]

News Report You are the anchor for the evening prime-time news in ancient Greece. Give a TV news report on Phaethon's chariot ride. Using diagrams and pictures, show the effects of this disaster on geography and the weather. If possible, videotape the report for your class. [Social Studies Link] [Science Link]

How Am I Doing?

Take a moment to write responses to these questions:

How did previewing the myth help me understand it? What other types of reading can I preview?

What does this ancient myth say to me about life today?

Djuha Borrows a Pot by Inea Bushnaq
All Stories Are Anansi's by Harold Courlander

Is it better to prove yourself through strength, skill, or intelligence?

Preparing Medicine From Honey, 1224 (detail)
Copyist Abadallah ibn ala-Fadl, The Metropolitan Museum of Art, New York

Reach Into Your Background

Perhaps you've known people who were so mentally quick they could outwit those who were bigger, stronger, and more skillful. With a group of classmates, try one or both of the following activities:

- Think of characters in films, books, and comic strips who succeed by fooling others. Compare the tricks they use to achieve their goals.
- Role-play a situation in which a person outwits someone who is bigger and stronger. Base your role-play on a situation you have witnessed or on a scene from a book or film.

Read Actively
Distinguish Between Reality and Appearance

In reading about characters who outwit others, you must tell the difference between **reality** (what is true) and **appearance** (what seems to be true). By distinguishing between reality and appearance, you will see clearly what is happening.

In these tales, Djuha and Anansi are characters who deceive others. To better follow what is happening, you might imagine you're a detective investigating their deceptions. As you read, prepare to write your report by noting differences between what appears to be true and what is true.

Djuha Borrows a Pot

from Syria

Inea Bushnaq

Bronze cauldron from Daghestan decorated with equestrian figure and two eagles Victoria and Albert Museum, London

One day Djuha[1] wanted to entertain his friends with a dinner of lamb stewed whole with rice stuffing, but he did not have a cooking pot large enough. So he went to his neighbor and borrowed a huge, heavy caldron of fine copper.

Promptly next morning, Djuha returned the borrowed pot. "What is this?" cried the neighbor, pulling a small brass pot from inside the caldron. "Oh yes," said Djuha, "congratulations and blessings upon your house! While your caldron was with me, it gave birth to that tiny pot." The neighbor laughed delightedly. "May Allah[2] send blessings your way too," he told Djuha, and carried the two cooking pots into his house.

A few weeks later Djuha knocked on his neighbor's door again to ask for the loan of the caldron. And the neighbor hurried to fetch it for him. The next day came and went, but Djuha did not return the pot. Several days passed and the neighbor did not hear from Djuha. At last he went to Djuha's house to ask for his property. "Have you not heard, brother?" said Djuha looking very grave. "The very evening I borrowed it from you, your unfortunate caldron—God grant you a long life—died!" "What do you mean, 'died'?" shouted the neighbor. "Can a copper cooking pot die?" "If it can give birth," said Djuha, "it can surely die."

---

1. **Djuha** (JOO uh)
2. **Allah** (AL uh): The name for God in the Muslim religion.

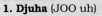

Respond
Would you like to have a neighbor like Djuha? Why?

Inea Bushnaq was born in Jerusalem and now lives in New York City. Beyond her collection of Arab folk tales, her other books include *The Arabs in Israel* and *Betrayal at the Vel d'Hiv*.

Storytelling has always been important in **Arab** culture. While Djuha is the most-beloved comic character in Arab folklore, perhaps the best-known collection of Arabic folk tales is *The Thousand and One Nights*, or *The Arabian Nights*. This group of about 200 stories includes the adventures of Aladdin, Ali Baba, and Sinbad.

All Stories Are Anansi's

from the Ashanti (Ghana)

Harold Courlander

In the beginning, all tales and stories belonged to Nyame,[1] the Sky God. But Kwaku Anansi,[2] the spider, yearned to be the owner of all stories known in the world, and he went to Nyame and offered to buy them.

The Sky God said: "I am willing to sell the stories, but the price is high. Many people have come to me offering to buy, but the price was too high for them. Rich and powerful families have not been able to pay. Do you think you can do it?"

Anansi replied to the Sky God: "I can do it. What is the price?"

"My price is three things," the Sky God said. "I must first have Mmoboro,[3] the hornets. I must then have Onini,[4] the great python. I must then have Osebo,[5] the leopard. For these things I will sell you the right to tell all stories."

Anansi said: "I will bring them."

He went home and made his plans. He first cut a gourd from a vine and made a small hole in it. He took a large calabash[6] and filled it with water. He went to the tree where the hornets lived. He poured some of the water over himself, so that he was dripping. He threw some water over the hornets so that they too were dripping. Then he put the calabash on his head, as though to protect himself from a storm, and called out to the hornets: "Are you foolish people? Why do you stay in the rain that is falling?"

The hornets answered: "Where shall we go?"

"Go here, in this dry gourd," Anansi told them.

The hornets thanked him and flew into the gourd through the small hole. When the last of them had entered, Anansi plugged the hole with a ball of grass, saying: "Oh, yes, but you are really foolish people!"

He took the gourd full of hornets to Nyame, the Sky God. The Sky God accepted them. He said: "There are two more things."

Anansi returned to the forest and cut a long bamboo pole and some strong vines.

---

1. **Nyame** (nee AH mee)
2. **Kwaku Anansi** (KWAH koo uh NAHN see)
3. **Mmoboro** (moh BAW roh)
4. **Onini** (oh NEE nee)
5. **Osebo** (oh SAY boh)
6. **calabash** (KAL uh bash) *n.*: A large fruit that is dried and made into a bowl or cup.

Words to Know

yearned (YURND) *v.*: Wanted very much
gourd (GAWRD) *n.*: Fruit from the squash and pumpkin family; the dried, hollowed shell of this fruit is used as a drinking cup or dipper

Then he walked toward the house of Onini, the python, talking to himself. He said: "My wife is stupid. I say he is longer and stronger. My wife says he is shorter and weaker. I give him more respect. She gives him less respect. Is she right or am I right? I am right, he is longer. I am right, he is stronger."

When Onini, the python, heard Anansi talking to himself, he said: "Why are you arguing this way with yourself?"

The spider replied: "Ah, I have had a dispute with my wife. She says you are shorter and weaker than this bamboo pole. I say you are longer and stronger."

Onini said: "It's useless and silly to argue when you can find out the truth. Bring the pole and we will measure."

So Anansi laid the pole on the ground, and the python came and stretched himself out beside it.

"You seem a little short," Anansi said.

The python stretched further.

"A little more," Anansi said.

"I can stretch no more," Onini said.

"When you stretch at one end, you get shorter at the other end," Anansi said. "Let me tie you at the front so you don't slip."

He tied Onini's head to the pole. Then he went to the other end and tied the tail to the pole. He wrapped the vine all around Onini, until the python couldn't move.

"Onini," Anansi said, "it turns out that my wife was right and I was wrong. You are shorter than the pole and weaker. My opinion wasn't as good as my wife's. But you are more foolish than I, and you are now my prisoner."

Pendant in the form of a snake catching a frog
Ebrie people, Ivory Coast,19th century, gold, Brooklyn Museum

Anansi carried the python to Nyame, the Sky God, who said: "There is one thing more."

Osebo, the leopard, was next. Anansi went into the forest and dug a deep pit where the leopard was accustomed to walk. He covered it with small branches and leaves and put dust on it, so it was impossible to tell where the pit was. Anansi went away and hid. When Osebo came prowling in the black of night, he stepped into the trap Anansi had prepared and fell to the bottom. Anansi had heard the sound of the leopard falling, and he said: "Ah, Osebo, you are half-foolish!"

When morning came, Anansi went to the pit and saw the leopard there.

"Osebo," he asked, "what are you doing in this hole?"

"I have fallen into a trap," Osebo said. "Help me out."

"I would gladly help you," Anansi said. "But I'm sure if I bring you out, I will have no thanks for it. You will get hungry, and later on you will be wanting to eat me and my children."

"I swear it won't happen!" Osebo said.

"Very well. Since you swear it, I will take you out," Anansi said.

He bent a tall green tree toward the ground, so that its top was over the pit, and he tied it that way. Then he tied a rope to the top of the tree and dropped the other end of it into the pit.

"Tie this to your tail," he said.

Osebo tied the rope to his tail.

"Is it well tied?" Anansi asked.

"Yes, it is well tied," the leopard said.

Stool with a leopard base Pace Primitive Gallery, New York

"In that case," Anansi said, "you are not merely half-foolish, you are all-foolish."

And he took his knife and cut the other rope, the one that held the tree bowed to the ground. The tree straightened up with a snap, pulling Osebo out of the hole. He hung in the air head downward, twisting and turning. And while he hung this way, Anansi killed him with his weapons.

Then he took the body of the leopard and carried it to Nyame, the Sky God, saying, "Here is the third thing. Now I have paid the price."

Nyame said to him: "Kwaku Anansi, great warriors and chiefs have tried, but they have been unable to do it. You have done it. Therefore, I will give you the stories. From this day onward, all stories belong to you.

Whenever a man tells a story, he must acknowledge that it is Anansi's tale."

In this way Anansi, the spider, became the owner of all the stories that are told. To Anansi all these tales belong.

Respond

Which of Anansi's accomplishments most impressed you? Why?

Harold Courlander (1908–) received a Guggenheim fellowship to study African culture. He has written versions of folk tales from many nations.

Anansi is a major figure in **Ashanti** (uh SHAHN tee) folklore. Some time before the thirteenth century, the Ashanti settled in a forested area of what is now the West African country of Ghana. They united their settlements toward the end of the seventeenth century and ruled a large empire during the 1700's and 1800's. Noted for their weaving and work in gold, the Ashanti play an important role in Ghanaian life.

Words to Know

acknowledge (uhk NAHL ij) *v.*:
Recognize and admit

Explore Your Reading

Look Back (Recall)

1. What do Djuha and Anansi gain and what tricks do they use to get what they want?

Think It Over (Interpret)

2. Why does Djuha's neighbor accept the idea that a pot can give birth but not the notion that it can die?
3. Why do the hornets, the python, and the leopard listen to Anansi?
4. Why do you think Anansi wants to own "all tales and stories"?

Go Beyond (Apply)

5. What lessons do these folk tales teach? Explain your answer.

Develop Reading and Literary Skills

Examine the Wise Fool and the Trickster

By distinguishing between reality and appearance, you weren't fooled by Djuha and Anansi. These characters represent two different types of deceivers who appear in folk tales, stories handed down by a group of people.

Djuha is a **wise fool**, someone who pretends to be foolish to achieve a goal. Anansi is a **trickster**, a character who relies on brains to outwit those who are bigger and stronger. These two characters are similar but not exactly the same.

1. Compare and contrast Djuha and Anansi. Consider the following points:
   - The goals they are trying to achieve
   - How they get others to trust them
   - Their attitude toward their victims
2. If people don't like to be fooled themselves, why do you think the trickster and the wise fool are such popular characters in folk tales?

Ideas for Writing

One reason ancient tales are read today is that the characters and situations they describe are still familiar to us.

Police Report You read these tales as if you were a detective investigating the schemes of Djuha and Anansi. Now write a modern police report on what happened. Name the victims and wrongdoers, describe the crimes, and recommend the charges to be brought.

Feature Story Write a feature story for your class book about a student who is a trickster or a wise fool. Base your account on a situation you witnessed or heard about. If you prefer, use imaginary characters and a made-up incident.

Ideas for Projects

Performance Write additional dialogue, or conversation, for one of these folk tales and perform it as a play for your class. Choose students to play the different roles and create costumes. If possible, videotape the performance.

Puzzle Challenge Become a math trickster by collecting number puzzles that will baffle your classmates. Research brain teasers in puzzle books, choose the best ones, and then challenge your classmates to solve them. [Math Link]

How Am I Doing?

Write your responses to these questions in your journal:

How did distinguishing between reality and appearance help me read these folk tales? How could this same strategy help me understand essays?

What have I learned about why we still read ancient tales today?

How does success change the way you feel about yourself?

Corn and Pumpkin Patch Gary Ernest Smith, Overland Gallery of Fine Art, Scottsdale, Ariz.

Reach Into Your Background

School competitions and fairs give you a chance to share your knowledge and talents with other students. Even if you don't win a prize, you can challenge yourself and be successful. With a group, do one or both of the following activities:

- List the scholastic fairs, athletic competitions, or other events that give you the opportunity to display your abilities.
- Imagine you are entering a fair. Gather ideas for a project or performance that would capture everyone's attention.

Read Actively

Identify a Sequence of Events

To enjoy a sports event, you have to remember the action and the order in which it happened. The same is true for reading. You must identify the **sequence of events** in a story to understand the action on the page.

In "A Ribbon for Baldy," a boy works on a science project that takes him four months to create. You might draw a time line like the one below and mark off sections labeled February, March, April, and May. While reading, fill in each area with the key events for the month.

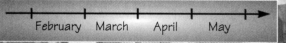

February   March   April   May

A Ribbon for Baldy

Jesse Stuart

The day Professor Herbert started talking about a project for each member of our General Science class, I was more excited than I had ever been. I wanted to have an outstanding project. I wanted it to be greater, to be more unusual than those of my classmates. I wanted to do something worthwhile, and something to make them respect me.

I'd made the best grade in my class in General Science. I'd made more yardage, more tackles and carried the football across the goal line more times than any player on my team. But making good grades and playing rugged football hadn't made them forget that I rode a mule to school, that I had worn my mother's shoes the first year and that I slipped away at the noon hour so no one would see me eat fat pork between slices of corn bread.

Every day I thought about my project for the General Science class. We had to have our project by the end of the school year and it was now January.

In the classroom, in study hall and when I did odd jobs on my father's 50 acres, I thought about my project. But it wouldn't come to me like an algebra problem or memorizing a poem. I couldn't think of a project that would help my father and mother to support us. One that would be good and useful.

"If you set your mind on something and keep on thinking about it, the idea will eventually come," Professor Herbert told us when Bascom Wythe complained about how hard it was to find a project.

One morning in February I left home in a white cloud that had settled over the deep valleys. I could not see an object ten feet in front of me in this mist. I crossed the pasture into the orchard and the mist began to thin. When I reached the ridge road, the light thin air was clear of mist. I looked over the sea of rolling white clouds. The tops of the dark winter hills jutted up like little islands.

I have to ride a mule, but not one of my classmates lives in a prettier place, I thought, as I surveyed my world. Look at Little Baldy! What a pretty island in the sea of clouds. A thin

Words to Know

surveyed (sur VAYD) *v.*: Looked over in a careful way; examined; inspected

ribbon of cloud seemed to envelop cone-shaped Little Baldy from bottom to top like the new rope Pa had just bought for the windlass[1] over our well.

Then, like a flash—the idea for my project came to me. And what an idea it was! I'd not tell anybody about it! I wouldn't even tell my father, but I knew he'd be for it. Little Baldy wrapped in the white coils of mist had given me the idea for it.

I was so happy I didn't care who laughed at me, what anyone said or who watched me eat fat meat on corn bread for my lunch. I had an idea and I knew it was a wonderful one.

"I've got something to talk over with you," I told Pa when I got home. "Look over there at that broom-sedge[2] and the scattered pines on Little Baldy. I'd like to burn the broom-sedge and briers and cut the pines and farm that this summer."

We stood in our barnlot and looked at Little Baldy.

"Yes, I've been thinkin' about clearin' that hill up someday," Pa said.

"Pa, I'll clear up all this south side and you clear up the other side," I said. "And I'll plow all of it and we'll get it in corn this year."

"Now this will be some undertakin'," he said. "I can't clear that land up and work six days a week on the railroad section. But if you will clear up the south side, I'll hire Bob Lavender to do the other side."

"That's a bargain," I said.

That night while the wind was still and the broom-sedge and leaves were dry, my father and I set fire all the way around the base. Next morning Little Baldy was a dark hill jutting high into February's cold, windy sky.

Pa hired Bob Lavender to clear one portion and I started working on the other. I worked early of mornings before I went to school. I hurried home and worked into the night.

Finn, my ten-year-old brother, was big enough to help me saw down the scattered pines with a crosscut.[3] With a handspike I started the logs rolling and they rolled to the base of Little Baldy.

---

1. windlass (WIND luhs) *n*.: A machine for raising and lowering a bucket on a rope.

2. broom-sedge (BROOM sej) *n*.: A coarse grass used in making brooms.

3. crosscut (KRAWS kut) *n*.: A saw that cuts across the grain of wood.

By middle March, I had my side cleared. Bob Lavender had finished his too. We burned the brush and I was ready to start plowing.

By April 15th I had plowed all of Little Baldy. My grades in school had fallen off some. Bascom Wythe made the highest mark in General Science and he had always wanted to pass me in this subject. But I let him make the grades.

If my father had known what I was up to, he might not have let me do it. But he was going early to work on the railway section and he never got home until nearly dark. So when I laid Little Baldy off to plant him in corn, I started at the bottom and went around and around this high cone-shaped hill like a corkscrew. I was three days reaching the top. Then, with a hand planter, I planted the corn on moonlit nights.

When I showed my father what I'd done, he looked strangely at me. Then he said, "What made you do a thing like this? What's behind all of this?"

"I'm going to have the longest corn row in the world," I said. "How long do you think it is, Pa?"

"That row is over 20 miles," Pa said, laughing.

Finn and I measured the corn row with a rod pole and it was 23.5 miles long.

When it came time to report on our projects and I stood up in class and said I had a row of corn on our hill farm 23.5 miles long, everybody laughed. But when I told how I got the idea and how I had worked to accomplish my project, everybody was silent.

Professor Herbert and the General Science class hiked to my home on a Saturday in early May when the young corn was pretty and green in the long row. Two newspapermen from a neighboring town came too, and a photographer took pictures of Little Baldy and his ribbon of corn. He took pictures of me, of my home and parents and also of Professor Herbert and my classmates.

When the article and pictures were published, a few of my classmates got a little jealous of me but not one of them ever laughed at me again. And my father and mother were the proudest two parents any son could ever hope to have.

Growing up in rural eastern Kentucky, **Jesse Stuart** (1906–1984) helped his father clear a cone-shaped hill named Old Baldy to use for farmland. Stuart actually did lay a furrow that went up the hill. He planted the longest row of corn in the valley "and maybe in the whole country," he wrote later. Like the narrator of the story, he wrote about the project for a science class.

Returning to Old Baldy years later, Stuart decided to write about his farming achievement again. He finished "A Ribbon for Baldy" in one day!

Respond

- How do you think the narrator's success changed the way he thought about himself?
- People have different ways of proving themselves. With a partner or a small group, explain the accomplishments or traits that make you respect others.

Activities
MAKE MEANING

Explore Your Reading

Look Back (Recall)

1. Why does the narrator say he started his project?
2. List the steps he takes to complete it.

Think It Over (Interpret)

3. How would you describe his personality? Explain.
4. Why are his classmates silent when he tells about his project?
5. How would you summarize his growth in the story?

Go Beyond (Apply)

6. The narrator plans a project to win others' respect. What other reasons might people have for taking on a challenging task?

Develop Reading and Literary Skills

Analyze Plot

Making a timeline helped you understand the sequence, or order, of events in this story. In literature, the sequence of events in a story is called the **plot.**

In many stories, like "A Ribbon for Baldy," events occur in order of time. The story begins with the earliest event and ends with the final one.

However, the plot can follow a different order. For instance, the narrator could begin the story with the final events and then tell about the events leading up to them. Still another way is to begin at the middle, go back to describe the early events, and then continue to the end.

1. Rearrange the time line you created and show a different way the writer might have told the same story.

2. Compare the original plot with the one you created. Which is better for keeping the reader guessing about the outcome? Why?

Ideas for Writing

Identifying a sequence of events is important in other types of writing besides short stories.

How-to Article Imagine you are Jesse Stuart and you want to turn your story into a how-to article. Step by step, explain how to plant a long row of corn on a hillside.

Movie Script Write a script for a brief movie about the achievements of students at your school. Include descriptions of camera shots and the words an announcer will say. Make sure you indicate the sequence in which pictures will be seen and words will be heard.

Ideas for Projects

Mobile Make a mobile that represents Baldy and its long row of corn. From the image of the hill, hang sayings, song titles, quotations, or other words that express the idea of working hard to achieve a goal—for example, "Climb Every Mountain" or "No Pain, No Gain." [Art Link]

Mathematics Problem Figure out about how many ears of corn the narrator could harvest from a row of corn 23.5 miles long. Hint: You will need to estimate how many cornstalks can be planted in a foot and to know how many feet make up a mile. Present your solution to the class. [Mathematics Link]

How Am I Doing?

List the activities you completed for this selection. Then ask yourself the following questions:
Where was I most successful?
What skills do I need to practice?

How far would you be willing to go to help a stranger in need?

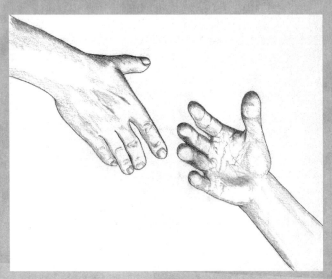

Reach Into Your Background

Whether you live in a large metropolitan area, a small town, or the country, you have seen people in need. Perhaps you have seen people who were seriously ill or out of work or too poor to be able to afford life's necessities. With a partner:

- List some of the needs of the people in your community.
- Discuss how you could realistically help in each situation.

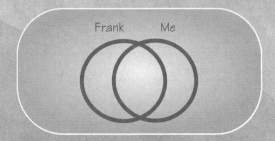

Frank   Me

Read Actively

Connect Nonfiction to Your Experience

Connecting to what you read means relating it to your own life. It means pausing over a passage and thinking "Do I know someone like that?" or "Would I do what he did?" Connecting to nonfiction, or true stories, will help you feel more at home with what you read.

In this true story, Frank Daily has to decide whether or not to help a stranger in need. Use a Venn diagram like the one on this page to connect your experiences to Frank's. Record Frank's feelings and reactions in the circle on the left. In the circle on the right, note how you might react in the same situation. Use the overlapping space to record feelings or reactions that you share with Frank.

Reaching Out to a Stranger

Barbara A. Lewis

Frank Daily stared down at the frozen ground. He kicked chunks of snow, blackened with car exhaust, to the side. He only pretended to listen to the chatter of his friends, Norm and Ed, as they all clambered aboard the Number 10 bus after school. He spouted out automatic answers to their questions: "Yeah, I aced the Milton test. . . . No, I can't tonight. I've got to hit the books."

Frank and his friends flopped down in the back of the Milwaukee city bus, along with several other high school boys, some from other schools. The bus belched a gray cloud out the back and headed west on Blue Mound Road.

Frank slouched into his seat. His hands hung from his two thumbs stuffed in the center of his belt. It had been another cold, gray day just a month ago in November when his world had come crashing down around him. He knew that his basketball skills were as good as the other boys'. His mom used to call him "the athlete of the season." When he was smaller, she

"Kojak" and Frank Daily

Words to Know

clambered (KLAM buhrd) *v*.: Climbed with effort

had nicknamed him "Search and Destroy." He smiled at the memory.

The bus lurched away from a curb, and Frank instinctively braced his Nikes against the floor. "It must have been my size," he thought. "That had to be it. Five feet four. Since I'm new at Marquette High and only a freshman, the coach must have taken one look at me and decided I was too small to make the basketball team."

It wasn't easy starting a new school, especially an all-boys' Catholic school. The older boys tended to be a bit clannish. It was especially hard for Frank, because he had been a star athlete in all the sports in elementary school. Now, it seemed, he was a nothing.

Not only had he excelled in athletics before arriving at Marquette; he had also come alive to politics and history in the fifth and sixth grades. He recalled the advice his teacher, Don Anderson, had given him: "Look, Frank, if you'd put as much time into books as you do into basketball, you can do great in both."

"Well," Frank thought, "Anderson was right about the books, at least. My grades have been A's and B's ever since. Basketball is another story."

A loud horn and a screech of brakes somewhere behind the bus startled Frank. He looked at Norm and Ed. Norm was leaning his head against the window with half-shut eyes, his warm breath creating a circle of fog on the glass.

Frank rubbed his own eyes. He still remembered his stomach chilling into a frozen knot as he approached the locker room last month. He had read the team list posted on the locker room door, hoping, searching frantically for his name. It hadn't been there. It was missing. No name. He had felt suddenly as if he had ceased to exist. Become invisible.

The bus jerked to a stop at the County Institutions grounds. The bus driver called to some noisy boys at the back to settle down. Frank glanced up at the driver, who had been dubbed "Kojak"[1] by some of the guys on the bus because of his bald head.

A very pregnant woman hung onto the silver handrail and slowly pulled herself onto the bus. As she fell backward into the seat behind the bus driver, her feet kicked up, and Frank saw that she was in stocking feet.

As Kojak steered the bus back into traffic, he yelled over his shoulder, "Where are your shoes, lady? It ain't more than 10 degrees out there."

"I can't afford shoes," the woman answered. She pulled her fraying coat collar around her neck. Some of the boys at the back exchanged glances and smirked.

"I got on the bus just to get my feet warm," the woman continued. "If you don't mind, I'll just ride around with you for a bit."

Kojak scratched his bald head and shouted, "Now, just tell me how come you can't afford shoes?"

"I got eight kids. They all got shoes. There's not enough left for me. But it's okay, the Lord'll take care of me."

Frank looked down at his new Nike basketball shoes. His feet were warm and snug, always had been. And then he looked back at the woman. Her socks were ripped. Her coat, missing buttons, hung open around her stomach, as swollen as a basketball and covered by a smudgy dress.

---

1. Kojak: Bald detective played by Telly Savalas in a television series that ran from 1973 to 1978.

Words to Know

instinctively (in STINK tiv lee) *adv.*: Doing something naturally or without thinking

clannish (KLAN ish) *adj.*: Sticking closely with one's group; staying away from others

fraying (FRAY ing) *adj.*: Wearing down; becoming ragged

smirked (SMERKD) *v.*: Smiled in a smug or conceited way

marginal (MAR juh nuhl) *adj.*: Close to the lower limit

Frank didn't hear anything around him after that. He wasn't aware of Norm or Ed. He just felt a warm thawing in his gut. The word "invisible" popped into his mind again. "An invisible person, marginal, forgotten by society, but for a different reason," he thought.

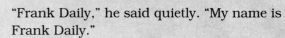

He would probably always be able to afford shoes. She probably never would. Under his seat, he pried the toe of one shoe into the heel of the other and slipped it off. Then the other shoe. He looked around. Nobody had noticed. He would have to walk three blocks in the snow. But the cold had never bothered him much.

When the bus stopped at the end of the line, Frank waited until everyone else had emptied off. Then he reached under his seat and picked up his basketball shoes. He walked quickly up to the woman and handed them to her, looking down and saying, "Here, lady, you need these more than I do."

And then Frank hurried to the door and stepped down. He managed to land in a puddle. It didn't matter. He wasn't at all cold. He heard the woman exclaim, "See, they fit me just perfect!"

Then he heard Kojak call, "Hey, come back here, kid! What's your name?"

Frank turned around to face Kojak. At the same time, Norm and Ed asked where his shoes were.

Frank's cheeks burned. He looked in confusion at Kojak, his friends, and the woman.

"Frank Daily," he said quietly. "My name is Frank Daily."

"Well, Frank," Kojak said, "I've never seen anything like that in the twenty years I've been driving this bus."

The woman was crying. "Thank you, young man," she said. She turned to Kojak. "See, I told you the Lord would take care of me."

Frank mumbled, "You're welcome." He smiled at the woman. "It's no big deal. Besides, it's Christmas."

He hurried off after Norm and Ed. It seemed to him that the grayness had lifted. On the way home, he hardly felt the cold beneath his feet at all.

Respond

- Would you have given the woman your sneakers? Why or why not?
- Would everyone agree that Frank did the right thing? With two classmates, role-play the conversation Norm, Ed, and Frank had as they walked home from the bus.

As a teacher **Barbara A. Lewis** (1943–) is dedicated to helping her students improve their world. She tells them that "the future belongs to you . . . you can choose to change your world for the better."

Her students must be listening because they have initiated the cleanup of a hazardous waste site near their school, proposed laws in their state legislature, and participated in many neighborhood improvement programs.

Activities
MAKE MEANING

Explore Your Reading

Look Back (Recall)

1. What adjustments did Frank have to make in his new school?
2. What happened to Frank that day to make him feel "invisible"?

Think It Over (Interpret)

3. Why does Frank decide to help the woman on the bus?
4. What details in the article suggest that Frank doesn't regret his decision?
5. How do the events of the day show that Frank has grown?

Go Beyond (Apply)

6. How do you think this experience will help Frank in the future?

Develop Reading and Literary Skills

Interpret Motivation in Nonfiction

Connecting to Frank may have given you a better understanding of his **motives**, the reasons behind what he did. The author helps you appreciate his motives by describing the feelings, physical details, and thoughts leading up to his unselfish deed.

For instance, she says he "slouched into his seat." This physical detail suggests that he was feeling sad, and his own sadness may have helped him understand the woman's distress.

1. Find examples of another physical detail, a feeling, and a thought that help explain Frank's motivations.
2. Use the examples you have found to explain why he did what he did. For each piece of information, ask yourself, "How does this show why he would want to help this woman?"

Ideas for Writing

Have you ever read about a true event and then wondered what happened next?

Feature Article Suppose that Frank is asked to tell his story for a magazine about students making a difference. Write the article as Frank, explaining what you did and how it has affected your life.

Poem You are Kojak, the bus driver. When you go home on the day Frank gave his shoes to the woman, you can't get the incident out of your mind. Write a poem about it to display inside your bus.

Ideas for Projects

Community Connection Visit one or two social service agencies in your community and find out whom they help and what services they provide. Take photographs, collect brochures, and ask who can volunteer. Present your findings to the class. [Social Studies Link]

Art Exhibit Many artists have tried to get people to reach out to those in need. Research photographers like Dorothea Lange, Jacob Riis, and Walker Evans. Investigate the work of painters like Jacob Lawrence and Ben Shahn. Find examples of their work to exhibit in class. To accompany your exhibit, write a brief description of how their work affected public opinion. [Art Link]

How Am I Doing?

With a partner, discuss these questions:
How did filling in the Venn diagram help me relate the story to my own experience? How else can I relate my experience to my reading?

What piece of work from this lesson do I want to save in my portfolio?

How Do I Show What I Can Do?

Think Critically About the Selections

The selections in this section give different answers to the question "How Do I Show What I Can Do?" Complete one or two of the following activities with a partner or small group to help you review what you've learned. Write your responses in a journal or share them in discussion.

1. List the ways in which different characters in these selections demonstrate their talents or beliefs. **(Summarize)**

2. Several of the selections feature characters who have reason to take action. Choose two characters and explain what prompts them to act. Then decide if their actions pay off. **(Identify Cause and Effect)**

3. Characters in these selections announce their identity in a variety of ways. Make a chart showing which characters choose positive methods and which choose negative ones. Defend your judgments. **(Classify)**

4. Choose a character who faces a serious problem and imagine that the solution presented in the selection doesn't work. What advice would you give that character? **(Solve Problems)**

Projects

Biographical Sketches With a partner choose at least two characters from this section and create Who's Who sketches that show how the characters express themselves. Display the completed sketches, along with illustrations, on posters in your classroom.

Student Art *Basketball* Luckshimi B. Balasubramanian, Sri Lanka

Community Service Journal Social service agencies, hospitals, and libraries often need help. Make some telephone calls to find out which places need help and when. Then volunteer for a few hours a week. Keep a journal of your experiences, feelings, and conclusions. Photographs and charts would make excellent additions to your journal. [Social Studies Link]

Informational Speech Think about your hobbies, special talents, or interests and select one to present orally to your class. Outline your speech and plan what you will say in each portion of it. Be sure to include definitions of any special terms associated with your interest. If possible, teach your classmates one of your special skills.

The Me You See

In this unit, you've been reading and thinking about these important questions:

- **Who Is the Real Me?**
- **Who Gives Me Inspiration?**
- **How Do I Show What I Can Do?**

Project Menu

Other people can give you new ways of looking at these questions, but no one can answer them for you. The answers that you build into your project will stay with you longer than anything you are told. Following are ways to create those answers:

Scientific Report on the Real You In a written and oral report to the class, show how you are unique as a physical subject. Explain fingerprinting, DNA and hair testing, and blood type. Consult your science teacher for tips on writing an objective report. In addition to book research, call a hospital blood laboratory and a crime laboratory. Use models, charts, and diagrams to support your presentation.

Book of International Names People's names are an important part of who they are. In a looseleaf book designed for your class, list names from different cultures, tell what they mean, and explain different ways in which children are named. Research your report by consulting books on naming and by calling local ethnic organizations. Illustrate your writing with original art or with pictures clipped from magazines. Include in your book a name wheel that can be spun to show different names and their meanings.

School Survey on Role Models Discover whom classmates, teachers, and other members of the school community admire. Use a questionnaire to find out who the most popular heroes are and ask people to

From Questions to Careers

How can I show what I can do? This question led Elizabeth Ericson to a career in architecture. Visiting the ancient Mayan city of Chichen Itza (chee CHEN eet SAH) in Mexico, she was stunned by the beauty of its geometrical limestone buildings.

Today, she uses her inspiration to design hospitals. She says, "I see no reason why these very important medical 'city states' are any different from those Mayan cities. . . . I like to bring daylight and gardens into medical treatment spaces. . . ."

How will you show what you can do? Chart out some of your interests and hobbies. Then ask teachers and members of your community to suggest careers related to your interests.

Elizabeth Ericson

explain their choices. Make a graph that shows your findings and share results with the class.

Your Inspirations in Multimedia
Show how your family, friends, and famous people give you inspiration. Use resources like home movies and videotapes, letters and other written material, photograph albums, recorded interviews, and important objects. Write a script for yourself so you know what you will say and how and when you will use each item in your presentation.

Class Yearbook
Imagine you are profiling your class for students of the future. Show how you and your classmates are similar and different by including predictions, mini-biographies, photographs, artwork, stories, poems, and humorous anecdotes. Make your class profile colorful and complete.

Community Project
You can show what you can do by contributing to your community. Give an oral presentation to the class on the goals and achievements of your project—a soup kitchen to feed the homeless, a clean-up brigade, or other useful work. Show how it made a difference in the community. Support your presentation with photographs, diagrams, charts, or the recorded comments of those who witnessed what you did.

Guided Writing

Autobiographical Incident

What is an autobiographical incident?

How did you become the person you are? Thinking back on your life, you can probably recall moments and events that helped shape you. Some might fit under the category famous firsts: learning to swim or meeting someone who would become a good friend. Others, like a quiet moment with a companion, might not fit so easily into a category but are memorable anyway.

Guidelines ● ● ● ● ● ● ● ● ● ● ● ● ● ● ● ● ● ●

In writing an autobiographical incident, you

- *tell the story of an important moment or event in your life.*

- *provide enough detail for readers to experience it as you did.*

- *suggest or say directly why the incident is important to you.*

Prewriting _____

How can I choose an incident and remember it clearly?

Talk with a friend. Recall some of your experiences and discuss them with a friend. Have your friend help you decide which of these experiences will interest a reader.

Use a time line. Choose a series of events with a clear beginning and ending and create a time line like this one. Which of the incidents on your time line would make a good topic?

Use a photograph. Find a photograph related to your experience and use it to jot down sensory details you can use in your writing.

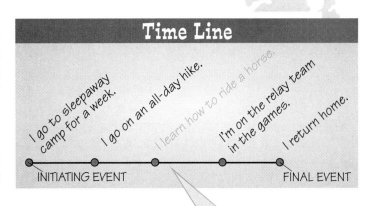

Time Line

I go to sleepaway camp for a week.

I go on an all-day hike.

I learn how to ride a horse.

I'm on the relay team in the games.

I return home.

INITIATING EVENT   FINAL EVENT

The writer focused on learning how to ride and created another time line to record what happened in this process.

sight—view from saddle like being on stilts
sound—rhythmic clop of hoofs
smell—leather of saddle
touch—bumpiness of ride

Drafting

What should I keep in mind when writing about the incident?

Draw in your readers from the start. You may want to ask an unusual question, make an interesting statement, or begin at a moment of suspense to get your readers' attention.

Give the necessary background. Ask yourself what a reader should know to appreciate the story you are telling. The student telling about her riding lesson, for instance, didn't describe her camp counselor. However, she did give some background on the riding instructor.

Tell your story dramatically. Bring your story to life by using specific names, sensory details, dialogue, and descriptions of action. Create suspense by keeping your readers guessing about the outcome.

Writing Model

Before my first riding lesson, the closest I had ever gotten to a horse was about five seats away—from a movie screen, that is.

The writer catches her readers' attention with an unusual statement.

Computer Tip

As you draft your essay, split your document window so that you can refer to your list of important details.

Revising and Editing

What should I look for when revising my incident?

Is the meaning clear? It isn't enough to tell an amusing or dramatic story. Readers should learn how the incident contributed to your understanding of yourself. You can suggest the meaning of the incident or state it directly.

The writer added the last statement to explain what the experience meant to her.

Writing Model

Why didn't Clint Eastwood and Kevin Costner tell me that I should always climb on a horse from the ~~right~~ left side? ∧Also, why didn't they tell me that trying something new, even if it's a little scary, can make you feel eight feet—or should I say twenty-four hands—tall!

Make sure you have used transitions to show a sequence.

Where appropriate, add words like *before*, *during*, *then*, and *after* to help readers understand the order in which events happened.

Prepare and proofread a final draft.

If your final draft contains errors in grammar, usage, and punctuation, readers may not come along for the ride. Carefully check over your paper. Pay special attention to the pronouns you have used. For instance, the writer changed "Me and the horse didn't get along" to "The horse and I didn't get along."

Checkpoints for Revision • • • • • • • •

- *What, if any, unimportant details can I eliminate to sharpen my focus on the incident?*
- *What, if anything, can I include to make my introduction interesting?*
- *What background information can I add to help readers appreciate the incident?*
- *How can I create more suspense and add vivid details?*
- *What can I include to make the meaning of the incident clearer to readers?*

Checkpoints for Editing • • • • • • • • •

- *Have I used transitions to show changes in time? (For practice in using transitions, see page F168.)*
- *Have I used pronouns correctly? (For practice in using pronouns, see page F169.)*

Publishing and Presenting

How can I share my autobiographical incident?

✔ Contribute your essay to a class bulletin-board display called *Up Close and Personal.*

✔ Ask family members to read and comment on your account.

✔ See if a local radio station will allow you to read your essay on the air.

✔ Submit your essay to the student writing magazine *Merlyn's Pen.*

How Did I Do?

Answer these questions to assess what you've learned:

What helped me gather details for my incident? How could I use this method for other types of writing?

Did writing about this incident give me a new way of seeing myself? Why or why not?

If you like your essay, consider adding it to your portfolio.

Develop Your Style

1 Use Transitions to Show Time

How can I show changes in time?

Use transition words to show the order of events. To help your readers follow the order of events, use words like the following:

first	when	at the same time
next	after	meanwhile
suddenly	before	the following
finally	while	as soon as
then	soon	last week
today	later	yesterday

Your transitions don't have to come at the beginning of sentences. Phrases that you weave into your sentences are also good. The point is to use words that make your meaning clear and keep your writing smooth.

Practice using transition words. Revise these sentences to include transitions. Use transition words different from those in the model.

> I went to sleep away camp. Each day was a new adventure. We went on a long hike. I learned to ride a horse.

Look at your autobiographical incident. Give your readers a break. Remember that they weren't there with you. If the order of events isn't clear, add some transition words and phrases from the list at the top of this page.

Writing Model

Last summer
∧ I went to sleep-away camp. Each day
                      On the first day,
was a new adventure. ∧ we went on a
       Later
hike. ∧ I learned to ride a horse.

Notice how a passage becomes much clearer when the writer adds transition words.

Writing Model

Before my first riding lesson,
   ∧ the closest I had ever gotten to
a horse was about five seats away—
from a movie screen, that is.

By the end of that lesson,
   ∧ the horse and I were great friends.

2 Use Subject and Object Pronouns

How can I refer to people without repeating names?

Use pronouns in your writing. A **pronoun** is a word that takes the place of a noun—the way a pinch hitter in baseball bats in place of someone else. By using pronouns, you won't have to repeat people's names, including your own.

> The horse and I is the subject of the sentence.

Use the right form of the pronoun. Some pronouns change form according to their function in a sentence. For example, you use the subject form *I* for the subject of a sentence, and you use the object form *me* for the object of a verb or a preposition.

> Use the object form, *me,* for the object of a preposition *(for)* or a verb *(asked).*

When using pronouns, refer to yourself last. When you're talking about yourself and someone else together, refer to yourself last, whether you're using a subject or an object pronoun. Don't say ". . . me and my friend." Instead, say ". . . my friend and me."

Practice using pronouns. Revise these sentences using subject and object pronouns correctly.

> The riding counselor and <u>me</u> had an argument. Later, she sent someone to look for Bill and <u>I</u>.

Look at your autobiographical incident. Have you avoided repeating names by using pronouns? Wherever you see a pronoun, check to make sure that you've used the correct form.

Writing Models

The horse and ~~me~~ *I* didn't get along at first.

The final ride was a good experience for the other campers and *me*.

The counselors asked my friend and *me* to help other campers dismount.

Word to the Wise

To help you decide whether to use a subject pronoun or an object pronoun, remove the word or group of words the pronoun is joined to. Your ear will tell you which sounds right.

Example: The counselors asked *my friend and* I/me to help.

Remove *my friend and.*

The counselors asked <u>me</u> to help.

This sounds right.

Book News

• • • • • • • • • • • • THE ME

Featured Review

Bearstone by Will Hobbs

This novel is the tale of a Native American boy who draws upon his heritage as he struggles to understand himself. His people, the Utes, lived among the stark peaks and lush valleys of southwestern Colorado, the region where this modern-day story takes place. The respect of the Utes for the animals around them is reflected in carvings like the bearstone, which lends its name to the title of this book.

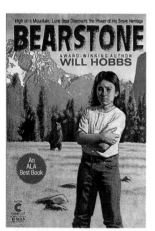

Cloyd's knowledge of his ancestors will help him deal with his problems in the present: his broken family and his own bitterness, which makes it hard for him to accept help. Someone who reaches out to Cloyd is an older white man named Walter Landis. However, you must read this exciting book to the end to find out whether Cloyd will take Walter's hand or succeed in the dangerous mission that awaits him.

Introducing the Author

Will Hobbs, who has written five novels for young people, lives in southwestern Colorado, where *Bearstone* is set. For Hobbs, "a novel begins with character and has to do with human relationships." When he began to think about writing

Bearstone, he had two characters in mind, a young Ute boy and an old man.

Will Hobbs wrote the first draft of *Bearstone* in six weeks. Then he spent another eight years writing five more drafts until he was satisfied. His patient work paid off. A young reader once sent him a fan letter saying, "The way you write, I can make my own movie in my head."

Pass It On: Student Choices

Catherine, Called Birdy by Karen Cushman

Reviewed by Melissa Lo, Lincoln Middle School, Santa Monica, California

Since this book is written in diary form, it really got me interested and I started to actually take Catherine's side. She says, "I utterly loathe my life." That phrase sometimes pops into my head when I'm upset or I'm in a fight with one of my friends, but it usually turns out okay. Catherine's life does, too. If you want to learn about the Middle Ages from a girl's point of view, you'll love this book.

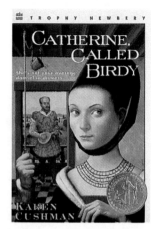

Journal

YOU SEE • • • • • • • •

Hatchet
by Gary Paulsen

Reviewed by Nick Merrill, Windham Middle School, Windham, Maine

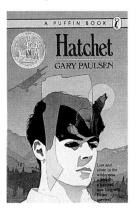

Brian survives a plane crash, winds up in the woods, and has to learn to keep himself alive while he waits for rescue. The author describes how the mosquitos attack Brian morning through night. Also, the author makes the wild animals such as the bear, wolves, porcupines, and moose seem realistic. The story is easy to read and believable. I would definitely recommend this book to other middle school students who like action-survival books.

Read On: More Choices

Jackal Woman: Exploring the World of Jackals **by Laurence Pringle**

Little by Little: A Writer's Education **by Jean Little**

A Boy Becomes a Man at Wounded Knee **by Ted Wood with Wanbli Numpa Afraid of Hawk**

Shadow of a Bull **by Maia Wojciechowska**

The Second Mrs. Giaconda **by E. L. Konigsburg**

My Brother, My Sister and I
by Yoko Kawashima Watkins

Reviewed by Sarah Drilling, Milford Junior High School, Milford, Ohio

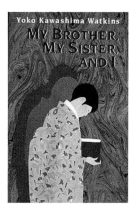

This book appealed to me. It tells about a young girl, her brothers, and their escape from Japan in a time of war. My only objection was the fact that this really happened to someone and was permanently imprinted on her brain; it now is on mine. This book deserves at least five stars. I wish more people would read it!

Share the Fun

Book Circles You can organize a book circle by finding a book you want to read and then finding several classmates who would also like to read it. Decide how many times you want to meet about the book and how much of it your group will read before each session.

Videotape Reviews Instead of writing a book review, have someone videotape you as you evaluate a book.

On the Internet Book discussions can be conducted in cyberspace. Find students in different parts of the country or the world who want to read and discuss the same book. Communicate with them using a Bulletin Board on the Internet.

GLOSSARY

Pronunciation Key

The vocabulary and footnotes in this textbook are respelled to aid pronunciation. A syllable in CAPITAL LETTERS receives the most stress. The key below lists the letters used for respelling. It includes examples of words using each sound and shows how the words would be respelled.

Symbol	Example	Respelled	Symbol	Example	Respelled
a	hat, cat	hat, cat	oh	no, toe	noh, toh
ay	pay, ape	pay, ayp	oo	look, pull, put	look, pool, poot
ah	hot, stop	haht, stahp	oy	boil, toy	boyl, toy
aw	law, all, horn	law, awl, hawrn	oo	ooze, tool, crew	ooz, tool, croo
			ow	plow, out	plow, owt
e	met, elf, ten	met, elf, ten			
ee	bee, eat, flea	bee, eet, flee	u	up, cut, flood	up, cut, flud
er	learn, sir, fur	lern, ser, fer	yoo	few, use	fyoo, yooz
i	is	fit	uh	a in ago	uh GO
ī	mile, sigh	mīle sīgh		e in agent	AY juhnt
				i in sanity	SAN uh tee
				o in compress	kuhm PRES
				u in focus	FOH kuhs

A

allocate (AL uh kayt) *v.*: To give; to set aside

apparent (uh PAR uhnt) *adj.*: Obvious; clearly seen

appraisal (uh PRAY zuhl) *n.*: Evaluation; decision about the value of an item

aptitude (AP tuh tood) *n.*: Natural skill; talent; ability

assumption (uh SUMP shuhn) *n.*: Idea accepted as a fact

B

balk (BAWK) *v.*: Stubbornly refuse

baptize (BAP tīz) *v.*: Give a name

behold (bee HOLD) *n.*: Look at; see

bow-legged (BOH leg guhd) *adj.*: Having legs that are bowed outward

broom-sedge (BROOM SEJ) *n.*: A coarse grass used in making brooms

bureaucrat (BYOO ruh krat) *n.*: Office worker who strictly follows rules and procedures

C

callus (KAL us) *n.*: Hardened, thickened skin on hands or feet that develops as the result of hard work

canvas (KAN vus) *v.*: To try to sell

capable (KAY puh buhl) *adj.*: Able to do things well; powerful, skilled

carnage (KAR nij) *n.*: A bloody scene; a slaughter

chandelier (shan duh LEER) *n.*: A lighting fixture hung from the ceiling with branches for several lights

characters (KAR ik terz) *n.*: Symbols used to write many languages, including Chinese

chasuble (CHAZ uh buhl) *n.*: A sleeveless outer garment worn by priests during mass

chrysolites (KRIS uh līts) *n.*: Green or yellow gems

clamber (KLAM buhr) *v.*: To climb with effort

clannish (KLAN ish) *adj.*: Sticking closely with one's group; staying away from others

congestion (kuhn JES chuhn) *n.*: Crowds; traffic

conscious (KAHN shuhs) *adj.*: Aware; alert

conservatory (kuhn SER vuh taw ree) *n.*: A school of music

conspire (kuhn SPĪR) *v.*: To plan together secretly

consumption (kuhn SUMP shuhn) *n.*: Tuberculosis, a disease that affects the lungs

conviction (kuhn VIK shun) *n.*: Belief

corporate (KOR puh rit) *adj.*: Business

crevasse (kruh VAS) *n.*: Deep narrow opening caused by a crack or split

crosscut (KRAWS kut) *n.*: A saw that cuts across the grain of wood

D

debut (day BYOO) *n.*: First performance in public

dejectedly (dee JEK tuhd lee) *adv.*: Sadly; showing discouragement

deter (dee TER) *v.*: To stop; to discourage

devastate (DEV uh stayt) *v.*: To destroy; to completely upset

disheartened (dis HART end) *adj.*: Disappointed; discouraged

E

embark (im BARK) *v.*: To begin a journey

emulate (EM yoo layt) *v.*: To imitate a person one admires

expansively (ek SPAN siv lee) *adv.*: Warmly; openly

exult (eg ZULT) *v.*: To rejoice; to celebrate

F

feat (FEET) *n*.: A remarkable accomplishment

fervent (FER vuhnt) *adj*.: Showing intense or strong feeling

fiasco (fee AS koh) *n*.: A complete failure

flaw (FLAW) *n*.: Problem; imperfection

fluke (FLOOK) *n*.: Strange bit of luck, either good or bad

forestall (for STAHL) *v*.: To prevent; to avoid

fraying (FRAY ing) *adj*.: Wearing down; becoming ragged

frenzied (FREN zeed) *adj*.: Wild; frantic; hurried; fast

G

genial (JEE nee uhl) *adj*.: Cheerful; pleasant

glower (GLOW uhr) *v*.: To scowl; to stare angrily

grieved (GREEVD) *adj*.: Saddened; overcome by grief

grueling (GROO ling) *adj*.: Very tiring; exhausting

gumption (GUMP shun) *n*.: Courage; enterprise

H

hallucinate (huh LOOS in ayt) *v*.: See or hear things around one that are not there

I

incentive (in SEN tiv) *n*.: Something that makes a person want to work or try

inconceivable (in kuhn SEEV uh buhl) *adj*.: Unthinkable; unimaginable

incorporate (in KOR puhr ayt) *v*.: To form into a legal business

incredulity (in kruh DOO luh tee) *n*.: Disbelief; complete inability to believe

inherited (in HER uh tuhd) *v*.: Received by custom, law or genetics from parents or an older generation

initiation (i nish ee AY shuhn) *n*.: The ceremony by which a boy is accepted as a man; a beginning

instinctively (in STINK tiv lee) *adj*.: Doing something naturally; without thinking

interrogations (in teh ruh GAY shunz) *n*.: Formal questioning sessions

J

jubilant (JOO buh luhnt) *adj*.: Joyful; proud

K

kiln (KILN) *n*.: An oven for drying or baking pottery

L

lance (LANS) *n*.: A long pole used as a weapon

listlessly (LIST luhs lee) *adv*.: Without interest or energy

locomotion (loh kuh MOH shuhn) *n*.: Movement

M

malady (MAL uh dee) *n*.: Illness; disease

malevolence (muh LEV uh luhns) *n*.: Spite; ill-will

marginal (MAHR juh nuhl) *adj*.: Close to the lower limit

maxim (MAKS im) *n*.: Short saying that expresses a rule of life or behavior

mesa (MAY suh) *n*.: Large, high rock with steep sides and flat top

mesmerizing (MEZ muh rīz ing) *adj*.: Hypnotizing

mettle (MET l) *n*.: Spirit or courage

N

neglected (ni GLEKT id) *v*.: Failed to take care of; failed to give enough attention

O

obscure (ahb SKYOOR) *adj*.: Not clear; hidden

ordained (or DAYND) *v*.: Ordered; commanded

ordeal (or DEEL) *n*.: A difficult or painful experience

P

parabola (pa RA buh luh) *n*.: A high curve

perplexity (puhr PLEK suh tee) *n*.: Confusion; doubt

pigeon-toed (PIJ uhn TOHD) *adj*.: Having the feet turned in toward each other

potential (puh TEN shuhl) *adj*.: Possible; capable of becoming

precise (pree SĪS) *adj*.: Exact; accurate

prodigy (PRAH di jee) *n*.: A child of unusually high talent

prolonged (proh LAWNGD) *v*.: Extended; made longer

prophecy (PRAHF uh see) *n*.: A prediction about the future

Q

quadruplicate (kwa DROO pli kit) *n*.: Four copies

R

raiment (RAY muhnt) *n*.: Clothing

refined (ree FĪND) *adj*.: Purified; polished

remedy (REM uh dee) *n*.: A medicine or treatment that cures illness

remote (ruh MOHT) *adj*.: Isolated; removed; far from people

reproach (rih PROHCH) *n*.: Disgrace; blame

reserve (ri ZERV) *n*.: Silent manner; self-control

reverence (REV uh ruhns) *n*.: Respect; awe; honor

reverie (REV uh ree) *n*.: Daydream; imaginings

rookie (ROO kee) *n*.: A first year player

S

sauciness (SAW see nes) *n*.: Liveliness; boldness; spirit

segregated (SEG ruh gayt ed) *adj*.: Separated; isolated by race

smirk (SMERK) *v*.: Smile in a smug or conceited way

spats (SPATS) *n*.: Heavy cloth coverings worn over shoes to keep the instep and ankle clean

spinet (SPIN it) *n*.: A small, upright piano

strife (STRĪF) *n*.: Trouble; conflict; struggle

survey (sur VAY) *v.*: Look over in a careful way; examine; inspect

susceptible (suh SEPT uh buhl) *adj.*: Easily affected; very sensitive

swaddled (SWAHD uhld) *adj.*: Wrapped

T

taboo (tuh BOO) *adj.*: Forbidden

talisman (TAL is muhn) *n.*: Any object thought to have magic power

timid (TIM id) *adj.*: Showing fear or shyness

tourniquet (TER nuh kuht) *n.*: Any device used to stop bleeding in an emergency, as a bandage twisted tightly to stop the flow of blood

transfixed (trans FIKSD) *adj.*: Unable to move, as if pierced through

tuition (too ISH uhn) *n.*: Money paid by someone to attend a private school

U

unintentional (un in TEN shun uhl) *adj.*: Not deliberate; chance; random

unrepentant (un ree PENT unt) *adj.*: Without feeling sorry for having done wrong

V

variation (ver ee AY shun) *n.*: Change; difference

W

wean (WEEN) *v.*: To draw away gradually from a habit or belief

windlass (WIND luhs) *n.*: A machine for raising and lowering a bucket on a rope

wretchedly (RECH id lee) *adv.*: Miserably; very unhappily

Z

zeal (ZEEL) *n.*: Great enthusiasm; strong interest; passion

zest (ZEST) *n.*: Gusto; strong enjoyment

Index of Fine Art

Index of Authors and Titles

Page numbers in italics refer to biographical information.

Index of Skills

Literary Terms

Autobiography, F110, F112, F119
    Characters in, F112
    Contrast Characters in, F112
    Looking At, F110
    Understand Autobiography, F119
Biography, F110, F120, F130, F160
    Interpret Motivation in, F160
    Looking At, F110
    Set a Purpose for Reading, F120
    Understand Biography, F130
Character, F17, F36, F48, F50, F60, F72, F74, F81, F112
    Characters in Autobiography, F112
    Characters in Drama, F74, F81
    Discover Theme Through Character, F72
    Dynamic and Static Characters, F48
    Make Inferences About Characters, F17
    Make Judgments About Characters, F60
    Observe a Character's Growth, F36
Conflict, F50
Connotation, F22, F27
    Appreciate Connotation and Denotation, F27
    Respond to the Connotations of Words, F22
Cultural Details, F88
    Identify Cultural Details, F88
    Interpret Cultural Details in a Folk Tale, F93
Denotation, F27
Drama, F74, F81
    Analyze Characters in, F81
    Visualize Characters in, F74
Dynamic and Static Characters, F48
Folk Tale, F88, F93, F149
    Trickster in, F149
    Wise Fool in, F149
    Cultural Details in, F88, F93
Humor, F8
Legend, F35
    Connect Social Studies to Legend, F35
Myth, F138, F143
    Preview a Myth, F138
    Analyze a Greek Myth, F143
Narrator, F50, F98, F108, F160
    First-Person Narrator, F108
    Make Inferences About, F98
Nonfiction, F160, F156
    Connect to Your Experience, F156
    Interpret Motivation in, F160
Plot , F50, F52, F59, F150, F155
    Analyze Plot, F155
    Recognize Plot Development, F52
    Sequence of Events, F150
    Understand Plot, F59
Poetry, F18, F21, F94, F97, F137
    Read Poetry Aloud, F18
    Similes in, F137
    Speakers in, F94, F97
    Stanza Form, F21
Sequence of Events, F150
Setting, F50
Short Story, F50
    Looking At, F50
Similes, F137

Speaker, F94, F97
    Identify the Traits of the Speaker, F94
    Understand the Speaker, F97
Theme, F50, F82, F87
    Discover Theme Through Character, F72
    Gather Evidence About, F82
    Use Evidence to Identify Implied Theme, F87

Reading and Thinking Skills

Analyze, F81, F143, F155
    Characters in Drama, F81
    Greek Myth, F143
    Plot, F155
Compare and Contrast, F112
    Contrast Characters in Autobiography, F112
Connect, F3, F28, F35, F156
    Literature to Social Studies, F28
    Nonfiction to Your Experience, F156
    Social Studies to Legend, F35
Connotation, F27
Contrast, F112
    Characters in Autobiography, F112
Denotation, F27
Distinguish Between Reality and Appearance, F144
Gather Evidence About Theme, F82
Interpret, F93, F160
    Cultural Details in a Folk Tale, F93
    Motivation in Nonfiction, F160
Make Inferences, F10, F17, F60, F98
    About Characters, F17
    About the Narrator, F98
Make Judgments About Characters, F60
Observe a Character's Growth, F36
Predict, F3
Preview, F2, F138
    a Myth, F138
Read Aloud, F21
    Read Aloud to Appreciate Stanza Form, F21
Respond, F3, F22
    to the Connotations of Words, F22
Sequence of Events, F150
Set a Purpose F2, F87, F120
    for Reading Biography, F120
Use Evidence to Identify Implied Theme, F87
Visualize, F3, F74
    Characters in Drama, F74

Ideas for Writing

Advertising Copy, F35
Advice Column, F17
Autobiographical Sketch, F119
Book Review, F130
Character Sketch, F97
Class-Book Feature, F21
Dialogue, F27
Diary Entries, F72
Dramatic Monologue, F81
Epilogue, F108
Extended Definition, F119
Feature Article, F160
Feature Story, F149
Folk Tale, F93
Gossip Column, F143
How-to Article, F155

How-to Manual, F59
How-to Memorandum, F81
Humorous Story, F8
Job Description, F48
Legend, F35
Letter, F87
Movie Script, F155
Musher's Journal, F130
Personal Letter, F17
Persuasive Dialogue, F93
Persuasive Letter, F8, F27
Poem, F87, F97, F108, F137, F160
Police Report, F149
Radio Sportscast, F137
Scene From a Story, F48
Science-Fiction Story, F59
Speech, F143
Story Sequel, F72
Tall Tale, F21

Ideas for Projects

Activities Survey, F59
Advertisement, F87
Animal Kingdom Report, F93
Art Exhibit, F160
Bar Graph, F72
Billboard, F21
Book of Names, F27
Career Cards, F119
Class Exhibit, F48
Coat of Arms, F35
Collage, F17
Comic Strip, F8
Community Connection, F160
Community Work, F17
Comparison of Self-Portraits, F119
Comparisons in Science, F137
Dance, F27
Debate, F35
Dramatic Scene, F72
Exercise Report, F130
Family Drama, F108
Family Scrapbooks, F108
Field Trip, F81
Inspirations Album, F87
Math Cards, F143
Mathematics Problem, F155
Media Review, F130
Mobile, F155
Model, F93
News Report, F143
Newscast, F35
Pantomime Routine, F21
Pen Pal, F81
Performance, F149
Puzzle Challenge, F149
Report on Timing in Music, F59
Song, F97, F137
Soundtrack, F48
Sports Interview, F130
Stage Name Report, F27
Stand-up Routine, F8
Storyboard, F21
Survey, F97

Student Review Board

Acharya, Arundhathi
Cecelia Snyder Middle School
Bensalem, Pennsylvania

Adkisson, Grant
McClintock Middle School
Charlotte, North Carolina

Akuna, Kimberly
Harriet Eddy Middle School
Elk Grove, California

Amdur, Samantha
Morgan Selvidge Middle School
Ballwin, Missouri

Arcilla, Richard
Village School
Closter, New Jersey

Arredondo, Marcus
Keystone School
San Antonio, Texas

Auten, Kristen
Bernardo Heights Middle School
San Diego, California

Backs, Jamie
Cross Keys Middle School
Florissant, Missouri

Baldwin, Katie
Bonham Middle School
Temple, Texas

Barber, Joanna
Chenery School
Belmont, Massachusetts

Bates, Maureen
Chestnut Ridge Middle School
Sewell, New Jersey

Bates, Meghan
Chestnut Ridge Middle School
Sewell, New Jersey

Beber, Nick
Summit Middle School
Dillon, Colorado

Becker, Jason
Hicksville Middle School
Hicksville, New York

Belfon, Loreal
Highland Oaks Middle School
Miami, Florida

Belknap, Jessica
Hughes Middle School
Long Beach, California

Bennet, Joseph
Conner Middle School
Hebron, Kentucky

Bennet, Joseph
Conner Middle School
Hebron, Kentucky

Birke, Lori
LaSalle Springs Middle School
Glencoe, Missouri

Bleichrodt, Angela
Beulah School
Beulah, Colorado

Block, Kyle
Hall-McCarter Middle School
Blue Springs, Missouri

Brendecke, Sarah Grant
Baseline Middle School
Boulder, Colorado

Brooks, Beau
Cresthill Middle School
Highlands Ranch, Colorado

Bruder, Jennifer
Nipher Middle School
Kirkwood, Missouri

Brunsfeld, Courtney
Moscow Junior High School
Moscow, Idaho

Burnett, Joseph
Markham Intermediate School
Placerville, California

Burrows, Tammy
Meadowbrook Middle School
Orlando, Florida

Calles, Miguel
Lennox Middle School
Lennox, California

Casanova, Christina
McKinley Classic Junior Academy
St. Louis, Missouri

Ceaser, Cerena
Templeton Middle School
Templeton, California

Chapman, Jon
Black Butte Middle School
Shingletown, California

Cho, Hwa
Miami Lakes Middle School
Miami Lakes, Florida

Chu, Rita
Orange Grove Middle School
Hacienda Heights, California

Church, John
Nathan Hale Middle School
Norwalk, Connecticut

Clouse, Melissa Ann
Happy Valley Elementary School
Anderson, California

Colbert, Ryanne
William H. Crocker School
Hillsborough, California

Crucet, Jennine
Miami Lakes Middle School
Miami Lakes, Florida

Culp, Heidi
Eastern Christian Middle School
Wyckoff, New Jersey

Cummings, Amber
Pacheco Elementary School
Redding, California

Curran, Christopher
Cresthill Middle School
Highlands Ranch, Colorado

D'Angelo, Samantha
Cresthill Middle School
Highlands Ranch, Colorado

D'Auria, Jeffrey
Nyack Middle School
Nyack, New York

D'Auria, Katherine
Upper Nyack Elementary School
Upper Nyack, New York

D'Auria, Patrick
Nyack Middle School
Nyack, New York

Daughtride, Katharyne
Lakeview Middle School
Winter Garden, Florida

Donato, Bridget
Felix Festa Junior High School
New City, New York

Donato, Christopher
Felix Festa Junior High School
New City, New York

Dress, Brian
Hall-McCarter Middle School
Blue Springs, Missouri

Drilling, Sarah
Milford Junior High School
Milford, Ohio

Fernandez, Adrian
Shenandoah Middle School
Coral Gables, Florida

Flores, Amanda
Orange Grove Middle School
Hacienda Heights, California

Flynn, Patricia
Camp Creek Middle School
College Park, Georgia

Ford, Adam
Cresthill Middle School
Highlands Ranch, Colorado

Fowler, Sabrina
Camp Creek Middle School
College Park, Georgia

Fox, Anna
Georgetown School
Georgetown, California

Freeman, Ledon
Atlanta, Georgia

Frid-Nielsen, Snorre
Branciforte Elementary School
Santa Cruz, California

Frosh, Nicole
Columbia Middle School
Aurora, Colorado

Gerretson, Bryan
Marshfield Junior High School
Marshfield, Wisconsin

Gillis, Shalon Michelle
Wagner Middle School
Philadelphia, Pennsylvania

Gonzales, Michael
Kitty Hawk Junior High School
Universal City, Texas

Goodman, Andrew
Richmond School
Hanover, New Hampshire

Granberry, Kemoria
Riviera Middle School
Miami, Florida

Groppe, Karissa
McCormic Junior High School
Cheyenne, Wyoming

Hadley, Michelle
Hopkinton Middle School
Hopkinton, Massachusetts

Hall, Katie
C.R. Anderson Middle School
Helena, Montana

Hamilton, Tim
Columbia School
Redding, California

Hawkins, Arie
East Norriton Middle School
Norristown, Pennsylvania

Hawkins, Jerry
Carrollton Junior High School
Carrollton, Missouri

Hayes, Bridget
Point Fermin Elementary School
San Pedro, California

Heinen, Jonathan
Broomfield Heights Middle School
Broomfield, Colorado

Hibbard, Erin
Willard Grade Center
Ada, Oklahoma

Hinners, Katie
Spaulding Middle School
Loveland, Ohio

Houston, Robert
Allamuchy Township Elementary
Allamuchy, New Jersey

Huang, Kane
Selridge Middle School
Ballwin, Missouri

Hudson, Vanessa
Bates Academy
Detroit, Michigan

Hutchison, Erika
C.R. Anderson Middle School
Helena, Montana

Hykes, Melissa
Meadowbrook Middle School
Orlando, Florida

Jackson, Sarah Jane
Needles Middle School
Needles, California

Jigarjian, Kathryn
Weston Middle School
Weston, Massachusetts

Johnson, Becky
Wheatland Junior High School
Wheatland, Wyoming

Johnson, Bonnie
West Middle School
Colorado Springs, Colorado

Johnson, Courtney
Oak Run Elementary School
Oak Run, California

Jones, Mary Clara
Beulah Middle School
Beulah, Colorado

Jones, Neil
Central School
Chillicothe, Missouri

Juarez, Sandra
Adams City Middle School
Thornton, Colorado

Juarez, Karen
Rincon Middle School
Escondito, California

Karas, Eleni
Our Lady of Grace
Encino, California

King, Autumn
Roberts Paideia Academy
Cincinnati, Ohio

Kossenko, Anna
Plantation Middle School
Plantation, Florida

Kurtz, Rachel
Paul Revere Middle School
Los Angeles, California

Lambino, Victoria
Henry H. Wells Middle School
Brewster, New York

Lamour, Katleen
Highland Oaks Middle School
North Miami Beach, Florida

Larson, Veronica
McClintock Middle School
Charlotte, North Carolina

Liao, Wei-Cheng
Nobel Middle School
Northridge, California

Lightfoot, Michael
Mission Hill Middle School
Santa Cruz, California

Lippman, Andrew
Thomas A. Blake Middle School
Medfield, Massachusetts

Lo, Melissa
Lincoln Middle School
Santa Monica, California

Lopez, Eric
Irvine Intermediate School
Costa Mesa, California

Lowery, Ry-Yon
East Norriton Middle School
Norristown, Pennsylvania

Macias, Edgar
Teresa Hughes Elementary School
Cudahy, California

Madero, Vanessa
Mathew J. Brletic Elementary
Parlier, California

Mandel, Lily
Mission Hill Junior High School
Santa Cruz, California

Manzano, Elizabeth Josephine
Hillside Elementary School
San Bernardino, California

Marentes, Crystal-Rose
Orange Grove Middle School
Hacienda Heights, California

Martinez, Desiree
Wheatland Junior High School
Wheatland, Wyoming

Massey,Drew
Union 6th and 7th Grade Center
Tulsa, Oklahoma

Matson, Josh
Canyon View Junior High School
Orem, Utah

Maxcy, Donald, Jr.
Camp Creek Middle School
Atlanta, Georgia

Maybruch, Robyn
Middle School 141
Riverdale, New York

Mayer, Judith
Burlingame Intermediate School
Burlingame, California

McCarter, Jennifer
Washburn School
Cincinnati, Ohio

McCarthy, Megan
Richmond School
Hanover, New Hampshire

McCombs, Juanetta
Washburn School
Cincinnati, Ohio

McGann, Kristen
Orange Grove Middle School
Hacienda Heights, California

McKelvey, Steven
Providence Christian Academy
Atlanta, Georgia

McQuary, Megan
CCA Baldi Middle School
Philadelphia, Pennsylvania

Mercier, Jared
Marshfield Junior High School
Marshfield, Wisconsin

Merrill, Nick
Windham Middle School
Windham, Maine

Miller, Catherine
Neil Armstrong Junior High School
Levittown, Pennsylvania

Miller, Kristen
Marina Village Junior High
El Dorado Hills, California

Montgomery, Tyler
North Cow Creek School
Palo Cedro, California

Mueller, Jessica
Spaulding Middle School
Loveland, Ohio

Mueler, John
St. Catherine School
Milwaukee, Wisconsin

Mulligan, Rebecca
Herbert Hoover Middle School
Oklahoma City, Oklahoma

Murgel, John
Beulah School
Beulah, Colorado

Murphy, Mathew
St. Wenceslaus School
Omaha, Nebraska

Neeley, Alex
Allamuchy Township School
Allamuchy, New Jersey

Nelsen-Smith, Nicole Marie
Branciforte Elementary
Santa Cruz, California

Ogle, Sarah
Redlands Middle School
Grand Junction, Colorado

Ozeryansky, Svetlana
C.C.A. Baldi Middle School
Philadelphia, Pennsylvania

Pacheco, Vicky
East Whittier Middle School
Whittier, California

Paddack, Geoffrey
Ada Junior High School
Ada, Oklahoma

Palombi, Stephanie
Marina Village Middle School
Cameron Park, California

Panion, Stephanie
Pitts Middle School
Pueblo, Colorado

Parks, Danny
West Cottonwood Junior High School
Cottonwood, California

Parriot, Cassandra
Orange Grove Middle School
Hacienda Heights, California

Paulson, Christina
Jefferson Middle School
Rocky Ford, Colorado

Perez, Iscura
Charles Drew Middle School
Los Angeles, California

Pratt, Lisa
Nottingham Middle Community Education Center
St. Louis, Missouri

Raggio, Jeremiah
Eagleview Middle School
Colorado Springs, Colorado

Raines, Angela
McKinley Classical Academy
St. Louis, Missouri

Ramadan, Mohammad
Ada Junior High School
Ada, Oklahoma

Ramiro, Leah
Magruder Middle School
Torrance, California

Raymond, Elizabeth
Julie A. Traphagen School
Waldwick, New Jersey

Recinos, Julie
Riviera Middle School
Miami, Florida

Reese, Andrea
Moscow Junior High
Moscow, Idaho

Reiners, Andrew
Redlands Middle School
Grand Junction, Colorado

Riddle, Katy
Willard Elementary School
Ada, Oklahoma

Rippe, Chris
La Mesa Junior High School
Santa Clarita, California

Robinson, Barbara
Wagner Middle School
Philadelphia, Pennsylvania

Rochford, Tracy
Louis Armstrong Middle School/IS 227
East Elmhurst, New York

Rodriguez, Ashley
John C. Martinez Junior High School
Parlier, California

Rowe, Michael
Washington Middle School
Long Beach, California

Sayles, Nichole
Hall McCarter Middle School
Blue Springs, Missouri

Schall, Harvest
Castle Rock Elementary School
Castella, California

Schellenberg, Katie
Corpus Christi School
Pacific Palisades, California

Schmees, Katherine
Milford Junior High School
Milford, Ohio

Schned, Paul
Richmond School
Hanover, New Hampshire

Schneider, Jennie
Parkway West Middle School
Chesterfield, Missouri

Scialanga, Michelle
Taylor Middle School
Millbrae, California

Shye, Kathryn
Happy Valley Elementary School
Anderson, California

Sirikulvadhana, Tiffany
Orange Grove Middle School
Hacienda Heights, California

Smetak, Laura
Orange Grove Middle School
Hacienda Heights, California

Smith, Shannon
Mary Putnam Henck Intermediate School
Lake Arrowhead, California

Smith-Paden, Patricia
Chappelow Middle School
Evans, Colorado

Sones, Mandy
Knox Junior High School
The Woodlands, Texas

Song, Sarah
Orange Grove Middle School
Hacienda Heights, California

Souza, Molly
Georgetown School
Georgetown, California

Stewart, Larry
Windsor Elementary School
Cincinnati, Ohio

Stites, Aaron
Redlands Middle School
Grand Junction, Colorado

Sturzione, James Van Duyn
Glen Rock Middle School
Glen Rock, New Jersey

Sundberg, Sarah
Milford Junior High School
Milford, Ohio

Swan, Tessa
Pacheco Elementary School
Redding, California

Swanson, Kurt
Allamuchy Elementary School
Allamuchy, New Jersey

Swihart, Bruce
Redlands Middle School
Grand Junction, Colorado

Syron, Christine
Nottingham Middle Community Education Center
St. Louis, Missouri

Taylor, Cody
Bella Vista Elementary School
Bella Vista, California

Thomas, Jennifer
Hoover Middle School
San Jose, California

Thompson, Robbie
Hefner Middle School
Oklahoma City, Oklahoma

Todd, Wanda
Hampton Middle School
Detroit, Michigan

Torning, Fraser
Allamuchy Elementary School
Allamuchy, New Jersey

Torres, Erica
Truman Middle School
Albuquerque, New Mexico

Tyroch, Melissa
Bonham Middle School
Temple, Texas

Ulibarri, Shavonne
John C. Martinez Junior High School
Parlier, California

Vanderham, Lynsey
Eagleview Middle School
Colorado Springs, Colorado

Vemula, Suni
Ada Junior High School
Ada, Oklahoma

Venable, Virginia
Chillicothe Junior High School
Chillicothe, Missouri

Vickers, Lori
Lake Braddock Secondary School
Springfield, Virginia

Vickers, Vanessa
Kings Glen School
Springfield, Virginia

Villanueva, Rene
John C. Martinez Junior High School
Parlier, California

Villasenor, Jose
Dana Middle School
San Pedro, California

Ward, Kimberly
Desert Horizon Elementary School
Phoenix, Arizona

Weeks, Josanna
Bellmont Middle School
Decatur, Indiana

West, Tyrel
Wheatland Junior High School
Wheatland, Wyoming

Whipple, Mike
Canandaigua Middle School
Canandaigua, New York

White, Schaefer
Richmond Middle School
Hanover, New Hampshire

Wilhelm, Paula
Wheatland Junior High School
Wheatland, Wyoming

Williams, Bonnie
Washburn School
Cincinnati, Ohio

Williams, Jason
Parkway West Middle School
Chesterfield, Missouri

Wiseman, Kristin
Glen Park Elementary School
New Berlin, Wisconsin

Wiseman, Megan
Glen Park Elementary School
New Berlin, Wisconsin

Yu, Veronica
Piñon Mesa Middle School
Victorville, California

Zipse, Elizabeth
Redlands Middle School
Grand Junction, Colorado

Acknowledgments (continued)

Bridgewater Books, an imprint of Troll Associates
"The Bear Boy" and excerpt from the "Introduction" of *Flying With the Eagle, Racing the Great Bear, Stories from Native North America*, Told by Joseph Bruchac. Copyright © 1993 by Joseph Bruchac. Reprinted with permission of the publisher, Bridgewater Books, an imprint of Troll Associates.

Siv Cedering
"Suppose" by Siv Cedering from *Color Poems* published by Calliopea Press. Copyright © 1978 by Siv Cedering.

Congdon and Weed Inc., and Contemporary Books, Inc.
"No Gumption" is reprinted from *Growing Up* by Russell Baker, © 1982. Used with permission of Congdon and Weed Inc. and Contemporary Books, Inc., Chicago.

Harold Courlander
"All Stories Are Anansi's" from The Hat-Shaking Dance and Other Ashanti Tales from Ghana by Harold Courlander with Albert Kofi Prempeh. Copyright © 1957 by Harcourt Brace Jovanovich, Inc.; 1985 by Harold Courlander. Reprinted by permission of the author.

Delacorte Press/Seymour Lawrence, a division of Bantam Doubleday Dell Publishing Group, Inc.
"The Lie," copyright © 1962 by Kurt Vonnegut, Jr. from *Welcome to the Monkey House* by Kurt Vonnegut, Jr. Used by permission of Delacorte Press/Seymour Lawrence, a division of Bantam Doubleday Dell Publishing Group, Inc.

Esquire, Inc.
"A Ribbon for Baldy," reprinted by permission of Esquire, Inc., © 1956 by Esquire, Inc.

Farrar, Straus & Giroux, Inc.
"basketball" from *Spin a Soft Black Song* by Nikki Giovanni. Copyright © 1971, 1985 by Nikki Giovanni. Reprinted by permission of Farrar, Straus & Giroux, Inc.

Free Spirit Publishing Inc.
"Reaching Out to a Stranger" from *Kids with Courage* by Barbara A. Lewis, copyright © 1992. Used with permission of Free Spirit Publishing Inc., Minneapolis, MN. All rights reserved.

Amanda Gross
"Snow Flowers" from *Snow Flowers* by Amanda Gross, © 1993. Reprinted by permission of the author.

Harcourt Brace & Company
"Seventh Grade" from *Baseball In April and Other Stories*, copyright © 1990 by Gary Soto. Excerpt from "preface" by Amy Tan in *Baba: A Return to China Upon My Father's Shoulders* by Belle Yang, preface copyright © 1994 by Amy Tan. Reprinted by permission of Harcourt Brace & Company.

HarperCollins Publishers Inc.
"The Highwayman" from *Collected Poems* by Alfred Noyes (J. B. Lippincott). Excerpt from "King Arthur: The Marvel of the Sword" from *The Book of King Arthur and His Noble Knights* by Mary MacLeod.

Kie Ho
"All Names Are American Names" by Kie Ho, first appeared in the *Los Angeles Times* in the spring of 1982.

Gary Hyland
"Their Names" by Gary Hyland, from *Just Off Main* (Thistledown Press, Saskatoon, Canada), copyright © 1982. Reprinted by permission of the author.

Alfred A. Knopf, Inc.
"Back to Back" from *25 Great Moments* by Geoffrey C. Ward, Ken Burns and S. A. Kramer. Copyright © 1994 by Baseball Enterprises International, Inc. "Mother to Son" from *Selected Poems* by Langston Hughes. Copyright 1926 by Alfred A. Knopf, Inc. and renewed 1954 by Langston Hughes. Reprinted by permission of Alfred A. Knopf, Inc.

Little, Brown and Company
"Susan Butcher" and an excerpt from the "Introduction" of *Champions: Stories of Ten Remarkable Athletes* by Bill Littlefield. Text Copyright © 1993 by Bill Littlefield. By permission of Little, Brown and Company.

McIntosh and Otis, Inc.
"The Captive Outfielder" by Leonard Wibberley, published in *The Saturday Evening Post*, 1961. Copyright © 1961 by Leonard Wibberley. Reprinted by permission of McIntosh and Otis, Inc.

New York Daily News
"Myself" by Abigail Friedman, as found in the *New York Daily News*, August 24, 1994. Copyright © New York Daily News, L.P., used with permission.

Pantheon Books, a division of Random House, Inc.
"Djuba Borrows a Pot" from *Arab Folktales* by Inea Bushnaq. Copyright © 1986 by Inea Bushnaq. Reprinted by permission of Pantheon Books, a division of Random House, Inc.

G. P. Putnam's Sons
Reprinted by permission of G. P. Putnam's Sons from "Two Kinds" from *The Joy Luck Club* by Amy Tan. Copyright © 1989 by Amy Tan.

Rethinking Schools Ltd.
"My Father Was a Musician" by Dyan Watson from *Rethinking Our Classrooms*, a special issue of *Rethinking Schools*. Copyright © 1994, Rethinking Schools, Ltd. Reprinted by permission of Rethinking Schools Ltd.

James D. Sanderson
"Dawn Discovery" (Daddy) is reprinted by permission of the author. Originally published by Sun Features, Inc. Copyright © 1985 by Sun Features, Inc. in *Sons on Fathers*, edited by Ralph Keyes.

Scholastic Inc.
"Me" by Linda Sue Estes from *Scope English Anthology*, Level 1. Copyright © 1983, 1979 by Scholastic Inc. Reprinted by permission of Scholastic Inc.

Signet Classics, an imprint of Penguin Books USA Inc.
Excerpt from *A Connecticut Yankee in King Arthur's Court* by Mark Twain, published by Signet Classics.

Simon & Schuster Books For Young Readers, an imprint of Simon & Schuster Children's Division
"Take My Mom—Please!" is reprinted with the permission of Simon & Schuster Books For Young Readers, an imprint of Simon & Schuster Children's Division from *If This Is Love, I'll Take Spaghetti* by Ellen Conford. Copyright © 1983 by Ellen Conford.

The Estate of William Stafford
"A Story That Could Be True" from *Stories That Could Be True*, copyright © 1977 The Estate of William Stafford. Originally published in *Stories That Could Be True* (Harper & Row, 1977), and is reprinted by permission of the estate.

Stone Soup, the magazine by children
"Scoring High" by Antoine Mack, II, age 11, is reprinted with permission from *Stone Soup, the magazine by children*, © 1995 by the Children's Art Foundation.

José Garcia Villa
"Lyric 17" from *Have Come, Am Here* by José Garcia Villa, Copyright 1942 by José Garcia Villa, copyright renewed © 1969 by José Garcia Villa. Reprinted by permission of the author.

Western Publishing Company, Inc.
"Phaethon and the Horses of the Sun" from *The Golden Treasury of Myths and Legends* by Anne Terry White, © 1959 Western Publishing Company, Inc. Used by permission of Western Publishing Company, Inc.

Note: Every effort has been made to locate the copyright owner of material reprinted in this book. Omissions brought to our attention will be corrected in subsequent printings.

Photo and Fine Arts Credits

Boldface numbers refer to the page on which the art is found.

Cover: *Untitled*, Tomas Sanchez, The Scholastic Art & Writing Awards; **Fv:** *Possibilities*, Jennifer Vota Scheidel, Artwork from the permanent collection of THIRTEEN/WNET's Student Arts Festival, 1978–1993; **Fvi:** *Celebration*,

Rudy Torres, The Scholastic Art & Writing Awards of 1995; **Fvii:** *Basketball*, Luckshimi B. Balasubramanian, 1994 UNICEF Wall Calendar. Collection of the Asahi Shimbun; **Fviii:** *El Pantalón Rosa* 1984, César Martínez, DagenBela Graphics; **Fix:** Courtesy of the author. Photo by Carolyn Soto; **Fx:** *Gemini I,* Lev T. Mills, Evans-Tibbs Collection; **F4:** Courtesy of the author; **F5:** Culver Pictures; **F7:** Walt Disney Co/Retna Ltd; **F9:** *Possibilities,* Jennifer Vota Scheidel, Artwork from the permanent collection of THIRTEEN/WNET's Student Arts Festival, 1978–1993; **F10:** *El Pantalón Rosa* 1984, César Martínez, DagenBela Graphics; **F13:** *San Pachuco* , Tony Ortega, Courtesy of the artist; **F14:** *La Morena Bakery,* Tony Ortega, Courtesy of the artist.; **F15:** *Vatos Parados 2,* Tony Ortega, Courtesy of the artist; **F16:** Courtesy of the author. Photo by Carolyn Soto; **F18–19:** (background) ©1988 Pete Saloutos/The Stock Market; **F19:** Thistledown Press Ltd.; **F20:** Photo © 1991 by Dan Labby. Courtesy of HarperCollins; **F20–21:** (background) ©1988 Pete Saloutos/The Stock Market; **F22:** *Latinoamerica* 1993, multi-media painting on Fabriano paper 22"x30", Orlando Agudelo-Botero, Engman International Fine Art, Coral Gables, Florida; **F23:** Shelley Rotner /Omni-Photo Communications, Inc.; **F24:** Myrleen Ferguson/Photo Edit; **F26:** Photo by Ruben Guzman; **F28:** Raymond O'Shea Gallery, London, Bridgeman Art Library; **F29:** The Granger Collection, New York; **F31:** The Granger Collection, New York; **F34:** *Arthur, from Lancelot du Lac f. 50r,* Bodleian Library, Oxford; **F36:** (top) Courtesy of the artist; (left) Andrea Brizzi/The Stock Market; **F38–39:** Carol Richman; **F39:** (br) *Storefront Window, Chinatown, N.Y.,* 1993, 40 x 54 inches, oil on linen, Don Jacot, Courtesy Louis K. Meisel Gallery, New York. Photo by Steve Lopez; **F40–41:** The Bettmann Archive; **F42:** *Mother and daughter. Leaf from a Manchu family album.* Ink and color on paper. H. 13-1/8 in. W. 14-1/8 in. Unidentified artist, Ch'ing Dynasty. The Metropolitan Museum of Art, Anonymous Gift, 1952. (52.209.3j). Copyright © 1980 by The Metropolitan Museum of Art; **F43:** *Twenty-one ancestors with spirit tablet.* Ch'ing Dynasty (1644–1912). Inscribed in Chinese: The ancestral tablet of the Honorable Madame Wu, the first wife. Ink and color on paper. H. 62 -1/4 in. W. 45-1/8 in. Unidentified artist. © 1980/95 by The Metropolitan Museum of Art, Gift of Mrs. F. L. Hough, 1969. (69.100).; **F44:** *Mandarin Square: Badge with peacock-insignia-3rd civil rank.* China, 17th–20th century. Yale University Art Gallery, Gift of the Estate of Schuyler V.R. Cammann; **F47:** (top) Courtesy of Amy Tan; (bottom) The Bettmann Archive; **F49:** *Possibilities,* Jennifer Vota Scheidel, Artwork from the permanent collection of THIRTEEN/WNET's Student Arts Festival, 1978–1993; **F51:** Harold Ober Associates; **F52:** (background) Joseph Palmieri/New England Stock Photo; (top) Peter L. Chapman/Stock Boston; **F53:** (tr) & (bl) The Bettmann Archive; **F54–55:** (background) Joseph Palmieri/New England Stock Photo; **F55:** Grace Davies/Omni-Photo Communications, Inc.; **F56–57:** (background) Joseph Palmieri/New England Stock Photo; **F57:** Dr. E.R. Degginger; **F58:** (br) Mrs. Leonard Wibberly; **F58–59:** (background) Joseph Palmieri/New England Stock Photo; **F61:** New England Stock Photo; **F62:** John Coletti /Stock Boston; **F64–65:** (background) Richard Pasley/ Stock Boston; **F68:** Gabe Palmer/Stock, Market; **F71:** P. Prince /Gamma-Liaison; **F73:** *Celebration,* Rudy Torres, The Scholastic Art & Writing Awards of 1995; **F74:** (left) New England Stock Photo; **F74–75:** (background) Dr. E.R. Degginger; **F76–77:** (background) Dr. E.R. Degginger; **F77:** (top) Jeff Isaac Greenberg/Photo Researchers, Inc.; **F78–79:** (background) Dr. E.R. Degginger; **F79:** (top) Courtesy of the artist; **F80:** Courtesy of the author; **F80-81:** (background) Dr. E.R. Degginger; **F83:** Focus on Sports; **F84:** *Hand and collage,* Fred Otnes, Courtesy of the artist; **F85:** Dr. E.R. Degginger; **F86:** (left) Chronicle Books. Photo by Arthur Furst; (tc) Florentine Films. Photo by Pam Tubridy Baucom; (tr) Villard Books, photo © John Isaac; **F88:** (center) *Mimbres bowl with human and bear design,* Swarts Ruin, Mimbres Valley, New Mexico. Mimbres: 705–1150 AD. Dia: 30cm. Copyright © Pres. and Fellows of Harvard College 1995. All rights reserved. Peabody Museum-Harvard University. Photograph by Hillel Burger.; **F89:** Jack Parsons/Omni-Photo Communications, Inc.; **F90:** Dr. E.R. Degginger; **F91:** *Bear Storyteller,* 1981, Louis Naranjo, (Cochiti). Photo by Guy Monthan from the book, *The Pueblo Storyteller,* by Barbara A. Babcock, and Guy and Doris Monthan, University of Arizona Press, Tucson.; **F92:** (center) *Mimbres bowl with human and bear design,* Swarts Ruin, Mimbres Valley, New Mexico. Mimbres: 705–1150 AD. Dia: 30cm. Copyright © Pres. and Fellows of Harvard College 1995. All rights reserved. Peabody Museum-Harvard University. Photograph by Hillel Burger; **F94:** (center) Focus on Sports; **F95:** Silver Burdett Ginn; **F96:** (tl) *Untitled,* Mark Fredrickson, Courtesy of Levi Strauss & Co.; (bl) *Langston Hughes,* 1939, Carl Van Vechten, Photograph copyright © Estate of Carl Van Vechten. Gravure and compilation copyright © Eakins Press Foundation; **F98:** Silver Burdett Ginn; **F100:** Joseph Nettis/Tony Stone Images; **F101:** Silver Burdett Ginn; **F102:** Silver Burdett Ginn; **F104:** (bottom) Fotopic/Omni-Photo Communications, Inc.; **F105:** Silver Burdett Ginn; **F106:** (top) Photo by Ken Karp; (bottom) John Lei/Omni-Photo Communications, Inc.; **F107:** Courtesy of the author. Photo by David Conford; **F109:** *Celebration,* Rudy Torres, The Scholastic Art & Writing Awards of 1995; **F111:** Salt Lake Tribune, photo by Lynn Johnson.; **F113:** Contemporary Books; **F117:** Contemporary Books; **F118:** The Bettmann Archive; **F120–121:** (background) Kim Heacox /Tony Stone Images; **F122** (tl) William R. Sallez /Duomo; **F122–123:** (background) © David Madison, 1995; **F124:** (tl) Wide World Photos; (left) © David Madison, 1995; **F125:** (tr) & (right) © David Madison, 1995; **F126–127:** (background) William R. Sallez/Duomo; **F128:** (top) William R. Sallez /Duomo; (left) & (bottom) © David Madison, 1995; **F129:** (tr) Jeff Schultz /Alaska Stock Images; (right) © David Madison, 1995; (bl) Courtesy of the author; **F131:** *Basketball,* Luckshimi B. Balasubramanian, 1994 UNICEF Wall Calendar. Collection of the Asahi Shimbun; **F133:** Outline Press Syndicate Inc.; **F134:** *Unfinished Man* 1968, Rupert Garcia, Courtesy of the artist and Sammi Madison-Garcia; Rena Bransten Gallery, SF; Daniel Saxon Gallery, LA; Galerie Claude Samuel, Paris. Photo by Ben Blackwell; **F135:** *Into the Future* 1987, Carborundum Gravure, 24"x31", Max Papart, Nahan Galleries, New York; **F136:** (tr) Courtesy of the author. Photo By David Swickard; (tl) AP/Wide World Photos; (bottom) New York Times Pictures; **F138–139:** The Bettmann Archive; **F144:** *Preparing Medicine from Honey,* 1224 (detail), Abadallah ibn ala-Fadl, The Metropolitan Museum of Art, Cora Timken Burnett Collection of Persian Miniatures and Other Persian Art Objects, Bequest of Cora Timken Burnett, 1957. (57.51.21). Copyright ©1986 by The Metropolitan Museum of Art; **F145:** *Bronze cauldron,* © The Board of Trustees of the Victoria and Albert Museum, London; **F147:** *Pendant in the form of a snake catching a frog,* Ebrie people, Côte d'Ivoire, 19th century, gold. Brooklyn Museum, Frank L. Babbott Fund; **F148** Pace Primitive Gallery, New York; **F150:** (top) *Corn and Pumpkin Patch,* 18x24" oil on canvas, Gary Ernest Smith, Overland Gallery of Fine Art; **F150–151:** (background) Jeff Greenberg /Omni-Photo Communications, Inc.; **F151:** Fotopic/Omni-Photo Communications, Inc.; **F152:** (top) G.R. Roberts/Omni-Photo Communications, Inc.; **F152–153:** (background) Jeff Greenberg/Omni-Photo Communications, Inc.; **F154:** (center) JesseStuart Foundation; **F154–155:** (background) Jeff Greenberg/Omni-Photo Communications, Inc.; **F159:** (top) Dr. E.R. Degginger; (bottom) Free Spirit Publishing; **F161:** *Basketball,* Luckshimi B. Balasubramanian, 1994 UNICEF Wall Calendar. Collection of the Asahi Shimbun; **F163:** (center) Photo by Marjorie Nichols; **F165:** Frederica Georgia/Photo Researchers, Inc.; **F170:** (left) Cover illustration only from "Bearstone" by Will Hobbs. Copyright © 1989 by Will Hobbs. By permission of Avon Books; (tr) Photo by Jean Hobbs; (br) HarperCollins-Children's Books; **F171:** (left) Penguin Group-Puffin Books; (right) Book cover of "My Brother, My Sister, and I" by Yoko Kawashima Watkins Macmillan Books for Young Readers.

Commissioned Illustrations

F156: Evelyn Magie

Electronic Page Makeup

Larry Rosenthal, Tom Tedesco, Dawn Annunziata. Penny Baker, Betsy Bostwick, Maude Davis, Irene Ehrmann, Alison Grabow, Gregory Harrison, Jr., Mike Huffman, Marnie Ingman, Laura Maggio, Lynn Mandarino, David Rosenthal, Mitchell Rosenthal

Administrative Services

Diane Gerard

Photo Research Service

OMNI Photo Communications, Inc.